Rival
Jacqui Rose

D0709735

avon.

Published by AVON
A division of HarperCollins*Publishers* Ltd
1 London Bridge Street
London SE1 9GF

www.harpercollins.co.uk

A Paperback Original 2020

First published in Great Britain by HarperCollins*Publishers* 2020

A catalogue copy of this book is available from the British Library.

ISBN: 978-0-00-836698-8

Typeset in Minion Pro by
Palimpsest Book Production Limited, Falkirk, Stirlingshire
Printed and bound in UK by CPI Group (UK) Ltd, Croydon CR0 4YY

MIX
Paper from
responsible sources
FSC C007454

This book is produced from independently certified FSC™ paper to ensure responsible forest management.

For more information visit: www.harpercollins.co.uk/green

This book is dedicated to my amazing nephew,
Jack Wimbleton.
Thinking of you, Jack, and marking off the days.
With love
J x

A common danger unites even the bitterest enemies.

Aristotle

THREE MONTHS AGO

'Alfie? Alfie? Pick up the phone. For God's sake, I know you're there. I don't know how many messages I've left, but we need to talk. Even if you're still angry with me at least call me back . . . *Please.*' Franny Doyle sighed as she cut off the call.

Despairing, she threw the phone on the white leather couch and took a large sip from the glass of Chardonnay she'd poured herself earlier. It was the same every time she tried to get through to Alfie. He'd just send it straight to voicemail . . . He was ghosting her, *big* time.

Walking across to the window of the front room of her large Georgian house in Soho Square, she looked out across the gardens, noticing the flickering of the street light.

It was late, gone midnight, and she could just make out a few passers-by as they hurried along the street through the rain and the cold. About to take another sip of her wine, Franny paused, the crystal wine glass resting on her lips. She was sure she'd just heard a noise coming from the hallway.

For a moment she stood still, wondering if it was just the sound of the wind hitting the gutter outside, which she'd neglected to get fixed. But no, there it was again.

Placing her glass on the hand-carved, black mantelpiece, Franny quietly walked towards the drawing room door as her heart began to race. She stopped at her silver bookshelf and as quickly and as carefully as she could, she slid her hand behind the row of the various first-edition hardbacks, pulling out a small handgun.

She could feel her heart racing faster as she gripped the gun and paused, listening once again before placing her hand on the solid brass door handle. She slowly began to open it, but the door was suddenly kicked open, sending Franny and the gun flying across the wooden floor.

Without bothering to look to see who it was, Franny scrambled desperately to reach the gun, but too late. She felt an agony in her hand as her fingers were crushed by the weight of someone's foot. The next moment she heard a gruff, gravelled voice.

'Hello, Franny; long time, no see. I've been meaning to come and visit you for a while, but you know how it goes, life gets busy. But hey, I'm here now.'

Face down, Franny let out a groan as the pain from the skin being torn open on her fingers rushed through her.

'What's that? Oh I'm sorry, Franny, am I standing on your hand? What a clumsy cunt I am. Is this better?' The foot stamped down even harder, and this time, Franny let out an agonising yelp as her blood squirted across the floor.

'*You bastard!*'

With a chuckle her hand was suddenly released and the next moment, Franny was staring a familiar face straight in the eye as he knelt down and glared at her. 'That hand looks nasty; you need to make sure you put something on that. You don't want to get it infected, do you?'

Sitting up and putting her hand underneath her armpit to try to stop the flow of blood, Franny gritted her teeth as she spoke. Her voice dripped with contempt. 'Hello, Harry, if you'd wanted an invite, you should've just told me – you didn't need to go to all this trouble. Cup of tea?'

Incensed by Franny's attitude, he grabbed hold of her face, squeezing as hard as he could. 'Listen to me, you silly bitch, you're walking a very *dangerous* line and if I were you, I wouldn't cross it.'

'What do you want, Harry?' Franny spat out.

'I understand that you've still got a hit out for Vaughn Sadler, and you're still looking for payback.'

'That's between him and me.'

'Oh no, but it ain't.'

Not wanting to show how much pain she was in to Harry, Franny took a deep breath before she spoke. 'What are you talking about?'

'I know that both you and Wan Huang have been wanting to have your day with Vaughn, but I've had a little talk with Wan. Made a deal. So, that's why I'm here. Wanted to tell you in person.'

Franny stared at Harry, knowing that she wouldn't like

3

what she was about to hear. Though Harry was right, Wan Huang, the new head of the Triads – a notorious South East Asian gang – also wanted to put Vaughn Sadler in the ground, albeit for an entirely different reason than Franny, though it came down to the same thing: revenge. 'My business with Vaughn is just that. *My business*.'

'As I say, I've made a deal with Wan. He's willing to let bygones be bygones, which means you're going to do the same; you back away from Vaughn. So any ideas you've got to take him out, well they're over now. Because *now*, he's got me in his corner. So, if I hear – if I even get a fucking whiff – that you're still planning to go after him, then, sweetheart, I'll be coming after *you*. And when I find you, I'll cut off those pretty fingers of yours one at a time, and after that, I'll bury you a-fucking-live. You understand me?' He got up and brushed down his expensive camel coat and smiled. 'Anyway, best dash, Franny, so if it's all the same to you, I'll leave that cup of tea. Maybe another time . . .'

TODAY

1

With the agonising sound of her own scream Tia Jacobs startled both herself and the disdainful-looking clerk of the court, who earlier in the morning had already shown his contempt for her as he'd stared at the short blue dress and black high heels she wore.

Not that it mattered now what he thought because that had been before. *Before* the judge had passed his verdict. The plain-looking man in the tired black robe with his pinched nose and overly dyed black hair, who had no idea what her favourite film was or why looking at the sea on an overcast day made her cry, had passed a judgement that would change her life forever.

Bent over, Tia wrapped her arms around her waist as if somehow it would stop the wailing sound that seemed to be resonating from every pore in her body. The only sight she could see through the pane of tears, which felt as if they were burning her face, was that of the out-of-focus passing shoes of the reserved British public, who, even when presented with a bent-over howling woman in the corridors of justice, still pretended all was well.

Suddenly, a pair of brown Gucci loafers brought Tia's eyes and mind into focus; though it could, she thought, be just as likely that the overpowering and over-applied after-shave that attacked all her senses had cleared her mind.

But there was no need to gaze upwards. Tia knew *exactly* who'd be standing in those shoes, the sneering smugness fashioned on his face, which always made her recoil in an attempt at self-protection from the toxic words that always followed.

'Stand the fuck up, Tia. You're making a show of yourself. You're a disgrace. I ain't surprised the judge said what he did. One look at you, he knows exactly what you are. You've got a fucking screw loose, you know that?'

Standing up to look at her husband, Tia wiped her nose on the back of her sleeve. 'You're loving this, Harry, ain't you? You got what you want. You won.'

Harry Jacobs stared at his wife and shook his head. The only emotion he felt at that moment was one of annoyance at the spectacle Tia was making of herself. If he stood in front of her any longer there was a strong possibility she'd snivel all over his favourite shoes.

Grabbing her arm tight enough for her to let out a little squeal, Harry snarled at his wife. 'I was always going to win. I told you what would happen if you took me on,

6

didn't I? I told that you were wasting your time, but no, you had to be a silly cunt and go ahead and try it anyway. You're my wife, Tia. Till death us do part, remember? But if you don't want to honour that, well, you have to pay the consequences, sweetheart.'

This last statement was like a bucket of ice-cold water being thrown over Tia. She shook off his grip and glared at her husband, looking directly into the blue eyes that at one time she'd found so mesmerising.

He hadn't aged that much over the years. At forty-four there was no middle age spread, no receding hairline, no lines around his eyes; he was as good-looking as he always had been, with the energy and body of a twenty-year-old man. He had it all: the looks, the money, the gift of the gab and the respect from all the other faces around Soho.

He had everything, everything except for a heart and she hated him for it, *especially* as it felt to Tia like he'd taken her heart away too.

She'd been brought up in a care home before being kicked out at the tender age of sixteen, having to turn tricks to make ends meet. And then out of what seemed like nowhere, she'd fallen head over heels in love and, stupidly, she'd thought she'd found her happy ever after.

But it hadn't worked out and although it hadn't been her choice to end the relationship, she'd consequently found herself back on the streets again. So when Harry had swept in, she'd thought all her troubles were behind her. Who had she been kidding – her troubles had only just started. At the time she'd wanted a roof over her head more than anything. She'd been vulnerable and she'd needed to be loved. And she supposed by then she certainly hadn't been picky.

Harry had promised her the world and of course she'd leapt at the chance even though all the flags had been there. Right from the start he'd been jealous, controlling and had been handy with his fists, but being with Harry was better than being on the streets like some of her other friends who'd left the care home at the same time.

Though it hadn't all been bad, especially at the beginning, and partly that had been the problem. Maybe it would've been easier to leave if at the beginning he'd been an out-and-out bastard, instead of saving it all for later.

They'd had laughs and they'd had times when they'd genuinely seemed to like each other and he'd bought her no end of presents and cars, but as the years rolled by the control, the jealousy, along with his cruelty, had become part of the fabric of her life.

Though if she were honest, those things alone wouldn't have made her go to the extremes she had. She would've stuck it out as she had done for all these years, put up with it all, told herself she was better off than some. But then there'd been the final straw. The final betrayal had come just over six months ago, and even now she didn't like to think about it, but it was that and that alone which made her pick up and leave.

'Oh, believe me, Harry, I've been paying the consequences for long enough now, don't you think?'

Hissing at Tia through his teeth, Harry grabbed hold of her arm again, pulling her down the corridor. 'Ain't you had enough of all the self-pity, Tia? You've stamped your feet enough now and wasted everybody's time. You're lucky I'm so understanding – most fellas I know would bury you in the nearest shallow grave and most men in my business wouldn't even let you step into a court, let alone try to say the crap you did. But I let you, Tia. I let you get it all out of your system, so don't give me the hard-done-by shit.'

Fighting back tears, Tia, not saying anything, shook her head as Harry barged into a couple coming the other way. Giving them a warning glare not to say anything, he continued to march Tia towards the exit as he spoke. 'What the fuck did you think you were doing, that's what I want to know? Leaving me and your home, then doing this shit. Why did you do it?'

Spinning around to look at him, she could hardly get the words out. 'You know why I did it, you know why I left, and me going to court is because I wanted my kids.'

Leaning down to her, Harry whispered nastily in Tia's ear. '*Our* kids, Tia. Don't forget that. They're *our* three kids. The way you talk, anyone would think I'm just some fucking sap paying for you, rather than your husband.'

With her hands shaking, Tia pulled out a cigarette from her denim jacket, finding it difficult to recall the judge's exact comments; her head was spinning too much.

Her solicitors, for all the good they'd been, had told her she'd stood a chance, but in the end the judge had only listened to Harry's lies and his expensive barrister, painting her to be someone she didn't even recognise. Painting her to be an unfit mother.

'Mrs Jacobs, after taking into account all the statements and hearing from both yourself and Mr Jacobs as well as

understanding more about your background and financial set-up, I feel it's in the children's best interest to stay with their father. I award him full and sole custody with you having weekly visitation rights.'

Blowing out a mouthful of smoke, Tia spoke slowly and softly in the hope she wouldn't lose control and start screaming again, because the next time she was afraid she'd never be able to stop. The pain in her voice clearly evident, she asked, 'What am I going to do, Harry? What am I going to do without the kids?'

Wrapping his expensive Fendi scarf around his neck, Harry glanced at his wife; she was truly stunning, even with her swollen eyes and red nose from all the snivelling she had insisted on doing, her beauty still shone through. Her skin was pale, her face held the darkest yet softest brown eyes, and her lips were full and red, which made the most faithful of men imagine what she could do with them.

To look at her, you'd never think she'd had three children. Her figure was tight and curvaceous, not to mention her fabulous, enormous breasts, but for all this beauty, he thought she was a fool. A fool to waste everyone's time and think that she could ever get custody of his kids and a fool to go up against him.

Though he'd stood back and let her do what she'd needed to do. And it'd actually amused him that she really thought she'd win. He'd let her think that she was getting somewhere, let her think that the solicitor she'd hired had been on her side, though the fact was her solicitor had been in *his* pocket, feeding *him* information, and as a result, he'd always been one step ahead of Tia.

Then when it'd come down to it, he'd made sure that his barrister had destroyed her. She hadn't stood a chance. Not one shred of a chance.

So as predicted, here she was in front of him, crying like her life was over, asking him what she should do.

She needed him and always would and even if she didn't, there was no way she was going anywhere.

Feeling the chill of the wind, he laughed as he put his powerful muscular arm around her shoulders, pulling her towards him as he led her down the stone stairs to the car park.

'Look, Tia, I think I've always been pretty fair to you. I've just about managed to put up with all the crap you've thrown my way, though God knows a lesser man wouldn't, including all that crazy shit at the beginning of the year. I've always been there for you—'

Interrupting, Tia snapped, 'That's crap, Harry – what you did, I hate you for it, so don't try to pretend you were there for me. We both know the truth.'

'There you go again, Tia, always pointing the finger at somebody else instead of taking a long hard look at yourself in the mirror. Isn't losing the kids enough for you for one day?'

Without thinking, Tia swung her hand in the direction of Harry's smug smile but he grabbed it and roared with laughter. 'I love it when you get angry; it gives me a real hard on. What do you say to giving me a quick blow job?'

The tears that had been threatening to escape again cascaded down her cheeks like a sudden cloud burst. 'I'm just a game to you, ain't I? Just leave me alone, Harry. You heard what the judge said, you've got what you wanted.'

Softening his face but hardening his eyes, Harry came to a standstill in front of a blacked-out Range Rover. Unlovingly he kissed her on the cheek. 'If you want the kids, Tia, you can have them. After all you're their mum.'

Tia stared up at Harry. 'What?'

'You heard me, you can have them.'

With her heart beginning to race, Tia blinked away the last of her tears. 'Don't play with me, Harry. Don't say that if you don't mean it . . . They're everything to me, you know that.'

He smiled, lighting up his handsome face. 'I know, darlin', that's why I'm saying it. I just wanted to teach you a lesson, show you you went about it all the wrong way.'

Shaking, Tia nodded. 'I'm sorry, I'm sorry, I just didn't know what else to do.'

Harry smiled, opening the Range Rover door. 'Good, well I'm glad we got that sorted out . . . Come on, get in.'

As quickly as Tia's smile had appeared, it went. 'What? What are you talking about?'

'Home. Let's go home.'

'But . . .'

Harry sniffed, his blue eyes narrowing. 'You want the kids don't you?'

'Yes, but . . .'

He smiled at her, showing off his perfect teeth. 'We all come as one big happy family, Tia, you should know that by now. You want the kids, then you come home.'

Tia stood and watched her husband get in the passenger seat of the car. Her head was telling her to turn around and walk the other way, but her heart – the part that counted – was moving her feet in the same direction as her husband. This was another chance, a chance to be with her children once again and her love for them was greater than anything.

She'd tried to battle her husband and it'd taken everything out of her in doing so. Now she supposed it was time to concede; Harry Jacobs had won . . . For now anyway, because as she'd thought so many times in the past, he'd left her no choice; one day, she was going to pay him back. Oh yes, Harry would get his comeuppance all right even if she had to kill him herself. For now though, she'd play the game. If being a player was good enough for Harry, it was good enough for her.

And with the tears streaming down her face, Tia, having made up her mind, slid slowly into the back passenger seat but immediately froze as she stared at the driver whilst Harry spoke. 'Ain't you going to say hello, Tia? You know Vaughn, don't you?'

With a tight smile, Tia nodded as she stared out of the window. She knew Vaughn Sadler all right, the problem was, she knew him too well.

2

'Franny! Franny! We need your help! Quick, please, you've got to come!'

Putting down her phone on the side, Franny Doyle looked up at Sasha – who was no older than eighteen – standing shaking in the doorway, her face pale and drawn.

Shocked at how upset Sasha was, Franny spoke, concern in her voice. 'What's happened, darlin'?'

The girl shrugged, wiping the tears from her face. 'I dunno really but Sophie's ill. She's vomiting. She was snorting some lines and then she just started convulsing.'

Without saying anything else, Franny nodded and jumped up, hurrying out of the office on the top floor of Foxy's nightclub in Greek Street. She followed Sasha – who was one of the club's newest recruits having only started working there seven months ago – down the stairs.

Getting to the lounge, Franny stopped and stared in

horror, muttering more to herself than Sasha. '*Jesus Christ.*' Then she rushed across the large, sparsely furnished white-washed room to where Sophie was lying naked on the floor.

Straight away, Franny could see Sophie was fitting and her eyes were rolling to the back of her head, a combination of vomit and spit foaming out of her mouth.

Kneeling down, Franny gently lifted Sophie's head onto her lap. 'It's okay, honey. It's okay. I'm here. We'll get you some help, darlin'.' She turned to Sasha and barked out her order. 'Phone an ambulance . . . Now!'

Still trembling and clearly in shock, Sasha nodded before disappearing out of the room. Turning her attention back to Sophie, whose breathing was becoming more and more staggered as her body violently convulsed, Franny moved her to the recovery position.

She brushed Sophie's long fringe back from her face, which was sprinkled with flecks of cocaine and vomit. 'It's okay, darlin', you'll be all right. You hear me? Sasha's calling the ambulance now. Hang in there, baby. Hang in there.'

Hearing a noise, Franny looked up and saw Sasha standing in the doorway with fear written all over her face.

'Did you call them, Sash? How long did they say until they get here?'

Unable to look at Franny, Sasha shook her head. 'No, I didn't call them.'

'What do you mean, you didn't? Go and call them. *Now!* For fuck's sake, Sash, she needs help! She's dying, now go and get help!'

With tears in her eyes, Sasha mumbled, her whole body shaking. 'I can't call.'

Worried for Sophie, who was looking paler and bluer, Franny glared at Sasha. 'I don't know what the fuck you're talking about or what's got into you, but you need to get an ambulance. *Please, Sash, go! Go, call them!*'

'She won't be doing that, Miss Doyle. No one's calling anyone.'

Franny stared up at the man, who she knew only from sight but was aware was one of the owner's henchmen, as he stepped into the room.

Franny snarled with anger and frustration running through her. 'She might die. Do you understand? If she doesn't get help soon, she is going to die!'

'Then she dies, Ms Doyle. That's what happens when you mess with drugs.'

As Sophie continued to convulse, Franny hissed through her teeth. 'Phone the fucking ambulance, you hear me? She's just a kid.'

The man, who spoke with a strong East End accent but was South East Asian by origin, pulled a face. 'Not my concern. If she snorts that shit up like it's on special offer, what do you expect?'

Placing Sophie's head on the floor, Franny scrambled up and rushed towards the door.

'You mean the shit that you feed her, because let's face it, what you expect them to do would be really fucking hard if they weren't out of their heads.'

The man glared at her, his brown eyes cold and menacing. 'I'd be careful what you say.'

Franny shook her head. 'Don't even try to threaten me . . . Now get out of my way, cos if you won't call for help, then I will.'

As she went to leave, the man blocked her way. 'I don't think that would be very wise, do you?'

'I don't care what's wise. I ain't your prisoner and I don't work for *you*, so just get the fuck out of my way, so I can get her some help.' Franny seethed.

'What's the problem, here?' Wan Huang spoke in a soft London accent as he came into sight and walked along the corridor towards Franny.

Glancing at him, Franny said, 'She needs help. I think Sophie must have overdosed, and this wanker won't let me call for the ambulance.'

Hurrying across to Sophie, Wan – tall and handsome, in his early twenties – knelt down, leaning his head towards her. He stayed there for a few moments before Franny watched as he put his fingers on the pulse of her neck and then on the pulse of her wrist. He looked up, shaking his head. 'It's too late, Fran . . . I'm sorry, she's dead.'

Sasha let out a piercing scream as Franny stared at Sophie lying motionless on the floor.

'What? No! No! She can't be! You must've got it wrong. She can't be.'

'She is, Fran, come and see for yourself.'

Unable to speak, Franny turned to the man standing at the door and without warning, slammed her fist into his face. 'You bastard! She was only seventeen years old!' Then she leapt at him, pummelling her fists into his head. She reached for her gun, which was hidden in her jacket, but

17

it was too late, the man fought back and Franny found herself being pushed up against the wall.

'That's enough! Break it up! I said, *enough!*' Wan shouted at the top of his voice as he dragged Franny off the man.

Without bothering to say anything else, she rushed down the stairs and out the exit to the fresh air, her heart breaking for Sophie and for Sasha who she could still hear wailing, and not for the first time she wondered how the hell it was she'd stepped into such a nightmare.

The past eight months had been an utter mess and that was putting it lightly. Everything had been well and truly screwed up. And the past three months had been even worse since the visit from Harry. After that, everything had become about collateral damage and her life now consisted of having to watch her back on top of not knowing who she was able to trust and wondering if she was going to make it through until tomorrow. And ultimately, it was all down to one person. Vaughn Sadler.

She'd needed to use all her powers of persuasion and negotiation skills not to find herself six feet under. Put there by the family and colleagues of Mr Huang, who'd been the head of a notorious South East Asian Triad gang. That was, of course, before Vaughn had put a knife through the back of his head.

At first the Triads had been all right but after Harry had started winding them up, stoking their fire, the finger of blame for Huang being killed had slowly begun to point towards her. Not because Wan and his associates thought that she'd actually killed him – they knew she hadn't – but because it had been *her* who'd arranged for Vaughn to meet

Huang at a secret location, and it was there it'd all gone wrong. Harry Jacobs had done a good job in stirring trouble for her.

And she was angry, so angry, because of course it was supposed to have been Vaughn with a knife in the back of his head or however Huang had decided to dispose of him on account of the fact that Vaughn had crossed *her*. The reason why she'd wanted Vaughn dead? He'd broken all the rules that they lived by; he'd snaked her out to the police by trying to frame her for a crime she *didn't* commit.

So, it was only right that he had payback, only right that she paid Huang to do his worst. But clearly, his worst hadn't been good enough.

When Huang had been killed, she'd expected his men to go looking for Vaughn, searching him out before chopping him into a thousand pieces. And they had . . . at first. But Vaughn had been smart; he'd sought protection from his long-term friend Harry Jacobs, who was not only a face, but also had a long, successful business history with the Triads. And she hated Harry nearly, *nearly* as much as she hated Vaughn.

Harry had always been well in with the Triads. He let them launder money through his clubs, provided weapons for them and used his network of contacts to bring cocaine and pills into the country.

Even so, she'd still been surprised and pissed off to say the least when Huang's half-brother, Wan, the new head of the gang, had agreed – as long as Vaughn was under Harry's wing – that they would leave Vaughn alone. Which meant he was untouchable for all concerned and that's when the heat had come onto her, leaving Harry and Vaughn to be able to do what they liked, including nearly taking her fingers off a couple of months back.

But though Wan had history with Harry, something didn't sit right. Why would he do a deal with Harry? Why would he essentially agree to let Vaughn off? It was true that Wan had hated his older brother and they'd never got along, but in her heart she knew that wouldn't stop Wan, or any of his associates for that matter. Wan's gang were hungry for blood, wanting to show everyone they weren't to be crossed.

So, Harry or not, why did they allow Vaughn to still keep walking around? Something wasn't right. There was *more* to it than met the eye, and she'd find out. *Somehow.* But for now, the irony was, it was her who had to watch her back. She didn't trust Harry and she didn't trust Vaughn, so a bullet in the back of her head was something she half expected.

And that's why no matter how much she didn't like it, no matter how much the things that Wan's men did made her sick to her stomach, if she wanted to stay alive the only option she'd had was to play Vaughn at his own game by seeking protection from the other side. From Wan and the Triads themselves. Not that she trusted them either, but with Alfie refusing to contact her, what else could she do?

Though it had cost her. To get Wan and his men to watch her back she'd handed over her shares in the club she'd owned along with her business contacts. She'd also agreed, or rather she'd been *forced* to agree, to work for them as well.

But more expensive than that, it had cost her her

self-respect. Grovelling apologies when she'd had to go to them begging, asking them to draw a line under what had happened to Huang. She'd been contrite, she'd agreed to their terms. She'd agreed to be someone she wasn't. And yes, she felt bitter.

All the years of power she'd had and worked hard for, worked *doubly hard* for because she was a woman and she'd had to be more ruthless, more hardened, more inflexible than the men. The loneliness and the sacrifices she'd had to make over the years. And for what? For it all to be thrown away because of Vaughn Sadler.

Well, as her father had always taught her, revenge was a dish best served cold. And if it turned out that she had to wait – one week, one month, one *year* – she would serve that dish no matter what it took. Vaughn, Harry and Wan.

Now, as she thought about Sophie, a girl who'd only been working for the gang for the past few months after coming down from up north, she hated Vaughn even more for putting her in this position – powerless, vulnerable . . . two qualities she hated nearly as much as she hated him.

She breathed in deeply again, inhaling the Soho air, gasping for breath and closing her eyes as she leant over, resting her hands on her knees.

She pushed down the feeling that she wanted to cry and instead – as she had done so many times before – she turned it into the feeling of hatred. Revenge. Payback. Feelings she'd had so much of recently. And she vowed sooner, rather than later, she'd be once again back on top. And when that time came, not one person who'd crossed her would live long enough to regret it.

3

It was already 4.30pm as Vaughn drove through the heavy traffic of Central London in silence, wondering if he looked as uncomfortable as he felt.

He'd tried not to glance in the rear-view mirror to avoid looking at Tia, who'd spent most the journey crying or trying to defend herself against Harry's constant jibes.

He couldn't believe that he'd ended up working for Harry Jacobs. He was grateful to be alive, of course, but he would rather be doing anything else than this. And there was only one person to blame for this mess he was in. Franny Doyle.

Franny had arranged for Mr Huang, Wan's brother, to have Vaughn killed, but it was Huang who was pushing up daisies. Though he hadn't killed Huang like everyone thought, he was more than happy to take the blame because Huang had actually been killed by Shannon Mulligan, who was no more than a kid, really. And an ex-junkie kid at that.

Shannon had saved his life, for no other reason than she cared for him – he'd looked out for her and put a roof over her head when no one else had. But things soon spiralled out of control and not only did Shannon end up killing her abusive uncle, she also got caught up with Huang and his men. Though in one way he would always be thankful that she did, because it was when Shannon had been working for Huang that she'd found out what Franny had been planning.

Instead of just leaving him to be set up, to be chopped up into pieces and thrown into the Thames, Shannon had come looking to warn him and had ended up driving a knife into the back of Huang's head herself to save Vaughn's life.

He'd never let on it was Shannon who'd actually killed Huang. He'd go to his grave with *that* secret.

Of course, they'd had to get away and lie low, and when they'd been hiding out in Spain, he'd wondered how he was going to make a comeback, earn money, but more importantly how he was going to live long enough to get his revenge. But then he'd run into Harry in Marbella, where they'd been holed up in a friend's villa.

Harry was someone he hadn't seen for years, someone he had a history with and someone he'd once helped get out of a tricky situation. And for all Harry was, for all Harry had done, he didn't forget a favour. So as much as he'd rather not be here working for Harry, the tables were turned and now Harry was helping *him* out of the trickiest situation he'd ever been in.

Though, in all fairness, he was surprised that Wan had

agreed to back down. He knew that Harry did business with him and they went back a fair way, but it was still saying something that Wan, who was known for being more ruthless than his brother, didn't want Vaughn's head on a plate.

With Shannon still tucked well away in Spain for now – both from the police who were looking to question her about her uncle, as well as being away from the mess that still circled around what had happened with Franny and to Huang – he could concentrate on sorting out the shit he was wading in without worrying about Shannon. And once he had, once he'd sorted everything out, there'd certainly be a happy ever after; Franny would get what was coming.

'Will you stop that fucking crying, Tia, you've done my nut in the whole journey. Poor Vaughn ain't said fuck all, cos he's probably wondering what the fuck he's got into and no doubt that bastard Wan and his gang probably seem a better bet to him right now. God knows they'd be quieter. Ain't that right, Vaughnie?' Harry's loud voice boomed around the Range Rover, cutting into Vaughn's thoughts as he pulled into a small mews just off Harley Street.

Vaughn gave a tight smile but didn't say anything, not wanting to get involved.

'You see that, Tia, Vaughn's too polite to say what a noisy cunt you've been.'

Tia stared at her husband wondering quite how she had so many tears. Harry was intolerable and she could see that he was enjoying tormenting her. She had a banging headache and the only thing that had got her through the journey was the thought of seeing her children. She was looking forward to getting out of the car and having a nice, long bath.

'Will you turn it in, Harry? Stop digging me out. You've made your point, so can you drop it?'

Roaring with laughter, Harry opened the car door after Vaughn pulled up outside the last house in the row. 'Drop it? Tia, after what you've done, I ain't even started, darlin'.'

He slammed out of the car and stalked towards the house with the pale pink front door as Tia wearily stepped out of the car. Though as she did, she quickly glanced across to Harry to make sure he wasn't looking as she spoke in a whisper to Vaughn. 'What the hell do you think you're doing?'

Vaughn stared ahead, not wanting Harry to see them talking. 'I didn't have a choice.'

'You had every choice!'

With his cheeks flushing with anger, Vaughn hissed, 'If I did, do you really think that I'd come here?'

'I dunno, Vaughn. I don't know what you'd do.'

'I was desperate.'

Grabbing her cream Prada bag, Tia snapped, 'Yeah, well we've all been that. It don't mean you needed to come here.'

With his anger getting the better of him, Vaughn swivelled around. 'If I hadn't, I would've been a dead man by now.'

'Well, it's a shame you're not.'

'*Everything all right? She ain't chewing your ear off is she mate?*' Harry's voice boomed out from the doorway of the house.

25

'No, it's fine. She just thought she'd dropped her phone!' Vaughn called back.

'*Dozy fucking cow. Just leave her to it. Come and have a drink!*'

Ignoring Harry's insults, Tia shook her head. She'd known that Vaughn had been in trouble, big trouble, but she never guessed that he would actually come and work with Harry. Leaning towards Vaughn, she hissed her words. 'I want you gone. Understand? But in the meantime, stay away from me, Vaughn. Don't talk to me. I don't want anything to do with you. You hear me? Just stay away from me.' And with that Tia Jacobs rushed into the house, crying again.

Tia's hand reached for the bathroom door just as it was abruptly swung open by a strikingly beautiful woman. Tammy Owens. It always amazed Tia how even though it was her house, with her children in it, over the past year or so it was Tammy opening the door from the inside, whilst she stood waiting to be let in, very much from the outside.

'Tia! Welcome home!' Tammy purred as she threw her arms over Tia pulling her into a steely embrace.

'Let me look at you. When Harry said you might be coming home, I couldn't believe it. Now we'll be able to catch up on all that girly gossip – it'll be like old times again. But first things first, we simply have to get you out of that hideous dress. You look like a tramp, darlin'.'

Tammy trilled with laughter, exuding the coldness that seemed always to be in her heart from her eyes. As Tia politely tried to free herself from Tammy's suffocating grip, it crossed her mind that for as long as she could remember, Tammy had always been a bitch. A bitch if she didn't get something, a bitch if she did.

They'd been close once, really close, and she would've done anything for her but Tammy had never acted like the same could be said of her. Tammy was selfish and so often mean, but Tia had always made some excuse for her behaviour.

But the real breaking point between the two of them had come last year when Tia's youngest child, Lily, who'd only just turned six, had been rushed into hospital after falling off a slide and smashing her head.

It had been touch and go for a while and the surgeons had had to rush her into surgery. She'd tried to get in contact with Harry and she'd tried to get in contact with Tammy but she hadn't been able to get in touch with either.

After a long, difficult night waiting to see if Lily would pull through, she'd come home exhausted from the hospital to get a fresh change of clothes, riding in the back of a filthy mini-cab.

She'd walked into the front room and what greeted her was a pair of size-eight La Perla knickers on the floor and a semi-clad Tammy entwined in her husband's arms. When they'd seen her standing there, Tammy had just lit a cigarette and told her how tired she looked.

And now, as Tammy stood smiling at her, Tia just shook her head. Rather than feeling anger towards her, Tia pitied her, because she was a fool if she thought that having Harry Jacobs would bring her any sort of pleasure. She knew well enough that Harry destroyed everything he came into contact with, and soon enough he'd destroy Tammy too. Yes, Tammy Owens, her *twin* sister, had a lot to learn.

4

'Where we going?' Sasha said sullenly as she looked at Wan from under her dark fringe. Immediately annoyed by the question, Wan grabbed her face, squeezing it hard so he could feel her jawbone pressing into his fingers.

He was already pissed off by what had happened to Sophie. A girl OD'ing was a pain, to say the least. Getting rid of a body was even more of one, and that wasn't even taking into account the fact they'd be a girl down now.

Still, like his brother and his father had always taught him, these girls were supposed to be disposable. Easy come, easy go. There'd always be another girl around the corner after all.

Faceless girls that nobody cared about. Runaways. Girls that no one would come looking for. Girls who'd been kicked out of their homes, girls who'd just come out of care. But the best kind of girls were the ones who'd already been abused so what he was asking of them, well, it had already become second nature to them. Oh yes, these girls were head and shoulders above the rest.

But that still didn't stop him from being irritated by the fact that Sophie had accidentally topped herself. Although she was new, the punters had clearly liked her. She was part of the latter group. Abused and unwanted, which had made it straightforward for him. A few kind words, a little bit of attention, a roof over her head and that had been basically it. It was all he'd needed to do to make her willing, willing to do whatever it was that was asked of her as long as she'd been fed some cocaine, which she'd taken to like a duck to water.

It was always helpful when they liked the taste of powder and the pills. Sophie couldn't get enough of it – clearly in hindsight *too* much of it. Unlike some of the girls who seemed to think that when he gave it to them he was trying to give them arsenic, Sophie had nostrilled it up like there was no tomorrow.

It was important that when he needed the girls to work for him they were high. That way they were loose, they didn't become frigid and tighten up, *especially* when they were being passed around a party. The last thing he needed was an uptight little bitch. It was bad for business. Plus, it helped them forget. The less they remembered, the better.

Though what he didn't like was the fact that Sophie had been the *second* girl recently who'd overdosed, and as much as they were disposable, he didn't want them falling like flies. More to the point, he was worried that the cocaine was too high a grade, too pure, though he'd been assured it wasn't, or that it was bad shit. The last thing he needed was to be letting the girls take what ironically *was* lines of arsenic.

Turning his thoughts back to Sasha, Wan growled, 'Don't question me. When I say we're going somewhere, that's all you need to know. You understand?'

Sasha, dressed in a skimpy white dress that skirted her pert bottom, nodded as she stared glassy-eyed at Wan.

'Good. Now get in the van,' said Wan as he stood surrounded by two of his henchmen in the private car park of his restaurant.

In the back of the blacked-out van, there were already two other girls sitting, spaced out on mats on the floor. Seeing Sasha hesitate, he gripped her arm, dragging her towards it. 'Get the fuck in. I haven't got time for this.'

'I . . . I . . . I just don't want to go after last time.'

Wan lunged for her, pulling her hair and twisting it around in his hand, causing her to let out a screech. He stared at her, his face inches away from hers. 'No one asked you to be here, Sasha. You're here of your own free will, remember that.'

'I know, I just don't like it, that's all. I don't like the parties. The men, they smell and, well, they're *old*.'

He continued to glare at her as he let go of her hair. 'You're not marrying them, so what's the problem?'

Sasha, who was barely five foot tall but tottering on high heels, looked up at Wan with tears in her eyes. 'I just—'

He interrupted, his cockney accent sounding stronger than normal. 'Do I put a roof over your head, Sash? Do I feed you? Let you eat in my restaurants anytime you like?

Order anything you want? Do I give you money to go out and about? To shop, to get your nails done? Even get your fucking hair extensions done?'

'Yeah.'

He took her face in his hands again, only this time, he stroked it gently. 'Well then, what's the sour look for? All I ask in return, is a few favours here and there. That's all, and that's not too much to ask, is it? My girlfriend doing me a favour . . . Tell me, Sash, who's treated you better than me?'

Sasha's green eyes stared up at him mesmerisingly. 'No one, Wan.'

'Exactly. No one. You've never had a better boyfriend than me, even your mum didn't want to know you, but I do, Sash. I want you but if *you* want, you can go back to where you came from. How about that, Sasha? Would that make you happy? You want to go back on the streets? I can take you there. I can take you back to the place I found you. Just say the word . . . Actually, let's just cut to the chase and why don't I take you back now? Save either of us any more heartache.' He began to pull her towards the gate.

'No, please! Please! I don't want to go back. Please, Wan! I'm sorry.'

He shook his head. 'But I don't think you are. I think it'd be better if you just went. No hard feelings, hey?'

'Please, please, don't make me go. I want to stay with you. I'll do it, I'll go to the party, and I won't complain, I swear. Give me another chance.'

'I'm all out of chances, Sash.'

Hysterical now, Sasha continued to beg. 'Please, please—'

'What's going on here?' Franny, her chestnut hair tied up into a ponytail, walked into the car park from the back entrance of the restaurant.

On seeing Franny, Wan dropped hold of Sasha who stood weeping quietly to herself. 'Go away, Franny, this is nothing to do with you. Just a boyfriend–girlfriend thing.'

Franny raised her eyebrows at the same time as hardening her gaze. She glanced at Sasha who looked distraught. 'Sash, sweetheart, are you all right? I've been thinking about you. I was worried.'

'I *said* this is nothing to do with you, so why don't you turn around and go and find something else to do,' Wan said.

Franny didn't move, instead she just stared at Sasha, seeing the dark circles under her eyes, and bringing down her voice, she spoke gently. 'Please, Sasha, talk to me.'

Standing under the grey London sky, tears came to Sasha's eyes and she opened her mouth to say something but it was Wan who spoke first as he turned to look at Sasha. 'Get in the fucking van . . . *Now!*'

Without hesitation, Sasha ran and stepped into the Ford transit, leaving Wan to stare at Franny with as much contempt as he could muster. His words snarled out as he pushed her hard in her chest, causing her to take a step back to hold her balance. 'Don't ever do that to me again. You hear me? You're overstepping the line these days. First back in the club and now this.'

Not showing the slightest hint of being intimidated, Franny, standing as tall as Wan, returned his stare *and* his contempt. 'All I was doing was asking how she was.'

'And I'm telling you, *not to.*'

'It was only a few hours ago that she watched her friend overdose. What the fuck is wrong with you? The girl's traumatised,' said Franny angrily.

Wan held a steady glare. 'Haven't you heard the saying, the show must go on?'

Barking out her words and feeling so much hatred towards Wan, Franny shook her head. 'This ain't a show though. You can't expect her to be okay. She's just a kid and that was her friend, Wan. She watched her friend *die* after your goon wouldn't even let her call for the ambulance.'

He shrugged. 'What can I say?'

Rolling her tongue around her mouth, Franny chuckled nastily. 'You really are something else. So what should I do, not bother when one of the girls is upset? Not bother when it's clear that Sasha's in shock?'

'That's exactly right.'

Nodding, Franny felt the surge of anger rush through her. Everything in her wanted to take her gun and shove it down his throat. But instead, she stayed still for a moment, not speaking, not moving, making sure that she was in control of her emotions before she did say anything.

Eventually, with an even tone, she asked, 'So where are you guys off to, anyway?'

Without warning, Wan slammed his hand around Franny's throat. '*Don't. Ask. Questions.*'

Then Wan stomped off towards the van, getting in it before speeding away.

Rubbing her neck, Franny closed her eyes for a moment. Anger, not pain, rushed through her veins. Yes, she'd paid for protection against Harry and Vaughn and yes, she'd had to hand over her shares to Wan and do any bit of dirty work he asked of her, but how long she could put up with it, she didn't know. If she was going to do anything about it, she needed help.

Pulling out her phone, Franny dialled the ever-familiar number and spoke to the ever-familiar voicemail. 'Alf, hey, Alfie, it's me. Call me back. *Please*. We need to talk. *I* need to talk.'

Putting the phone back in her pocket, Franny decided that although she'd made some stupid mistakes in her life, none were as stupid as allowing Wan to make an enemy of her.

5

Standing in the bedroom of his friend's large, luxurious flat situated on the banks of the River Thames, with stunning views of both Tower Bridge and the Tower of London, Alfie Jennings listened to the message from his on-off lover Franny Doyle and, as was his habit, he threw his mobile across the room. The phone crashed against the wall where it fell on the bed, waking up the hooker he'd had his friend send over to him last night.

'Bloody hell, Alf, what happened to a gentle wake-up kiss?'

'What happened to a silent whore?'

The hooker, who'd known Alfie for the past ten years, shrugged, clearly not taking offence. 'What's ruffled your feathers this morning?' she said laughing. 'And for your information, if you want me to keep my mouth shut, it'll cost you another fifty quid.'

He rolled his eyes at her. 'Do me a favour, Jan, just shut the fuck up. I'm happy to pay you a bull's-eye for some peace.'

He sighed and broke open the new bottle of whiskey, pouring it generously into a crystal glass.

'Alfie, why don't you come and take some lines with me, relax a little.'

He turned around and stared at Jan. 'I thought you were going to shut your mouth.'

She shrugged and giggled. 'You never used to be such a grouch. Come on, let's have some fun.'

Alfie stared at the cut-up lines of cocaine on the cream Ralph Lauren nightstand. He could almost taste it, almost feel the burn in his nose, and he could almost hear it calling his name. After the last couple of years of indulging to excess, he was trying to knock it on the head. Or at least cut down on it. But that didn't mean he wasn't tempted and it certainly didn't help his cause that Jan was noisily snorting it up.

'Drop me out, Jan, and if I were you and wanted to get paid at all, I'd stop chewing my fucking ear off.' And with that, Alfie shot one last angry glance at the lines of coke, took a huge swig of whiskey and stepped outside onto the balcony, feeling the drips of water run down his handsome face from where he hadn't bothered to dry his hair after his shower.

With the cold air somewhat taking away the urge to snort some gear, absentmindedly watching a tugboat on the river, Alfie thought of Franny. In actual fact, she was the only thing he could think of. No matter what he did

– even when he was getting his dick sucked by some whore or having a threesome – Franny was the only thing on his mind. And since he'd met her all those years ago, it had always been the same.

In the messages she'd left for him, he could hear the tone in her voice and he knew her well enough to realise that she was struggling. What with, exactly, he wasn't sure, though from a good source he knew she was somehow caught up with Wan. But he was damned if he was going to come running, playing a knight in shining armour. After all, she had fucked him over. She had fucked everyone over, come to think of it.

Franny had not only set Vaughn up, she had set *him* up by giving him no alternative than to do her dirty work.

Last year his daughter, Mia, had been kidnapped and he and Franny had gone looking for her and it had taken them down a very dark road. He'd thought that Mia had been taken by a paedophile ring and whilst they'd been searching, they'd come across a little boy who was about to be auctioned off to the worst kind of human beings. Worse still, the boy's own father had been part of the sale.

And of course, once he knew about the boy there'd been no way he could've left the kid; he could never have that on his conscience. But he'd also known the sort of money that the boy was going for, being young and innocent – fresh meat, as they called it – was the sort of money he didn't have to hand. His business hadn't been doing great, *especially* after Franny had taken two million quid of his money. Though he knew that was another story entirely, one he didn't want to think about now.

The bottom line was he'd needed nearly half a million pounds quickly so, foolishly, he'd gone to Wan's brother for a loan. A loan that had interest written in blood on it.

He knew that when he'd gone there. He knew that he was putting his life on the line for it when he'd asked Huang, knowing that getting the money was the easy part. The hard part was paying him back in time. But what else could he have done? And looking back, if it meant saving the boy, he would do the same thing all over again.

Afterwards, after it was all over, he'd asked Franny for help. For money to pay Huang back. But she'd pretended her money was untouchable. All tied up in trusts, which she couldn't access. That had turned out to be bullshit. And he'd found out it was bullshit too late.

In effect, what Franny had done was play him. She'd been desperate for him to do her dirty work, something he wouldn't normally agree to. But she'd told him that if he did help her she'd somehow help him find the money for Huang.

In truth, she'd already paid off his loan to Huang. Paid it to stop Huang slashing his throat and cutting him up in pieces. Behind his back, she shelled out almost three-quarters of a million pounds to Huang, which had been his original debt of half a million pounds plus the exorbitant amount of interest Huang charged. Though no part of him felt he needed to be grateful; after all she'd only done it to keep him alive.

But not because she loved him. Oh no, he didn't think that the ice queen was capable of that. She'd kept him alive merely because it was convenient for her. She needed him to get her out of a mess and let's face it, dead men weren't much good at that.

Dangling the carrot of helping him with the loan had kept him on his toes, because at one time, he wouldn't have cared. He would've taken his chances with Huang, cos bottom line, that was the business they were in. Kill or be killed. At one time even, he thought he was lucky to get to forty without having had a bullet in his head. But his attitude to all that had changed since he found out he had a daughter. And Franny had known that; she'd known he'd do anything to stay alive, even being her puppet.

So yes, that had given her power over him. Gave her the power of making him think that if he refused her requests she wouldn't help him, which ultimately meant he was a dead man. So, she'd thrown him a bone and he'd snapped at it like a fucking mug, not knowing that once again Franny was playing him.

She'd even insisted on him trying to set Vaughn up. Not that Vaughn hadn't deserved it, because after everything they'd been through, for Vaughn to try to bring Franny down was against every rule in their books. Not that he necessarily wanted Vaughn to have a bullet in his head, a punishment gangland style, maybe, but he'd never wanted him dead.

Though he knew as far as Vaughn was concerned, because Alfie had sided with Franny, he and Vaughn were now enemies too.

So no, fucking no, he wasn't going to go running to help her, he wasn't going to pick up the pieces cos he'd been fucked over by her too many times, and not only that, he'd also had his heart broken by her too many times. He was best off away from her. She was like a black widow spider; she devoured her mates. So, for all he cared, Franny Doyle could go to hell.

So why, then, was he here in London? Why the fuck had he jumped on a plane and left his daughter with her nanny if he didn't care? Why, when he'd known she was in trouble despite everything she'd done to him, would he bother to be on hand if she really needed him?

Taking another large sip of his glass of whiskey, Alfie continued to stare at the river, gritting his teeth as he drank it down, not because of the bitter taste – no, it was quality stuff, smooth and velvety – oh no, the only thing that was bitter was him, because he knew only too well why he was here. He knew why he'd come back to London. He loved her. It was as simple as that.

And no matter how much he tried not to love such a manipulative, cold, conniving, heartless bitch, he couldn't help it. She was under his skin and God, he hated her and loved her in equal measure for it. Though this time loving her wasn't going to make him go charging in and pick up her pieces.

He was here, in London, without anyone knowing, and that was enough for now. Maybe she'd never know that he'd come. But if she *really*, *really* needed him he was close enough. After all, she could hold her own, though ultimately he wasn't going to let anyone hurt her; that was his job and his job alone. Whether he liked it or not, whether he'd tried to break away from her or not, and no matter how many whores he fucked, he was a one-woman man and Franny *was* his woman.

He was the one who had spent the last few years loving her and hating her, so if anyone was going to kill her, it was him. That was *his* prerogative. But he couldn't kill her, no matter how much he wanted to, so that meant no one else could either. That meant if they wanted to kill her, they would have to kill him first.

But for now, he would just wait and watch . . .

6

Tia heard her husband's breath before she saw him in the dark of the large, cream-coloured bedroom, and as she felt his touch, she tried to roll away.

'Stop playing games, Tia. You're my wife for fuck's sake.'

Sitting up in bed, Tia switched the bedside lamp on and stared at her husband. Her long, blonde hair tumbling in waves over her shoulder. 'Let's have it right, Harry. I'm your wife in name only. I ain't here cos I want to be – we both know that, so why don't you just go back to your room and get cosy with my sister.'

Harry's mouth curled up into a sneer. 'What do you expect, if you won't give it out? I'm a man, Tia, and I've got needs.'

Raising her eyebrows and wondering what she ever saw in him, Tia snapped angrily, 'What I expect, Harry, is for you not to screw my twin sister. It's hardly much to ask, is it?'

'You make it sound like I forced her. Your sister couldn't get her knickers off fast enough. She was gagging for it. I was only doing her a favour.'

'No, Harry, you wanted to play games like you've always done. Admit it; you get off on hurting me, don't you? I mean, when I found out about you and Tammy, you hated the fact that I didn't kick off and give you the reaction you'd hoped for. So you had to go one better and move her in, didn't you?'

'She means nothing to me. I don't want her, it's you I want.'

'You amaze me, you know that? What do you do, Harry, get Tammy to lie there looking like me but saying nothing, so you can pretend she *is* me? You're one sick fuck, you know that?'

Grabbing her roughly, Harry slapped Tia hard across the face. She squealed in pain as she felt the blood from her nose trickle into her mouth. With tears in her eyes, she shook her head. 'Is this why you brought me back, so you can knock me around?'

'I brought you back cos you wanted to be with your kids and besides, this is where you belong. You ain't going anywhere, Tia. And if you do, you'll never see your children again. So, take that miserable look off of your face and get used to it. I love you, Tia. You just got to start behaving, that's all.' He leant in for a kiss but she pulled away and, breathing hard, Harry said, 'Stop being such a cock tease.'

He pulled her towards him and she tried to push him off but the sheer power of his body on top of her made it impossible for her to move. 'Get off me, Harry, just get off me!'

Pushing his hand hard over Tia's mouth, Harry used the other one to rip her lace knickers off, the elastic tearing into her flesh as they ripped around her thighs.

Feeling she couldn't breathe properly, Tia panicked and thrashed her legs about, fighting to get him off. He whispered gruffly in her ear, 'Stop pushing me away! I want to make love to you. Maybe if you learnt not to be so uptight you'd enjoy it more.'

She felt the force of him entering her and it sent a searing pain throughout her whole body. He thrust deeper and harder inside her, growling inaudible words into her ear as he took his hand off her mouth only to put it tightly round her throat, gripping it to the point of her feeling she was going to black out. Then, within moments, as the sweat poured down Harry's face, he groaned loudly before rolling off Tia.

Propping himself up on his elbow, he stared at her, moving her hair away from her eyes.

'For fuck's sake, Tia, you don't have to look like that. Do you know how many women would love to be in your position? Come on, darlin', don't do this to me . . . just give me a kiss, will you?'

She turned her face away as she felt Harry get up from the bed. 'You're one cold bitch, Tia, but until you realise that, nothing's going to change . . . Oh, and by the way, I forgot to tell you that tomorrow and from here on out, you're going to have your own little babysitter.'

Tia spun around to look at Harry, who was now standing by the door of their bedroom.

'What are you talking about?'

'I'm talking about not being able to trust you and because I can't watch you every minute of the day, I've got someone else. Vaughn.'

'No, you can't. Harry, I ain't having Vaughn around.'

Harry gave a tight smile before walking back over to Tia and kissing her on the top of her head. 'You'll have whoever the fuck I say looking after you, and if you don't like it or if you try anything, you'll be sorry.'

7

The next day – a Thursday afternoon – Selfridges on Oxford Street seemed busier and hotter than ever as Vaughn trudged around carrying a multitude of shopping bags. Feeling trickles of sweat running down his back, he muttered to himself, cursing Harry who'd asked him, or rather *told* him that his job for the next couple of weeks was to keep an eye on Tia.

That was bad enough but becoming her new skivvy, lugging about designer shoes and knickers, was taking the absolute piss. It was a joke. A fucking joke. What kind of muppet Harry had him down as, Vaughn didn't know, but playing keeper to his missus certainly wasn't in any of his job descriptions.

'I need to go and try this on.'

Vaughn sighed loudly, letting his irritation show and be heard, though he didn't look Tia directly in the face. He wanted to avoid doing that for several reasons, but mainly because he didn't want to see the fresh, angry bruise on her cheek, which hadn't been there yesterday.

Knocking women about wasn't and would never be his thing, and even being around it made him feel uncomfortable. But the problem was, Harry was handy with his fists when it came to men or women, and there wasn't much Vaughn could do about it, not if he wanted to stay alive.

For now he needed Harry way more than Harry needed him and knowing that made him feel shit and angry in equal measures.

Taking his frustration out on Tia, Vaughn growled, 'Do you have to, Tia? We've been trudging about most of the day. How many dresses does anyone need?'

Staring at him and noticing that he wouldn't look at her, Tia shrugged her shoulders. 'And you wonder why you're single.'

Chewing on his lip, probably to stop himself exploding, Vaughn shook his head furiously as he glanced round at the various shoppers, his handsome face lined with stress. 'No, Tia, I don't and I'm single because I *choose* to be, cos I don't ever want to have to do this shit. This sensitive, new-age guy that goes shopping, for manicures, pedicures and any other fucking cure you lot do. Just drop me out, darlin' . . . Now come on, let's go.'

Holding the Attico zebra-printed dress in her hand, Tia – although feeling miserable after what had happened with Harry last night – laughed warmly. She stood in front of Vaughn and gave him no choice *but* to look at her. 'You don't change, do you?'

'No, and I ain't got any intentions to either. I'm happy as I am, now come on. The sooner I get out of this fucking place, the better.'

He turned, heading towards the escalators but Tia began to walk in the other direction.

'Well wait outside for me then.'

Fuming at how things had spiralled to this point, Vaughn marched back across to Tia. 'I told you that you don't need another dress.'

'Vaughn, I don't like this any more than you do. Like I told you yesterday, I'd rather you not speak to me or be around me for that matter. Yes, Harry has made you my keeper so neither of us have much choice, but that don't mean you can tell me what I can or can't buy.'

Gazing down at her, Vaughn could feel the pulse in his temple throbbing. 'I ain't telling you that, I'm telling you that you're not going into the changing rooms to try it on.'

'Fine, I'll do it here then.' Holding Vaughn's stare, Tia took off her jacket before beginning to unbutton her shirt at which point, grabbing her arm not too roughly, Vaughn pulled her towards the changing rooms. 'Okay, you win. Go on, just hurry up. But I'm warning you, Tia, don't mess me about.'

Inside the changing rooms Tia sat down on the bench, feeling the grey, luxury carpet under her feet. She stared at herself in the mirror under the harsh glare of the lights, seeing the worry lines around her eyes.

She still hadn't seen the kids – Harry had made sure of that. They hadn't been at home when she'd come back from court as they'd been staying with Harry's mother, and even though he'd promised that he'd bring them back in the morning so she could take them to school, he'd broken his promise as usual.

Everything was a game. Harry's game. But one day, she knew that Harry's game would be over because she'd promised herself she'd make sure that sometime soon he'd be speaking his last words. And *that* would be a promise that certainly wouldn't be broken.

Suddenly her phone beeped, breaking her out of her thoughts. She pulled it out of her pocket and saw that it was a text.

Can you come around? I need to see you.

Texting back, Tia wrote:

Give me half an hour. I'll see what I can do.

Making sure that the text had gone through, Tia quickly deleted it before pushing her phone back into her pocket. She got up and headed out of the cubicle where at the entrance of the changing rooms she could see Vaughn standing impatiently waiting for her.

Moving back out of sight, Tia leant on the slate-grey wall of the changing room and tried to think. There was no way she could sneak out without being seen and there was certainly no way she was going to tell Vaughn where she was going.

Suddenly, an idea came to her and she turned to the tall,

pretty assistant who rather than putting the clothes back on the hangers was texting on her phone.

'That man out there is hassling me. I'm worried to go back out. Can you call security, please?'

The assistant looked up from her phone and smiled sympathetically at Tia before glancing across to Vaughn discreetly. 'The one in the Barbour jacket?'

Still staying out of sight, Tia nodded. 'Yeah, that's him. Just tell them that he's been bothering me.'

'No problem. They shouldn't be long.' The assistant picked up the walkie-talkie on her desk with her perfectly manicured fingers, and set about radioing security.

Ten minutes later, Vaughn, full of hostility at having been accosted by two large security men, stared at them. 'What the fuck are you talking about? I'm waiting here for someone, so if I were you I'd get your fucking hands off me, mate.'

'I'm sorry, sir, but we've had a complaint.'

'I'm telling you, you've got the wrong fucking person,' Vaughn snarled.

'There's no need to swear and I'd appreciate it, sir, if you kept your voice down.'

'And I'd appreciate it if you weren't such a cunt. Now get off my arm, otherwise . . . *Oi, Tia! Where you going? Tia! Is this down to you? Are these two jokers to do with you! Tia! Tia!'* he shouted angrily across the store as he noticed Tia darting towards the escalators. '*Tia, I'm talking to you. Come back! Don't try and pretend you didn't hear me! Tia! Tia! Don't you fucking go anywhere! You hear me! Tia!'*

Looking over her shoulder as she hurried down the escalator, Tia saw Vaughn getting into a scuffle with the security guards as he tried to break away from them.

She sighed, knowing that ditching Vaughn was one more thing she had to worry about, though the main problem now was how the hell she was going to explain this to Harry . . .

8

Wan Huang cut a line of cocaine with the edge of his Amex black card. He leant forward on the mahogany wooden chair and smiled, his handsome face lighting up as he stared intently. 'Here you go. It's yours.'

Smiling back, the girl dressed in a tight black jumpsuit giggled as she took another sip of vodka from the plastic tumbler. 'I don't know, I've never had any before.'

Wan's eyes twinkled. 'Then this is your time to try some. Come on, Shelby, there's nothing to it.'

A glint of hurt passed over her face. 'My name's not Shelby. It's Ellie.'

Standing up, Wan's shoes squeaked on the sticky, beige lino floor as he walked towards her. He kissed her gently on her neck and ran his fingers through her shoulder-length dyed red hair. Then, feigning innocence at the same time as thinking that he didn't care less what her name was, he winked. 'What do you take me for, hey? Of course I know it's Ellie, I was only joking.'

Glancing up at him, Ellie looked hurt. 'Why do you do that to me? It's not funny.'

Wan shook his head. 'You need to have more of a sense of humour.'

'I don't see the joke in forgetting me name.'

Ruffling her hair, Wan laughed. 'Oh come on, Ellie, how could I forget it? We've been seeing each other for a while now, haven't we? If I didn't know your name by now, I think that would make me a pretty rotten boyfriend, don't you?'

Hearing the word *boyfriend*, Ellie visibly glowed with happiness. 'I guess it would.'

'So come on then, what do you say – why don't you take a couple of lines, help you relax?'

Pouting her full red lips, Ellie shook her head. 'I ain't into drugs; you know that. Not powder, anyway. I don't mind them pills you give me and I don't mind alcohol either, but not that, especially after what happened to Sophie.'

Wan raised his eyebrows. 'She's nothing to do with you.'

'I know but . . .'

'But nothing, El. How many times have I told you not to listen to rumours? If you must know Sophie was too greedy. She liked to do everything in excess. I'm not asking you to do that, I'm asking you just to have a little fun with me, for fuck's sake. That's all.'

'I don't know.'

Wan nodded as he glanced out of the window of the small, grubby flat above the Golden Dragon Chinese takeaway in Brewer Street, a place his family had owned for the past eighteen years.

Ellie was becoming hard work and from what she'd told him about her background, he was genuinely surprised at how unwilling she was to just roll over and please. Most girls like her were easy, like putty in his hands, but for some reason Ellie was different, and from what he had heard she was also quite jealous of him giving attention to the other girls. Which made it even more frustrating that she didn't just sit up and beg when he told her to.

Picking up his jacket he sighed and nodded. 'No problem, Ellie. If you're not interested in having a bit of fun, that's okay. I'm not going to force you, am I; you know I'm not like that. Your choice. Always. Listen, just let yourself out when you're ready. There's no rush.'

He headed for the door and although he didn't let Ellie see, he smirked when she called after him.

'Wait, Wan! Where are you going? I thought we were going to spend the afternoon together?'

He turned around, putting on his best sympathetic smile. His dark brown eyes, twinkling. 'I think it's best if we don't. I can see that you're uncomfortable with the whole thing and I'm not into making you feel awkward.'

Ellie, just like Sasha had earlier, shook her head and rushed across to him, her big green eyes full of vulnerability. 'I'm *not* uncomfortable. I love being with you. It's just that I don't want to do powder, that's all.'

Wan held her gaze, knowing *exactly* how to play it. Play her. After all, he'd played this game with dozens of other girls before.

He took her face gently into his hands and kissed her again, this time on the lips. Long and sensual. 'Look, I don't know what sort of boyfriends you've had in the past but I'm not going to force you to do anything you don't want to. I love the fact that you've got your own mind. You should never let anyone push you into anything.'

Ellie's eyes filled with tears, her pretty face crumpling up. 'None of them have been like you. They've just treated me like shit.'

Wrapping his arms around her, he held her tight, then drew her away and spoke in a hush. 'And it makes me sick to hear that. You didn't deserve that. And that's why I don't want you to do this. I don't want to be like the rest of the men in your life.'

'They weren't men. They were boys, not like you. You make me feel safe,' Ellie said in a rush of panic.

'I'm glad to hear it, but I think we should just be friends. We can still hang out, do stuff together, but in all honesty, you're probably a bit young for me anyway.' Then pretending he'd forgotten, Wan added, 'How old are you again?'

'Fifteen.'

'That makes me feel well old. I'm almost eleven years older.'

Ellie shrugged. 'But that's okay. I don't mind. I like it.'

Wan turned again for the door. 'It's not though. I keep forgetting your age cos you act so maturely. Of course you don't want to take a line of coke. I get it. I'm just so used to dating someone my own age who wouldn't think twice about taking a few lines. To them it would be no big deal;

taking a few lines of coke is just the same as having a drink . . . I'm sorry, okay?'

Ellie's voice was filled with desperation. 'I don't want you to be sorry, you ain't done anything. I don't even know why I'm making such a big deal out of it . . . Look.' She hurried across to the small, wooden table where the lines of cocaine sat.

'I don't know if you should,' Wan said, as he absentmindedly touched his short, black, gelled hair.

'Well I do. I was just being stupid. Come on, give me another chance. *Please.*'

Taking out a ten-pound note from his pocket, Wan began rolling it up. 'If you're sure, cos I'd hate it if you were only doing it for me . . . but then, I guess it would be nice to spend the afternoon together.'

'Yeah it would and I want to do this. You're not forcing me to do anything,' Ellie said with a smile on her face.

Laughing warmly, Wan shrugged. 'Well in that case, just snort it up through that.'

Without saying anything, Ellie took the rolled-up ten-pound note from Wan then proceeded to bend over the lines where she snorted one after the other. As Wan watched her he saw her eyes roll back. 'What do you think, Ellie? You like it?'

But Ellie didn't answer. She staggered across the room, holding on to the table and then to the chairs and the words that did try to come out sounded garbled and incoherent. A moment later she dropped to the floor.

Wan stared at her and smiled. He kicked her side to see if there was any response. There was nothing. It always amazed him at how fast the ketamine he'd secretly cut into the cocaine worked. It was a matter of seconds before they collapsed into an almost catatonic state. Not that having a girl almost comatose was to everyone's taste, but for what he wanted now, it did the trick nicely.

Leaving Ellie on the floor, he walked out of the small lounge, taking his phone out of his pocket as he did so. He dialled a number and almost immediately it was answered. 'She's spark out now, you can bring him up.'

As he made his way down the stairs, a small, fat Turkish man in his mid-sixties walked up and met Wan who nodded, and without bothering to stop continued on down the stairs as he barked out his instructions. 'You've got fifteen minutes. I don't want you making any marks on her face or her body. Nothing too rough – you got that? But anything else, enjoy yourself. I'll see you in a bit . . . Oh, and no photos of her either.'

Outside in the fresh air, Wan's phone rang in his hand. He looked at it and saw it was Franny. The last thing he wanted to do was speak to her. She was asking too many questions and just the way she looked at him made him feel uncomfortable. The less she knew the better because he hadn't quite decided what he was going to do with her yet.

For the time being though he'd just get her to look after running the clubs and the girls, because he had to give it to her, she was good at that. Profits were up since she'd taken over running things. The promotions she ran and her overall knowledge of the club game made her an asset, at least for the time being. Because as much as he'd made a deal with her, a good, lucrative deal for *him* anyway, and a promise to protect her, he had a feeling that Franny Doyle might spell trouble. And if that turned out to be the case, well, he wouldn't hesitate to get rid of her. After all, promises were just there to be broken.

9

At the same time as Wan was having a cigarette outside the Golden Dragon, a few streets away Tia hurried down Shaftesbury Avenue.

She touched the large, red bruise on her cheek and winced. She was sick of it, sick of being a punching bag for her old man, but what other choice did she have for now?

Life was bad enough with Harry without her sister Tammy adding to the mix. But for all that Tammy was, she didn't blame her. Tammy had suffered just as much growing up in the abusive care home as she had, and Tia supposed that her sister behaving the way she did was her way of surviving. Though she hoped one day that they could put everything behind them and just start again.

Sighing, she pulled out a packet of cigarettes from her jacket pocket and dashed across the road.

'Look where you're fucking going, will ya?' An irate cab driver leant out of his window, waving his fist at Tia but, ignoring him, she lit the cigarette and continued to hurry along the street, feeling her mobile phone buzzing in her pocket.

She had no doubt it was Vaughn and without bothering to even think about answering it, she rushed down Wardour Street, weaving in and out of all the milling tourists.

At the corner of St Anne's Court, Tia curled up her nose at the smell of urine, jumping over a pool of vomit as she arrived at the entrance to a block of flats.

Seeing the silver buzzer covered with dirt and specks of blood, she used her knuckles to press it, speaking into the intercom breathlessly. 'It's me.'

A moment later the door was opened and Tia made her way slowly up the rubbish-strewn stairs, trying not to inhale the stench of alcohol and dirt.

Panting and feeling her phone constantly vibrating, Tia – too scared to look to see if it was Harry calling as well as Vaughn – walked to the end door, which was covered in graffiti.

She knocked softly, calling out at the same time. 'Only me.'

The door was immediately opened by a young girl who smiled, her hazel eyes twinkling as she spoke. 'Hi, Mum, thanks for coming.'

Immediately, Tia wrapped her arms around her oldest daughter, hating the fact that it was here, in this filthy block of bedsits, that she had to come and visit her. 'No problem, darlin', you know I'm always here for you, Milly,'

Tia said as she took off her jacket and cream cashmere scarf.

Giving her mum a half-smile, Milly threw herself back down on the second-hand, tatty brown couch. 'I'm surprised he let you out.'

Not wanting to think about the grief she'd get once Harry knew that she'd given Vaughn the slip, Tia forced another smile. 'He's not all bad.'

Silence fell between Milly and Tia with them both knowing what Tia had said was a lie.

'He's bad enough to do that to your face, ain't he?' Milly said as she finished off the satsuma she'd been eating.

Automatically, Tia touched the bruise on her cheek. 'It wasn't him, I banged into—'

Interrupting, Milly, worried and upset for her mum, spoke angrily. 'Stop, Mum! Stop trying to cover for him. The only thing you banged into was his fist. I don't know who you're trying to mug off – yourself or me?'

'Mills, come on.' Tia reached out for her daughter but Milly quickly snatched her hand away.

'Enough, Mum, you know what a pig he is. I hate him and it's not just because he threw me out.'

Taking off her jacket, Tia stared at her daughter. 'Problem was, Mills, you gave him the excuse he was looking for. Always out partying, hanging out with right wrong 'uns.'

'Yeah well it was better than coming home to him.'

'Oh, Mills, it wasn't that bad,' Tia said, knowing that was just wishful thinking.

Milly shook her head, her long blonde hair, so similar to her mother's, dropping over her eyes. She bit her lip not wanting to cry, not wanting to upset her mother either. 'It was and you know it was . . . And anyway, he was always going to kick me out when I turned sixteen.'

Frustrated at the fact that what her daughter was saying was true – after all, Harry had threatened it so often everyone knew where they stood – Tia turned her anger for Harry onto her daughter.

'Yeah, but like I say, you didn't have to go and make it easier for him, did you? Fuck's sake, Milly, why play into his hands? Why stay out late? Why get yourself into trouble?'

'Cos that's what teenagers do, Mum. They go out.'

'Yeah well, maybe if you hadn't—'

'If I hadn't, every night I would've had to stay around listening to him treat you like dirt and watch him sleep with anything that moves just to wind you up. So, *my bad* for not wanting to be around for that, Mum,' Milly said sarcastically.

'Mills, all I'm saying is if you hadn't done what you did, who knows – things might've been different.'

Milly's eyes filled with the tears she tried not to show. 'Oh, that's right, I forgot, it's my fault he dragged me out of the house by the hair. But thanks, Mum, thanks for being on my side.'

Hating to be reminded of that day, Tia went over to switch on the kettle. She felt so inadequate, so useless and certainly so undeserving to have such wonderful kids. She'd let them all down, but especially Milly.

Milly had always been the butt of Harry's anger and spiteful words, and although she'd tried to protect her, she knew Milly had not only been unhappy a lot of the time, she'd also been frightened.

She'd longed to give her kids what she didn't have, but simply put, she'd failed. And the final blow had come three days after Milly's sixteenth birthday, when Harry had *literally* kicked Milly out.

Although it had happened six months ago, the painful memory of seeing her daughter begging and pleading with Harry not to turn her out made it feel like it'd happened only yesterday. And it'd been *that*, not Tammy moving in, not the constant cheating and not the way he treated Tia, which had made her move out of the house and try to win custody of her other kids.

At the time she'd managed to take out a few thousand pounds from the various safes in the house as well as money from the bank before Harry had realised and put a stop on all her cards. Most of the money had soon gone on legal fees, for all the good that had done, as well as on hotels, so she hadn't even been able to help Milly as she'd have liked to and now this filthy bedsit was where Milly had to call home. Even now, if Harry found out about Milly living here or the fact that Tia was still in contact with her, she was certain somehow Harry would run Milly out of town.

Tia turned and looked at her daughter. 'Sweetheart, I love you so much and you know I'm on your side. I'll do anything for you.'

'Then get me out of this place. I hate it and I hate being around here. I hate this area, Mum.'

'Why? I mean, I understand why you'd want to get out of this place but Soho's all right, isn't it?'

Milly shook her head, not wanting to go into it so instead she said, 'I just hate it, that's all. Please, Mum, just get me out of here.'

Turning away from her daughter to stop Milly seeing *her* tears, Tia nodded as she made the tea. 'I am, I'm trying, babe. I promise. I promise somehow I'll get you out.'

It was a moment before Milly said warmly, 'I know you will, Mum, and I'm sorry. I know you're trying.'

Wiping the tears from her eyes, Tia picked up the mug of tea and took it to her daughter. She passed it to her, smiling. 'So anyway, how are you doing? You're looking really well.'

'I'm looking really pregnant.'

Bending down to touch her daughter's large, round tummy, Tia nodded. 'Well it's not long now and I can't wait to meet him or her.' She stood back up, trying to hide her worry. Because as much as she wanted to support her daughter and be fully there for her, she hated to admit it but this baby had already caused trouble and she was certain it was going to cause a whole lot more.

10

Like a lithe feline, Tammy stretched out naked on her sister's bed and lit a cigarette as she looked around the plush bedroom, wondering how her sister could have so little respect for herself.

Whenever Tammy thought of Tia she saw her as someone who was weak. Someone pitiful. She was one of life's doormats, letting Harry treat her the way he did. And in her mind the only person to blame was Tia herself.

In all the time Harry and Tia had been together, she'd never put her foot down when it came to the way he treated her. Right from the beginning of their relationship, Harry had cheated and lied, humiliated her and been easy with his fists. And from what she could see, her sister had either just turned a blind eye or had to cover a bruised one. Tia's need for security, for a life away from the streets, surpassed everything else.

But men didn't like weakness and in her opinion Tia didn't deserve to have a man like Harry if she didn't know how to handle him. He was powerful and yes, he was difficult and arrogant but he deserved a strong woman by his side to complement him, not a snivelling, ungrateful cow like her sister.

After all, Harry had thrown money at her sister, given her every luxury she'd wanted. He'd spoilt her and Tia still couldn't see how lucky she was. All she'd done was sit in her own silent misery. No wonder he'd treated Tia like he had done. No wonder Harry had come to seek her out and unlike Tia, she'd shown him how a woman should treat a man.

However, when it came to her kids, Tia was a different woman. She was a lioness. She would do anything for them. And if Tammy thought about it, she'd guess that was the main reason Tia was still here.

The idea of her children being pushed from pillar to post, going from one shabby place to another – like they'd done when they were kids before eventually being taken into care – was something she knew that Tia wouldn't ever contemplate.

So, whilst all the time Harry had treated the kids well, Tia had been willing to stay and put up with anything Harry threw at her. But when things had taken a turn for the worse, and Harry had kicked out Tia's oldest daughter, Milly, then finally Tia had tried to stand up to Harry. Though it was too little, too late.

Harry had wiped the floor with her and when Tia had walked out, Tammy had been sure that Harry would never forgive her. She'd been sure that Harry would never want to lay his eyes on her sister again and she'd thought that over time Harry would've forgotten about her completely. But she'd been wrong. So wrong. Because weakness was weakness and, predictably, her sister had come crawling back to Harry.

And it hurt. It bloody well hurt that once again Tia was the one who'd come out on top. And Tammy *hated* her for it. She hated the fact that Harry wanted someone as pathetic, someone as weak as Tia instead of her.

Oh yes, Tia may look identical to her, but when it came down to their personalities, they were as far apart as a spider was to a fly and if she had anything to do with it, not too far in the future, Tia would be gone again, but this time *permanently*.

'What the fuck are you doing?' Harry stood at the door staring with total contempt at Tammy.

Taking a long drag of the cigarette, Tammy pouted out her full red lips. 'Waiting for you.'

'In my wife's room? Get the fuck out.'

Tammy flinched at the words, smarting at the fact that Harry wasn't pleased to see her. Though of course she didn't show it; she just smiled seductively. 'Harry, baby, come on, let me help you unwind.'

Incensed, Harry ran towards her, dragging her off the bed by her long, blonde-streaked hair. His face twisted up in rage. '*This is my wife's room!* I don't want you in here. Understand? You may think this is some kind of joke, you little slut, and you may think it's okay to wind up your sister, but don't you fucking dare try to wind up me. You understand?'

Holding on to his hands to try to stop him pulling her hair so hard, Tammy nodded and gave a tiny squeal as the pain ripped through her head.

'Okay, good, I'm glad we've got that sorted and if I find you in here again, I won't be responsible for my actions. Understand?' He let Tammy go, pushing her across the floor where she fell into a heap, and he stared at her hard.

Looking at Tammy of course made Harry think of Tia, which in turn made him feel angry.

Since Tia had come home yesterday, she'd been more distant with him than ever before, and that was saying something.

He was under no illusions and knew that Tia wouldn't be within a mile of him if it wasn't for the kids. When he looked at her, he could see the cold hatred in her eyes and the unhappiness that exuded from her. But what was he supposed to do? He'd tried with her, given her everything and still she was a cold-hearted bitch towards him. Yet she still had a way of getting under his skin. She always had done.

And it wasn't just because she was his wife and in his eyes that meant forever or at least until he said so. It was more than that, so much more. She had a hold on him. He'd asked himself many a time why he didn't just let her go, and each time he came up with the same answer, *he couldn't*.

He just couldn't let her go because he wanted her. Every minute of every hour of every day he wanted her, and he hated her for it. Hated the fact that she was right there in his head.

It wasn't just her beauty. He knew that because her sister had the same face, the same nose, the same-shaped body but unlike Tia, Tammy meant nothing to him. She was just a bit of sport.

Taking Tammy as a lover, he thought it might have broken the spell Tia had unknowingly had over him but instead it'd only made it worse. It'd fucked with his head seeing the face and body of Tia without her actually being there.

And when Tia had actually found out he was sleeping with her sister, she hadn't said anything. She hadn't kicked off at all, which had made him want to hurt her all the more. He'd wanted her to scream and shout and show him she cared but all she'd done was look at him with even more contempt.

Even when she'd come home from court yesterday and found that he'd moved Tammy in, she still hadn't reacted, and it pissed him off to no end. He wanted to get under Tia's skin as much as she got under his; he wanted her to suffer like he did. And he did. He suffered because he hated her and was captivated by her in equal measures, which in turn gave way to an all-consuming jealousy, which was why he needed to know where Tia was at all times.

The thought of any other man even looking at her made him want to kill someone. It made him irrational with anger which, ironically, was directed at Tia. Though it wasn't as if she didn't deserve suspicion. It wasn't as if she was purely innocent. Oh no, his wife was a slippery cow and she certainly couldn't be trusted.

He hadn't known anything about her plan to walk out on him until it actually happened, though looking back all the signs had been there. She'd disappear for hours on end and when he questioned her about where she'd been she was evasive. For some reason he couldn't explain now, he'd just let her get on with it, never imagining she'd be brave enough to do anything stupid.

And the only reason Tia was still breathing, still alive today, was because she left him not for another man, but to fight some silly battle she could never win, and he could just about forgive her for that. *Just about.* Because if she *had* left him for another man, that would be an entirely different matter. She knew there'd be no hiding place for her then because however long it took, he'd find her, fuck her, and finish her. After all, she was *his* wife and in his eyes that meant doing what he wanted with her.

Having wound himself up, Harry – leaving Tammy on the floor – angrily stalked out of the bedroom as he pulled his mobile out of his pocket. He dialled a number but it went straight to voicemail. Then almost shaking with rage, he pressed another number, waiting for it to dial out, but after a few rings it went to voicemail as well. He growled down the phone.

'You better have a good fucking reason why you ain't calling me back cos I need to have a word with my wife and she ain't answering and now you're not either and I don't want to talk to some cunt's answer machine, so you need to call me back *now* . . . Oh, and remember, Vaughn, we have a deal. I gave you my word I'd keep Wan and his men off your back. But if you think that you can fuck me off, fuck me over, then I'd think again, mate, unless of course you want that lot to come and get you. So if I were you I'd answer your phone so I can speak to my FUCKING WIFE!'

11

Lamb's Conduit Street was as busy as ever with café goers and ambling tourists as Tia made her way towards Russell Square.

Turning into a small street, she headed towards a house with a large, freshly painted blue front door, which stood next to a florist's.

Under the grey sky of London, feeling a cold chill, Tia shivered as she stood on the doorstep and rang the bell. She glanced around, more out of habit than thinking she'd been followed, though she knew she couldn't be too careful.

Within moments the door was opened by a heavily made-up woman who was wearing a ruched red dress and a warm smile. She greeted Tia cheerily.

'Hello, darlin', you look like you're freezing your tits off. Come in, sweetheart.' But then she stopped and stared at

Tia. Her lips pursed. 'What's that on your face? Harry been knocking you about again?'

Tia touched her cheek, and shrugged. 'It is what it is, Lydia. It ain't so bad.' She followed Lydia into the house which, like the front door, had been freshly painted but in muted colours of grey and pink. Wanting to get the topic of conversation away from herself, Tia asked, 'You been all right?'

'Not too bad, shouldn't grumble though we fucking do, don't we?' Lydia said as she cackled warmly.

Going through to a room at the back – which always reminded Tia of the bedroom she'd stayed in the first night she'd been put into a foster home – she sat down wearily as Lydia, house proud as always, fluffed the pink cushions on the bed.

'I wasn't sure if I'd be able to make it today,' Tia said as she took off her jacket in the excessively hot room.

Lydia raised her eyebrows and came to sit opposite Tia on one of the cream flowered couches. 'I'm sorry to hear about what happened at court. But it don't surprise me. He was never going to let you go. We both know that.'

Trying to stop the tears pricking at her eyes, Tia absent-mindedly picked up the teddy bear that was next to her on the sofa. 'I know it was stupid but I had to try. I just thought if I could get the kids, then I could get a place for us all and Milly would have some kind of home again. You should see the place she's in, Lydia. It's a dump and I feel so guilty cos I know she needs me. She's sixteen and eight months pregnant and she ain't got a pot to piss in either.'

Looking sympathetic, Lydia reached out and held Tia's

hands. 'But she's got you ain't she, lovie? And that's the main thing. She's not the first kid who's got no money and is having a baby in some shithole and she won't be the last. Look at us – weren't much older than her when we got up the duff. You had Milly young, and you not only survived, you did a bloody great job with her.'

Allowing the tears to come, Tia shook her head. 'I want more for her though.'

'I know, darlin', and you'll get more. It'll work out, I know it will, but it's just going to take time. I'm only sorry I can't offer Milly a place to stay here, but you know what my poxy landlord's like; he's a right bastard and well, let's face it, it ain't really the right environment for Milly, is it?'

Tia looked at Lydia and smiled. She was grateful for a friend like Lydia. Someone who was always there for her, someone who never judged her no matter what.

She'd known Lydia for years, since she was a teenager, and although she was ten years older, Lydia had always looked out for her. Though of course, Tia kept her friendship with Lydia a secret from Harry. He didn't want her to have friends; he didn't want her to have anyone in her life apart from him.

'I know, it's just I hate seeing her where she is. But it's the only place I can afford and you know as well as I do, even that's a scrape. And it's not like I can get any money from Harry. He checks all the bank statements and even if I buy a whole heap of designer gear, I can't even sell it cos he ain't stupid; he wants to see that as well. Harry basically thinks if I've got money, I've got power and that's something he's never wanted me to have.'

Nodding sympathetically, Lydia stuffed a piece of gum in her mouth. 'He's got you proper locked down, darlin', but you know you'll always have here.'

'I appreciate that, Lydia. But the problem I've got now is trying to get out. It was bad enough before, him never letting me come or go as I please, but now I've got me own babysitter.'

Getting up and walking towards the door, Lydia asked. 'What you talking about?'

'He trusts me less than he did before, so he's given me my own minder. And you'll never guess who it is . . . It's Vaughn.'

A look of shock crossed Lydia's face. 'What? You kidding me?'

Tia shook her head. 'No. It's Vaughn. Vaughn Sadler.'

Whilst Tia was talking to Lydia, a mile and a half away Vaughn was stomping across Oxford Street, barging angrily through the crowd of tourists sauntering across the road. He sighed as he felt his phone going off again. *Fuck.* It was the sixth time that Harry had called him and it was the sixth time that he'd ignored it. And each time he did, each time he *didn't* answer it, he didn't even need to try to imagine how Harry was feeling – he *knew.*

Harry would be gunning for him big time, ready to read him the riot act, which was something he knew that he couldn't afford for Harry to do. He had to keep him on side, had to be some sort of frigging lap dog because he knew only too well that if Harry decided to drop him, to go back on the decision to help him out, then Wan and his men would sweep in like vultures. *Then*, it'd only be a matter of time before he was a dead man.

Hurrying along, he thought about switching off his mobile. There was a temptation to do so but he had no doubt that such an action would incite Harry's anger even more and at the moment it was all about damage limitation.

Hearing a text buzz through, he pulled his phone out of his Hawes & Curtis taupe suede jacket to read it.

Where the fuck are you, you cunt?

Shoving it back in his pocket, Vaughn, seething with anger at the situation he was in, made his way through to Ramillies Street, contemplating the bollocking he'd give to Tia as well as trying to figure out how the hell he was supposed to tell Harry that on the first day of minding her, he'd lost her.

And the truth was, walking along the street now, he had no idea where he was supposed to find her; he was really only going from street to street to make himself feel better, to make himself feel like he was one step closer to laying his eyes on her and one step closer to being able to phone Harry back and feed him some bullshit about why he hadn't answered in the first place.

Approaching Great Marlborough Street, Vaughn suddenly froze as he caught sight of a familiar person. A person he wanted to speak to. But it wasn't Tia, it was Franny. Franny Doyle, the person he hated more than he'd ever hated anyone in his life and the person who'd caused all this mess in the first place.

And even though he knew he probably shouldn't, even though he knew he would be better off just searching for Tia, Vaughn couldn't help himself and he began to follow Franny. For now, Harry and Tia would just have to wait.

12

Back at Lydia's house, Tia stood and looked into the mirror. She sighed, hating what she saw, though it wasn't the tiredness or the tiny lines around her eyes that she hated, and it wasn't the fact that she'd lost too much weight from all the stress. It wasn't even the fact that her long, blonde hair looked dull and tired, it was herself she hated. It was what she'd become . . . *again*.

There was a knock at the door and Tia, not feeling it but sounding it, shouted cheerily, 'Hi, come in.'

Lydia put her head around the door and grinned. 'You ready, darlin'?'

Nodding, Tia finished putting on her red lipstick. 'To tell you the truth, I just ain't in the mood.'

Lydia cackled and nodded. 'I haven't been in the mood for the last forty years, pet . . . You all right?'

Tia spun around on the stool. 'Ignore me, it's just one of

them days. I guess I just have to think of the kids but Harry's not even letting me see them really. He's playing games with me. Still, at least I'm not cut out of their life completely.'

Lydia gave a genuine smile. 'That's right, darlin', look on the bright side and one day them kids will be big and Harry won't have a hold on you anymore, not like the way he does now.'

Tia put her head down and absentmindedly pulled at the hem of her dress. 'I just feel so shit at the moment, Lyds. I don't know if I'm doing the right thing anymore. Maybe the kids would be better off with just Harry, and at least that way they wouldn't be moved from pillar to post. Harry's using them as pawns. It's not fair for them. First they're at his mum's and then at his sister's. It's not right, and anyway, look at me. I'm hardly going to make mum of the year, am I?'

'You listen to me, Tia Jacobs, you're a good mum, and don't you think or let anyone tell you otherwise. Sometimes we just have to do what we have to do for our kids,' Lydia said firmly. 'So put that smile back on your face and hold your chin up, cos you ain't got nothing to be ashamed of.'

'Thanks, Lydia . . . Thanks for everything.'

Giving another tiny nod, Lydia smiled. 'I'll send him up, shall I? It's one of your regulars. Alan. So it should be over in a matter of minutes.'

'More like seconds.'

Lydia winked. 'That's my girl. That's what I want to see. And remember why you're doing this. Milly. You're doing this for her.'

* * *

With Lydia gone to get Alan, Tia stood in the middle of the room on her own and took a deep breath, forcing a smile: something she'd had to do through her marriage with Harry, something she'd had to do when she'd been on the game before, something she'd had to do when she'd been in care. The smile she'd learnt to paint on when her heart had been broken into tiny pieces when the only man she'd ever loved had walked out on her.

But then, she supposed Lydia was right, she *was* doing this for Milly, and for her kids she would do *anything*. Even this. Even having the likes of Alan maul her. She would just lie there and smile as if it was for them.

After all, the way she figured it, she'd done that for years with Harry – just lying there and letting him do what he liked to her whilst she hated every moment of it. So what was the difference? Harry, Alan, they were all the same. They didn't care how she felt and at least Alan was paying for it whilst *she* was paying for it with Harry.

It had only been these last few months she'd been back working for Lydia, though of course she'd thought this life was just a bad memory from the past. But the combination of the legal fees and Milly's rent and living expenses had given her no choice other than to go back to what she knew.

Milly had tried to get help with housing but there'd been none available. The council lists were full to heaving and besides, when they'd questioned her about her previous accommodation, she'd been too afraid of Harry to mention him, too afraid to tell them about him kicking her out, so instead, she'd told them she'd just left. And as such, they'd decided she'd made herself intentionally homeless, telling her they couldn't help her anyway.

So, Tia had called Lydia and asked to come back and work for her and of course Lydia had been more than delighted. Tia had been grateful because she certainly couldn't stand on the corner touting for work, and she certainly couldn't have a pimp or work in a brothel. She couldn't work anywhere she might be seen. Because if she ever *was* seen, Harry would probably kill her right there and then.

Therefore, all things considered, Lydia was the best bet, especially as she did *mates rates*. She took a nominal fee from Tia, rather than the big cut she could do. And not only that, she made Tia feel safe here and cared for. She guessed Lydia was right; she had to look on the bright side.

So, standing in the bedroom with its flowered pink wallpaper and matching pink sheets, Tia held her smile as Alan came through the door.

She purred. 'Hi, Alan, how are you? You haven't been for a while. I thought you might have found someone else . . . I missed you.'

A small, tubby, ruddy-faced man in his sixties with a shiny bald head, round glasses and a large moustache shuffled towards her. He spoke in a West Country accent. 'Have you, Bernie?'

Nodding and always grateful that she'd never given her real name to any of her punters, Tia continued to hold that smile, trying to push away how much she hated what she was doing, trying to push away her hatred for Harry, and instead keep thinking on the bright side. To focus on the fact she was earning money to pay for Milly's rent.

She leant forward and caressed his face. 'Of course I have, Alan, you must know by now you're my favourite? You make me feel special, like no other man I've ever had.'

Alan's pudgy face lit up, his vein-lined cheeks going even redder as he spoke, sounding breathless. 'Really?'

'Of course. Ain't it obvious?' Tia said at the same time as trying not to wince as Alan kissed her on her neck, feeling the slobber of saliva all over her skin.

Self-satisfied, Alan smirked as he continued nuzzling her, his hands beginning to wander onto her large breasts. 'I suppose it is now you come to mention it. I wish my wife was as grateful as you are – she never wants me anywhere near her. We sleep in separate bedrooms now.'

Thinking what a smart move that sounded by Alan's wife, Tia continued to play the game.

'Well, that's not nice. If I had someone like you, Alan, I certainly wouldn't be sleeping in the next room . . . Now what can I do for you today?'

Grinning widely, Alan proceeded to take his erect penis out of his trousers. 'You can start by sucking this tinker here. Then, Bernie, you can sit on my face and call me Daddy. Now how does that sound?'

Trying her hardest not to shudder in disgust, Tia, almost unable to get her words out nodded as she fought back her tears. 'Oh, I'd like that, Alan, I'd like that very much.' And as Tia got down on her knees, the bright side seemed to be pretty dark.

13

It began to rain as Vaughn charged down Carnaby Street, keeping Franny in sight. As he raced along, bashing into the crowds of people coming the other way, everything inside him told him to hang back, to leave it, to stick to the deal that he'd made with Harry and ultimately that Harry had made with Wan. But he couldn't. He just couldn't. And he *wouldn't* because whether they'd made a deal or not, he'd *never* forget what she'd done. He'd never forget that she'd set him up and if it wasn't for the fact the gods had been on his side, he'd be long dead and buried by now.

Racing into Ganton Street, Vaughn picked up his pace, not wanting to lose this chance to speak to Franny; after all he hadn't seen her since before the set-up and he wasn't about to miss this opportunity.

He began to jog as he saw her cut into Marshall Street and then he turned his jog into a sprint and, catching her up, he grabbed her jacket, roughly dragging her past the dry-cleaner's and down the side of the newspaper shop into a tiny alleyway.

With his cheeks red with anger, he spun her round and slammed her against the wall so she was facing him. 'I want a word with you.'

Franny stared at Vaughn, a look of panic passing over her face, but as usual she managed to quickly get her emotions under control. 'Keep away from me, Vaughn.'

Looking at her as hard as she was looking at him, Vaughn shook his head as he pushed her again against the wall as she tried to step away. 'Don't think so . . . Why, what's the matter, Franny, you ain't feeling so brave now you ain't got your men around you?'

Franny, never one to back down, sneered. 'I could say the same about you. How is Harry?'

Seething with hatred, Vaughn leant nearer to her, his handsome face veiled in scorn. 'Oh he's fine, unlike you.'

'How do you make that out?'

He whispered in her ear, making it seem to any passers-by they were simply lovers in the street. 'Because one day, Franny, I'm going to get you, cos I know Wan and his men, and they ain't going to be looking out for you forever. You're going to piss them off. That fucking mouth of yours that you can't keep shut is going to get you in trouble.'

Franny laughed ruefully. 'Like I say, the same thing could be said about you. You think that Harry is going to keep watching your back forever? He ain't, but you'll wish he was, cos the minute I hear he's dropped you, I'll be coming and finishing off the job that Huang started.'

Infuriated by Franny's attitude, Vaughn, unable to help himself, grabbed her jacket collar and slammed her hard against the brick wall. But as much as it had hurt Franny, she showed nothing to him apart from contempt.

Franny's dark brown eyes narrowed as her long, chestnut hair fell over her face. 'Temper, temper, Vaughn. I'd be careful if I were you. You wouldn't want me running back and telling Wan you attacked me, would you? Because he won't like the fact that you disrespected him. He wouldn't appreciate it that I'd made a deal with him to look out for me and yet you just blatantly ignored it. It won't look good for you *or* for Harry, come to think of it, and I can't imagine Harry would like that.' She paused for a moment and then added thoughtfully, 'How did he do it?'

'Do what? What the fuck are you talking about?'

'I'm talking about Harry. How did he persuade Wan not to kill you? I mean, let's face it, Wan's brother's dead and it's your fault, yet he's still letting you walk around. There must be something else to it. Harry's good with the gift of the gab, and he and Wan might even have done business together, but that still ain't a good enough reason for Wan not to come after you. There's something else to it; I just know it. And I'll find out. Mark my words.'

It was Vaughn's turn to sneer. 'Sorry if I spoilt your plans.'

'I like to see it as just a hiccup, because you won't be around for long. So enjoy life whilst you can.'

Vaughn took a step back and stared at Franny. She was beautiful but she was cold and dangerous and it didn't seem to matter who she hurt as long as she came out on top. 'You're poison, Franny. Look around you. Everyone has left;

they've gone. You ain't got no one. You pushed them all away. And you're so desperate you've had to pay Wan to look out for you. He and his men are scum and I didn't think even you would want to be around them. You're one sad bitch, you know that?'

'And you know what you are?' She paused for a moment before quickly kneeing Vaughn in the balls, causing him to double over in pain. He coughed and spluttered as Franny leant over him, rubbing his back in a condescending way; then she reached down and grabbed hold of his balls, squeezing them tight. 'What you are, Vaughn? You're a dead man, but you just don't know it yet.'

Upon which, Franny Doyle marched away, leaving Vaughn curled up in a ball on the floor as his phone began to ring again.

14

Deep in thought, Franny stormed along Berwick Street. She was still shaking from the confrontation with Vaughn, more from anger than anything else. However, something Vaughn had said had rung true with her. She *was* alone. She didn't have *anyone* around her. Not anymore. And as much as she pretended she didn't care, she did. And it hurt like hell no matter how much she tried to ignore it.

She was lonely and, looking back, she wasn't sure how along the way it had all gone so wrong. The past couple of years had been a nightmare. Everything seemed to have trickled through her fingers. Everyone who'd been close to her had gone. And although she and Vaughn had never really seen eye to eye, there had never been an all-out war between them until now.

There had certainly been a snowball effect. She knew if Vaughn hadn't set her up for a murder she hadn't committed in the first place, then likewise, she would never have put a hit on him and neither of them would've been in this position.

Worse still, she'd lost her best friend, her business partner, her lover, Alfie Jennings, who seemed not to want to have anything to do with her. It was painful even to think of his name.

After the failed hit on Vaughn, Alfie, angry with her and not wanting to get into the middle of the war that was brewing up between her and Vaughn, had taken his daughter to Marbella to get away from it all. To get away from *her*.

Though she supposed him going away wasn't just down to the bad blood with her and Vaughn. Even *before* he'd gone things had been tense between them, and Alfie had a huge part to play in that. Mainly because a couple of years ago whilst she'd been in America, Alfie, thinking she was never going to come back, had gotten together with an old flame, and it had been *then* that he'd fathered his child, his beautiful daughter.

And although she'd been mad at him – angry and hurt – she'd hidden her feelings as usual, burying them as she'd always been taught to do since she was a child. So, in that respect, it'd been relatively easy to forgive him. Though as much as she didn't feel many things, as much as she'd learnt over the years to be tougher and stronger than any man, any face around – which had meant turning off any kind of emotion – she *had* felt something for Alfie. She'd loved him, and when his daughter was born, surprising herself, she'd fallen in love with her too. A huge unconditional love, which had shocked and frightened Franny, especially as she'd never taken an interest in children before. Yet with Alfie's daughter, she'd been besotted.

But now they'd both gone away and she didn't know if they were ever going to come back. And Christ it hurt – big time. At times she felt she couldn't breathe. She missed him so much. She just wanted him back. And for what it was worth, behind her tough exterior, behind the fight for survival in the dog-eat-dog world that she'd been born into, her heart was broken into thousands of pieces.

Yes, she'd made mistakes. A hell of a lot of them. And she was sorry, really sorry, but it just didn't seem like Alfie was going to be as forgiving in return. He could barely call her back when she left a message, and when he *did* speak to her, a coldness was there in his voice.

Though if ever she needed him, God, she needed him now. Her problem, though, was that she would never admit it. *Couldn't* admit it to him. In truth, she didn't know how to reach out for help, because being vulnerable was something she wasn't very good at . . .

Suddenly, Franny's thoughts were broken and she froze by the Endurance pub, on the corner of Berwick Street, as she stared down Kemps Court – though it was more like an alleyway than anything else. She could see yellow police tape halfway down, cutting off access, and there were police officers milling around, putting up a white forensic tent.

But it wasn't them Franny was staring at, it was the girl lying behind one of the large bottle recycling bins. And as much as she'd only been able to get a quick glimpse of her before the tent had gone up, and despite her body being twisted and crumpled up, Franny knew *exactly* who it was. It was Sophie, the young girl who'd overdosed yesterday at Wan's club. Seventeen-year-old Sophie.

She felt sick and with her heart racing, unable to look anymore, Franny stepped back into the shadows and hurried away.

She didn't know what she'd expected. But it wasn't this. Not this. Not for some young girl to be thrown and stuffed down a dirty alleyway like she was rubbish. So yes, there was one thing Vaughn had been *totally* right about. Wan and his men *were* scum, and somehow she needed to stop them in their tracks.

15

'Where the fuck have you been?' Vaughn snarled at Tia as he ran up to where she was standing on the corner of Park Crescent. 'Where the *fuck* have you been?'

Having texted Vaughn half an hour ago to let him know where she'd be waiting, she stared at him and shrugged. 'I . . . I've been busy. I just needed to get some fresh air and I walked around for a bit. Anyway, I'm here now, ain't I?'

Vaughn stared at Tia. He stepped forward, fighting the temptation to wring her neck. He glanced at his Rolex. 'When has *now* been five hours later? Do you know how many times Harry called me?'

Not in the mood to be questioned by Vaughn, and certainly not in the mood to think about Harry, or any man come to that, *especially* after the afternoon she'd had with Alan and another punter who seemed to think that rough, violent sex was something she wanted, Tia shrugged again. 'A few times I'm guessing.'

Vaughn exploded in rage, giving the elderly couple walking by a fright. 'A few? A fucking few? Try more like *thirty-four* times. Thirty-four *fucking* times, Tia. That ain't a man who's happy, is it?'

She stared at him coolly. 'To tell you the truth, Vaughn, right now I couldn't care less if he was happy or not.'

Enraged and still wound up by Franny as well as having a painful throb in his balls from where she'd kneed him, Vaughn flushed red as he hissed with fury through his teeth.

'Oh, but you'll care when you see him. You will care when he smacks you about some more and gives you another crack in the face.'

The minute Vaughn had said the words he regretted them as he saw Tia flinch.

'Fuck off, Vaughn, and thanks by the way, thanks for your concern. But then, I shouldn't expect better from you, should I? You are who your friends are.'

With Tia angry with him, Vaughn's temper continued to flare, and leaning inches away from her face, he growled, 'You *know* that I ain't like him, you *know* I'd never do that.'

With the noisy sound of the Marylebone Road behind them, Tia shook her head and raised her voice, her big brown eyes full of pain. 'I wouldn't know would I? I wouldn't put *anything* past you.'

'That ain't fair, Tia.'

Laughing bitterly, Tia fought back her tears. She didn't want to show Vaughn how upset she was; in fact she didn't want to show him any kind of emotion at all. 'Don't talk to me about fair. Don't you *ever* talk to me about fair. You wouldn't know the first thing about it.'

She turned to walk away but Vaughn grabbed her arm, pulling her back. 'You ain't going anywhere, darlin'. I'm taking you home. And *you* can face the music and tell him why you ran off.'

'I will and I'll tell him exactly what I told you. I'll tell him I just needed some air, that ain't a crime, is it?'

Vaughn's eyes flashed with anger. He was *sick* of women trying to manipulate him, he was *sick* of lies and he was certainly sick *already* of having to mind Tia. Even after less than one day, this job seemed like it was going to turn out to be much, much harder than he could've imagined. 'Wind it in, darlin'. He ain't stupid and I ain't a mug. So don't start treating me like a cunt; I ain't in the mood. I don't know what you were doing, but you certainly weren't looking for air.'

'I was. It was crowded in the shop and—'

'Stop the lies, Tia,' Vaughn interrupted her. 'You better tell me the truth, otherwise I will tell Harry.'

A wave of relief passed over Tia's face. She sounded breathless. 'So . . . so . . . so you haven't told him?'

Tightly, Vaughn said, 'No, I should've done but like a fucking fool, I was looking out for you.'

'Or were you looking out for yourself?'

Glancing at a cyclist nearly being knocked off his bike, Vaughn sighed wearily. 'Don't push it, Tia. You should be thanking me.'

With her face clearly strained, Tia's voice was full of pain.

'Understand this, Vaughn, I will *never* thank you for *anything*.'

They held each other's stares and with his jaw clenched in anger, Vaughn nodded and spat out his words. 'Whatever you say, Tia, but I ain't letting you off that easily . . . So, come on then, tell me: where were you?'

Tia continued to stare at Vaughn, her gaze darting across his handsome face. She couldn't believe Harry had lumbered her with him. Had she known otherwise, she would've thought that Harry had done it on purpose just so he could wind her up.

Part of her wished she could go right ahead and blurt out what was going on with her. What she'd been doing. That she'd spent the whole of the afternoon being mauled and literally fucked over by men who made her skin crawl. But obviously she couldn't. No matter how much she felt like screaming and telling someone, the fact was, if she wanted to stay alive, nobody could ever know. 'I was upset, okay.'

'Upset? For five hours?'

'Yeah, Vaughn, it happens. Maybe you should try it one day. Oh no, you couldn't, could you, cos to be upset would mean you'd have to care about something.'

Ignoring her comments, Vaughn, not wanting to be drenched by the puddle the black cab coming up the road was about to drive through, stepped back from the pavement slightly as he said, 'What about? What were you upset about?'

'Are you joking?'

'Do I look in a joking mood?'

Pulling her jacket around her, Tia, just wanting to go home and have a bath, snapped, 'Well where shall I start? Oh yeah that's right, my daughter was kicked out, I lost my kids, I had to come back home, my twin sister is fucking my husband, the same husband who thinks it's okay to knock me about, and then of course there's you. I've got *you* as my babysitter.'

Not quite knowing what to say but uncomfortable with the fact Tia was clearly hurting, Vaughn muttered, 'Look, come on, let's go. Let's face the music, but let me do the talking.'

'Really? What are you going to say?'

It was Vaughn's turn to shrug. 'Fuck knows, but hopefully I'll think of something.'

Before Tia could say anything, a text came through. She pulled her phone out of her pocket and stared at it.

'Is it from Harry?' Vaughn said.

She looked at Vaughn and nodded, her voice sounding strained. 'Yeah, to add to all the others he's sent me.'

'Come on, let's go then. The quicker we put his mind at rest, the better.'

As Vaughn walked in front, Tia looked back down at her phone. The text hadn't been from Harry at all. It had been from Wan. And it simply said:

Where is it? I'm not interested in waiting.

Suddenly beginning to shake, Tia shoved the phone back into her pocket and hurried to catch Vaughn up, wondering what the hell she was going to do now.

16

It was late the same evening as Franny sat full of concern next to Ellie in one of the empty rooms above Wan's club in Greek Street. The place wasn't yet open and most of Wan's men weren't about, so the only real noise was the buzz of traffic from outside.

'Tell me what happened, Ellie.'

With her eyes red from crying, Ellie, still dressed in the same black jumpsuit she was wearing earlier on in the day, shrugged as she glanced at Franny. 'I don't know.'

Warmly, Franny said, 'What do you mean, you don't know?'

Sniffing loudly and wiping her nose on the back of her sleeve, Ellie burst into tears again. 'I don't feel well.'

'Do you want me to make you a coffee?'

Miserably, Ellie shook her head. 'I just want to see Wan.'

Franny frowned. She didn't know much about Ellie, and

had only seen her a couple of times but she did know that something was troubling her. She'd been surprised to find Ellie sitting on her own, shaking and looking completely miserable, and close up she could see that Ellie was really no more than a kid. 'How old are you?'

Ellie's green eyes darkened with mistrust. She shrugged as she glanced out of the window, seeing the rooftops of Soho. 'Twenty.'

Giving a sad smile, Franny, not unkindly said, 'I ain't stupid, Ellie, just tell me how old you *really* are.'

Crossing her arms, Ellie pouted. 'Why? What's it to do with you?'

Keeping her patience, Franny tried again. 'I just want to *help* you, that's all. I don't like to see you upset.'

Ellie shrugged. 'I don't need any help, I just need to see Wan.'

'Wan?'

'Yeah, why's that so strange? He's my boyfriend in case you don't know.'

Franny stood up and walked across to the window. She couldn't afford for Wan and his men to catch her grilling Ellie, but it was clear there was something very wrong. The whole set-up with the girls made her feel uncomfortable but she had no one to talk it through with. If Alfie was here or at least even if he was returning her calls, she'd be able to get everything straight in her head. But then, maybe she should just follow her gut, because it was when she didn't that things went badly wrong.

It wasn't as though she'd been a stranger to employing prostitutes and escorts in her own club, but this was different. These were *young*, inexperienced girls and although she didn't know exactly what Wan was doing, it was clear that these girls were vulnerable and Wan and his men were taking full advantage.

God, didn't she just hate the fact that she'd been forced to hand over her shares of the club, a huge part of her livelihood, to Wan and his men for protection from Vaughn and Harry, as well as being made to work for them. Which meant it was hard or maybe it was impossible for her to walk away unless she wanted to walk away with nothing, having to spend the rest of her life looking over her shoulder. That was something she couldn't afford to do.

The whole thing was a circle of a mess. Vaughn needed protection from Wan and had sought it from Harry, which meant *she* had to get protection herself and, ironically, that had been in the form of Wan. So in one way, she and Vaughn were in very similar positions: up shit creek with neither of them wanting to be there. Stale fucking mate.

'Is that what he told you, Ellie? He told you that you were his girlfriend?' Franny said.

Ellie spun around and glared at Franny from under her red fringe. 'What are you getting at?'

Knowing she had to tread carefully as she certainly didn't want Ellie alerting Wan she was asking questions, Franny played it cool. She feigned a smile. 'I'm not getting at anything. I'm just surprised that's all, cos you seem so young and pretty, and well, Wan seems so much older.'

Defensively, Ellie barked. 'He's only ten years older. That ain't a lot, and anyway that's how it's supposed to be. The man older than the woman.'

Franny nodded her head, not letting Ellie see how angry she was. She knew exactly how old Wan was, and if like Ellie said, she was ten years younger, that would make her fifteen. *Christ*. She was just a baby.

Taking a deep breath, Franny continued to play it coolly. 'So how come you were crying? Did you have a lovers' tiff with Wan?'

Suspiciously, Ellie scowled. 'What's that?'

Franny gave a genuine laugh and tried her hardest to push the thought of Alfie out of her mind. 'A lovers' tiff? It's when you have an argument with your boyfriend but it ain't really a serious row . . . Is that what happened, Ellie?'

Seemingly putting her defensive wall down, Ellie looked coy. 'Kind of.'

Taking a can of 7Up out of the mini fridge, Franny continued to play the game with Ellie. 'Look, you can tell me, it won't go any further. We're just all girls together, ain't we? I've been there with my boyfriend so I know what it's like.'

'Do you?' said Ellie after a few moments.

'Yeah, of course . . . So come on, what was it about?'

Fifteen-year-old Ellie, desperate to talk, stared at Franny with her eyes wide open, dropping her voice into a whisper. 'You promise you won't tell him?'

'Of course – guys don't need to know everything that us girls talk about, do they?'

Then smiling, Ellie began to talk. 'This morning, I was with Wan and he . . .' She trailed off but within moments, she started speaking again, playing nervously with her hands in her lap. 'He wanted to know if I would do a few lines of coke.'

Franny, without saying anything just nodded, wondering if her face let on how much she hated Wan at that moment. But she stayed silent and continued to listen to Ellie talk.

'I didn't want to do it at first, cos I was a bit nervous. I ain't done drugs like that before. I've done pills he's given me – he's always giving me pills, but not coke. And after Sophie, I was a bit nervous.'

'And did you tell Wan that?' asked Franny as she took a sip of her drink.

'Yeah, but he said it was fine.'

Franny muttered, 'I bet he did.'

'But he didn't make me, I swear; in fact he said that I shouldn't take it and maybe he was asking too much of me . . . You know, like maybe it would be better off if we were friends. He was dead nice about it. He gave me a choice.'

Franny, seeing how Wan had clearly manipulated Ellie, couldn't help herself saying, 'If you say so.'

Bursting into tears, Ellie raised her voice. 'He did! He did! He did give me a choice!'

Not wanting to upset Ellie more than she already was, Franny put down her drink and walked back to where Ellie was sitting. 'I'm sorry, I'm sure he did. I shouldn't have said that.'

With Franny appeasing her, Ellie continued in between sniffing. 'Anyway, I took a line and I don't remember anything else, but when I woke up, Wan weren't there. No one was, so I let myself out and came over here looking for him, cos I wanted to know why . . . cos—' She stopped and buried her face in her hands at which point Franny spoke softly to her, genuine concern in her voice.

'What is it, Ellie? What's the matter?'

'I've got bruises and I'm sore.'

Franny frowned. 'I'm not following you.'

Slowly taking her hands off her face, Ellie stared at Franny. 'When I woke up, it's like . . . well, it's like I've had really, really rough sex and, I dunno, I guess I'm just upset that Wan didn't stay or . . . or maybe he was busy and had to go.'

'So he had sex with you and you can't remember it?'

Ellie nodded her head. 'And the thing is . . .' she said with her green eyes full of panic. 'You won't say anything will you?'

'Of course not.'

'Well he's never usually rough, not like that anyway. And it's not like, well it's not like I haven't done favours for him before.'

'What do you mean?'

'You know, sometimes he wants me to keep his friends entertained. It's no big deal, but this is different – I can't even remember what happened.' She sniffed loudly again as Franny sat in thought.

'Let me see the bruises, Ellie.'

With only a moment's hesitation, Ellie began to take off her black, skin-tight jumpsuit, rolling it down to her knees.

'Jesus Christ, Ellie, when you said bruises, I thought you meant just a few,' Franny said as she stared in horror at Ellie's inner thighs, which were covered in huge, red and purple bruises, so much so, she could barely see the real colour of Ellie's skin. 'What's that?' She leant towards Ellie's skinny legs, getting a better look. 'They're bite marks . . . Do you—' Suddenly hearing a noise, Franny looked up at Ellie. 'Quick, get dressed. And don't worry, El, I won't say anything. I won't tell him you told me.'

'Told you what?' Unexpectedly, Wan stepped into the room, just as Ellie was zipping up her jumpsuit, giving even Franny a fright. His face, good-looking and chiselled, was drawn in a stern line.

'Just girl's stuff, Wan,' Franny said casually as she held his gaze.

Looking suspicious, Wan looked from Franny to Ellie. He glared at her as he spoke.

'What are you doing here, anyway?'

Ellie blushed, clearly uncomfortable, and glanced at Franny before saying, 'Oh, I was just looking for you. I-I-I wondered where you'd gone and then I got chatting to Franny.'

Wan lit a cigarette. He could see her eyes were red and it looked like she'd been crying, though it could, of course, have been the fact that she'd been passed out on the keta-mine. It pissed him off that his men hadn't just taken her back to the house in Whitechapel. Sighing, he blew out the smoke. 'I don't appreciate you just turning up like this, Ellie. But I guess now you're here, you might as well go downstairs to get a drink. I'll come and find you in a minute.'

Ellie nodded and quickly dashed out of the room, leaving Franny to stare at Wan. She could feel the tension in the air and it was all she could do to hold back her temper. Tightly, she said, 'Ellie tells me she's your girlfriend. Seems like you've got a lot of those. I think Sasha thought the same . . . and Sophie, come to think of it.'

Wan's face curled up into a grimace. 'What the fuck's that got to do with you?'

Franny stood back up and began to walk out of the room. 'Well, Ellie especially, she just seems young that's all. I just wondered what you'd see in her.'

Wan stepped forward, blocking Franny's way. He took her long chestnut hair in his hands and sniffed it, his face dark and dangerous. 'Let me tell you something. Keep out of my business, Franny, because if you don't, you'll regret it. I'll make Vaughn look like a fucking pussy cat.'

17

'You're trying to tell me that both your phones weren't fucking working?'

Vaughn nodded as he stared at Harry whose face had *literally* turned to red in front of his eyes. He shrugged. 'What can I tell you, Harry?'

Pushing Vaughn hard against the expensive grey slate kitchen table, Harry snarled, 'You can fucking tell me what was going on.'

Opening and closing his fists to stop himself beating Harry to a pulp, Vaughn chewed on his lip. It was going to be even worse than he thought it would be, and the tension in the air was strained, to say the least.

As he stared at Harry, once more hating the fact he was in this position, Franny came into his head, but he shook the thought away quickly, knowing that thinking about her wouldn't help matters, especially as no doubt she was sitting pretty.

Irritated even more now but unable to show it, Vaughn said, 'I ain't saying they weren't working, Harry, I'm saying that the basements of those stores Tia likes to go in, well they ain't got much reception.'

Harry's face – as handsome as Vaughn's – was screwed up in anger. 'So, you're telling me that you were stuck down a poxy basement for nearly six fucking hours? Do I look like a cunt to you?'

Vaughn shrugged. 'Again, I ain't saying that, I just didn't think to look at me phone. It's that simple really.'

Harry spun around to Tia, walking up to her and grabbing her arm, squeezing it hard. She squealed in pain. 'But you know, you know that you need to keep in contact, don't you?'

Vaughn, not wanting Harry to lay his hands on Tia but not wanting to wind Harry up either, walked over to them and gently peeled Harry's hand from Tia's arm. 'Look, mate, this ain't her fault, it's mine. I'm sorry, I should've checked me phone, called you, kept you in the loop basically. Next time I'll know.'

Not liking the fact that Vaughn had stepped in between him and his wife, Harry shoved Vaughn hard in the chest. 'You should've known *this* time.'

The temptation to grab Harry by his face and smash it over and over again against the kitchen units was overwhelming, to the point where Vaughn had to take a quick gulp of air to try to calm himself down. 'I know, Harry, and I'm sorry. I really am.'

Harry stared at Vaughn and then at Tia, trying to work

out how big a problem he should have with Vaughn for the fact that not only had he corrected him but he'd also corrected him in front of Tia.

But then, he had to see Wan later and he needed all his energy for that, so instead, he just nodded. 'Fine. But next time, I ain't going to be so fucking charitable.'

Vaughn and Tia turned to walk out of the door but Harry grabbed Tia and said, 'Not you, darlin', I need another word with you.' He pulled her close and then his hands roamed over her body, moving down to between her legs. She stiffened at the same time as trying to back away and as she did so, she caught sight of Vaughn, who looked at her before he hurriedly turned and looked away.

'Not now, Harry. Please.'

He stepped back and glared at her. 'You're a frigid bitch, you know that. What's your problem, Tia?'

'I'm . . . I'm just tired, that's all and I wanted to read the kids a bedtime story.'

Harry laughed bitterly as he turned to Vaughn. 'You hear this? This is what I have to put up with. A wife who thinks it's all right not to put out. A wife who's too busy giving her kids attention to give any attention to me . . . But don't worry about that because tomorrow, I'm packing them off to my sister's. Then you've got no excuses.'

'Harry, *please*, don't do that, I came back because of them. Don't send them away the minute I'm back.'

He grinned nastily. 'Be a good girl and I won't have to, will I? Give me what a woman should give a man, and then they'll be back before you know it . . . Now come here, give me that kiss. Let's start where we mean to go on.'

'Harry, don't . . . Vaughn's here,' Tia muttered.

Putting his hand under Tia's chin to lift her head up higher, Harry grinned. 'Vaughn's a big man, I think he's seen it all before. He knows all about the birds and the bees – don't you, Vaughn?'

Vaughn, not liking how being around the situation was making him feel, walked towards the door. 'Look, I'll leave you to it. I'll see you tomorrow.'

As he reached the kitchen door, he raised his eyebrows in surprise at Tammy who was walking down the hallway towards him. It had always shocked him how extraordinarily alike she was to Tia, in looks anyway. In anything else, they were as far apart as a cat and a mouse.

'Hello, Vaughn, you're looking as handsome as ever,' purred Tammy. 'Maybe you should drop by one day. Catch up on old times or maybe you could come and babysit me instead of my sister. What do you say?'

Vaughn stared at her, wondering what the hell Harry was playing at bringing Tammy back. Though he guessed it was just to wind Tia up. To hurt her. Harry had always had a dark streak when it came to his wife.

And if he was being honest with himself, well, it was a shame. A damn shame. He knew how much Tammy being here would hurt Tia, though not because Tia wanted Harry to herself. He knew that Tia had always wanted her sister to be just that. A sister, not a prize bitch. *Shit* . . .

He didn't want to even think about their domestic set-up. It was totally screwed up but ultimately it wasn't anything to do with him and he certainly wasn't interested in getting involved. He needed to get his life back on track; anything else would take a back seat.

It was at this point that Vaughn, not bothering to answer Tammy, walked away, leaving them all standing in the kitchen as he tried to ignore the overwhelming feeling of sadness.

18

It was late and already felt like it had been a long day when, at the corner of Beak Street, Vaughn, deep in thought about Harry and Tia, suddenly felt a rough grip on his arm.

He spun around ready to drape up whoever it was that seemed to think it was all right to hold on to him, and came face to face with a tall black man in his mid-forties who wore a supercilious smile. 'Hello, Vaughn, I think you and I need a word.'

Vaughn stared at the man – someone he'd known for a long time, *too long*. 'What about?'

'Perhaps we can go in and talk?' The man nodded to the café that was directly across the street from them.

'I ain't got anything to say to you,' Vaughn growled menacingly.

'No, but the thing is, I've got something to say to *you*. I understand that you've been working with Harry Jacobs.'

Vaughn shrugged, and said in a hostile tone, 'I've already told you, I ain't got anything to say to the likes of you.'

The tall gentleman dressed in a plain, grey mac, stepped forward. 'And as I've already told *you*, I have something to say. So if I were you, I'd let me buy you a coffee. Unless of course you want to talk out here. Or we could go and talk down the station, if you'd rather.'

'Sounds like you ain't giving me a choice.'

Detective Carter nodded. 'You're not as stupid as I thought you were . . . Shall we?'

Carter gestured to the café before marching across the road giving Vaughn no other option but to follow.

The café was hot and a cloud of steam seemed to be sitting in the air along with the smell of frying eggs and bacon, the sound of laughter and voices filling the whole place. The cream walls, looking somewhat grimy, were adorned with photographs of famous British landmarks.

The Turkish couple behind the counter waved a familiar greeting to Vaughn who nodded in recognition as he sat down on one of the green, faux leather benches.

Sliding into the bench opposite, Carter picked up the menu. 'Can I get you anything, Vaughn?'

'I think I'd choke.'

'Food that bad here?' said Carter sardonically.

'You know exactly what I mean. I ain't here for a social, so just say what you need to, then you can piss off out of my face.'

Carter placed the menu very slowly down on the table. He stared at Vaughn, taking him in, and it was a good few moments before he spoke. 'All right then, tell me about Harry Jacobs.'

Vaughn stared back at Carter as if he'd lost his mind. 'I don't speak to coppers.'

Carter sat back and whistled. 'That's not what I heard, though I must say I *was* surprised to hear that you'd been working with one of my ex-colleagues to get Franny Doyle sent down.'

Vaughn shook his head. Part of him would always be ashamed he'd ever spoken to the police; after all it *was* breaking every rule in the world he lived in. No one snaked, no one grassed but, and here was the thing, *he'd* been prepared to break those rules to get Franny once and for all.

And it'd been a good plan, a plan that *should've* worked. The problem had been not only did Franny have one of the best gangland solicitors around, the copper he'd been speaking to and had worked with had been bent to the point that a lot of his cases had been ruled unsafe and that had fucked Vaughn off no end, to say the least.

So once again Franny had slipped through the net. Yes, she hadn't actually really killed anyone, but that didn't mean she hadn't deserved all that had been coming to her. It didn't mean that he shouldn't have tried to get her sent down. Not that his failure to get rid of her had put him off attempting it again. Oh no, if anything the combination of having to work with Harry and Franny's obvious smugness had made him even more determined. It was just a question of when.

'I don't want to talk about Franny. Just tell me what you want, Carter.'

Carter stared down at his perfectly manicured fingernails then, having made Vaughn wait long enough, he said, 'I'm here to clean this place up. I'm going to get Soho back to how it should be and unlike my predecessor I'm not willing to take any short cuts. I'm not willing to be in *anyone's* pocket. So here's the thing, Vaughn, you can either work with me or I bring you down with all the others.'

Like Carter, Vaughn rested back on the faux leather bench. He'd known Carter for a long time, and at one point they'd even been friends. Good friends. They'd knocked about as teenagers, but now, things had certainly changed. They were on different sides of the track and whether they'd once been close friends or not, that was then, and *this* was certainly now.

'You can forget me helping. Do what you have to do cos no matter what you've heard, I ain't a grass and besides, I don't know anything.'

Carter nodded. 'So, you can't tell me anything about Harry Jacobs.'

'Nope.'

'But you're working for him, right?'

Vaughn stared at Carter evenly. 'As they say in the trade, *no comment*.'

Not giving up, Carter glanced out of the window for a moment, then he turned back to stare at Vaughn intently. 'That must be strange.'

'What the fuck are you talking about now?' snarled Vaughn impatiently.

'Well, Harry, he's married to Tia, isn't he?'

Vaughn didn't move. The only thing that gave away any

kind of emotion was the pulse in his jaw. The tension was palpable.

'And you can't tell me anything about Wan?'

'Nope.'

Leaning forward, Carter said evenly, 'And you can't tell me anything about Sophie?'

Vaughn looked surprised. 'Sophie? Who's Sophie?'

'A seventeen-year-old girl.'

Still confused, Vaughn shrugged. 'And what's she to do with me?'

'I don't know, that's what I'm hoping to find out. She was found dead in Kemps Court.'

Not showing any emotion but genuinely saddened hearing about the young girl, Vaughn asked, 'How did she die?'

'There's going to be an autopsy, but it seems like she might've overdosed.'

'Shame.'

Carter tilted his head as he put the menu back behind the tomato ketchup bottle. 'The thing is, she's the second girl in two weeks who's overdosed. Two young girls both dead. What a waste of life, don't you think?'

In agreement but certainly not willing to be drawn in by Carter on any emotional level, Vaughn sat in silence listening to Carter continue.

'So that's why I want to talk to you.'

'What's it got to do with me? This is Soho if you ain't remembered. That's just the way it is.'

As cool as Vaughn, Carter spoke. 'You're right, these things do happen but *only* if there are scumbags out there selling drugs.'

Not wanting to stay and talk any longer, Vaughn began to get up. 'Whether you like it or not, people will always take drugs.'

'That might be the case, but when it seems the drugs have been laced with crap, then it's my job to look into it. And as you hang around with the likes of Harry and Wan . . .'

'Let me stop you right there,' said Vaughn. 'I don't *hang* out with Wan.'

Carter blinked. 'Seems like he's a touchy subject. Any reason?'

'Listen, do all your detective shit elsewhere. I ain't interested.'

Vaughn turned to go but Carter, still sitting at the table, grabbed him by his sleeve as he walked past, though he didn't look up at Vaughn as he spoke quietly. 'I meant what I said. I don't want to bring you down, Vaughn, but I *will* if I have to, so it'd be in your best interests to work with me, because otherwise, there'll only be one loser, and I promise you, it won't be me.'

19

Wan and Harry leant back on the red couches in one of the private rooms of Wan's West End club. The music was turned up loud and the lights were turned low and even through the leather, padded door, Harry could still hear the hum of the punters on the other side.

Taking a large drag of his cigar, Harry, feeling more relaxed after his run-in with Tia, yawned. 'I hear that you had a problem with one of the girls the other day.'

Wan shrugged, his handsome face not showing any emotion. 'Problem, how?'

'You had a blow-out, one of them keeled.'

Thinking about Sophie overdosing immediately turned Wan's good mood into a foul one. 'That's the problem with shit gear, it has a way of biting you in the arse.'

Harry raised his eyebrows. 'You sure it's the gear? More likely the ketamine you cut in it. That stuff knocks out horses.'

Wan gave a wry smile before taking a large sip from his glass of brandy. 'Yeah but how else am I going to knock them out?'

'Have you tried a cosh?'

Both men laughed and Wan said, 'The problem is they get greedy for it. Once they like the taste, they're snorting it up like it's oxygen. Sophie did anyway.'

'You just need to be careful, that's all. I remember how good a worker you said Sophie was. It's a shame to kill off all the good ones,' Harry said with a grin and a wink.

Wan shrugged. 'Maybe I'll change suppliers just to be on the safe side . . . You sure you don't want to get back in the business? Your powder was always good. Quality coke.'

Taking another drag from the cigar, Harry shook his head. 'I'd rather not step on any toes. The Russians won't like it if I mess around in their territory. I already had a little warning last year from one of the bosses, or rather, an ultimatum,' Harry said. 'Still, if things change, or I get desperate, I've still got a few kilos I can get rid of, but until then, I don't fancy having my face blown off.'

Wan regarded Harry and for a moment he didn't say anything as different thoughts raced through his head. Then with a cloying smile he asked, 'So how is that lovely wife of yours? How's Tia?'

Trying to hide the bristle of irritation he felt when any man asked about his wife, Harry nodded. 'Same as usual. Still chewing me ear off, but then that's women for you, ain't it?'

'Well it's certainly Tia.'

Not enjoying the familiar way he was speaking about her, Harry sniffed and shrugged. 'It is what it is.'

'Yeah, but it's good to see that you've got your house back in order. You know, with her doing a runner. You should've put your foot down with her a long time ago. It's a dangerous thing having such a beautiful wife.'

Wan was trying to wind him up and doing a good job of it. Harry narrowed his eyes. He leant forward, locking the other man's stare as he spoke through gritted teeth. 'Women and marriage are complicated things, Wan, and although I appreciate your input, I'd rather you save the advice for someone who *fucking* wants to hear it.'

Before Wan could answer, two girls walked in, wearing only flimsy G-strings. It was Ellie and Sasha.

Wan winked, tapping his knee. 'Hey, Sash, why don't you come and give me one of your massages.'

With a delighted look in her eye, Sasha walked across to Wan, sitting down on his knee. She wrapped her almost naked body around him and began to massage his shoulders, much to the disgust of Ellie who raged inside, giving Sasha daggers.

She hated Sasha; she was a bitch, trying to take Wan from her. Who the hell she thought she was Ellie didn't know, but what she did know was it should be *her*, not Sasha, sitting on Wan's knee. After all, *she* was Wan's girlfriend, not Sasha.

Maybe he was trying to punish her for chatting to Franny the other day. He'd certainly been angry with her. He'd even given her a slap. Not that she'd told him that she'd shown Franny the bruises on her legs, but for some reason he'd been pissed off that she'd told Franny that they were boyfriend and girlfriend.

As Ellie stood there in her red G-string, Wan, playing with Sasha's hair, looked up at her. He frowned as he saw the look on her face. 'Aren't you going to say *hello* to Harry? Anyone would think you had no manners and didn't want to be welcoming to my friends.'

With a tight smile, Ellie shrugged. 'It's not that . . .' She trailed off, fighting the urge to cry, fighting the urge to scream at Sasha who was busy kissing Wan's neck. She loved Wan and Sasha was trying to get in the way and it wasn't fair.

She'd never had anyone care for her in her life. Not her mum – she didn't even know her dad – and certainly not the social workers who'd come in and out of her life. So no, she wasn't going to give Wan up without a fight. He made her feel loved and that was something she wasn't ready to let go.

'Well go on then, be nice. We had this chat earlier didn't we, El? About giving a little bit and helping me out now and then.' Wan paused then winked at her adding, 'I thought we had an arrangement, but like I said to you before, it's your choice.'

Wanting to please Wan above all else, with one last glare at Sasha, Ellie, without saying anything, went to move towards Harry who grinned and stubbed out his cigar in the nearby silver ashtray before dragging her onto his lap, groping her breasts.

He pulled her into him, nuzzling his face into her neck at the same time as pulling at her G-string before growling,

'Like Wan says, you could make me feel a bit more welcome. You're acting like I'm fucking contaminated,' Harry said as he stopped to look at her.

'Sorry,' Ellie muttered as she felt Wan's glare on her.

As Tia suddenly came into his head, Harry snarled, 'Yeah well, you know how to cock block don't you?' He gave her a hard shove, pushing her onto the floor, and she let out a yelp as he stood up and looked at his watch. 'Anyway, fuck this, I've got to get on.'

'You have to excuse Ellie. Sometimes she needs a bit of something to help her relax, don't you, El?' Wan said as he gave Ellie another hard stare.

Nearing the door, Harry shrugged. 'Whatever. I ain't got time for this shit.'

'I tell you what, Harry, how about I get Ellie to make up for it? Leave it with me; you're in for a treat . . .'

20

Franny crept up the back stairs of the large house in Whitechapel, one of the places in which Wan kept his girls. This was the first time she'd been here, though she'd been to the other places he had, and to all intents and purposes the houses felt like homes. Bright and clean, each girl with her own bedroom and bathroom, or only having to share with one other girl. PlayStations, Xboxes, Apple televisions, gadgets galore and free access to come and go as they pleased.

There was no doubt that the place seemed a safe haven to a lot of these girls. Maybe the best place they'd ever been able to call home . . . *At first, anyway.*

Of course she knew there'd always be hookers and whores; she certainly wasn't standing in any kind of judgement. It didn't make a bit of difference to her. Hookers were just part of the life she was in; women were friends with them and men slept with them. It was as simple as that. But this, this was different. What Wan was doing was darker. Much, much darker.

She knew there was an air of secrecy around it because when she asked the girls anything, they clammed up. The problem was that she knew it was a dangerous line she was walking by asking questions. A lot of the girls were vulnerable and she would go as far as saying a lot of them were brainwashed. Brainwashed into thinking that Wan was their saviour.

She guessed that compared to the life they'd been in, he might be. Wan Huang, redeemer and rescuer. It was a joke. A fucking joke; feeding them drugs, proclaiming undying love to girls who were so desperate for it, it was hypnotic to them. *Wan* was hypnotic to them.

When she'd first started working for Wan, she'd thought the girls were *only* working in the clubs. She'd also thought the girls were much older than they were. Slapped with make-up, hair extensions and designer gear that could make the most innocent of teenagers look like young women with experience.

But as more time went on, being around Wan and the clubs – and especially around the girls – the more she heard and found out the more sinister it all felt.

Of course she didn't know everything – very little in fact – but she was beginning to put the pieces together. And the truth was, no matter what they were or weren't doing, having underage girls was and always had been a big no-no to her.

And the worst thing was, if they chose to, they could

just walk out of the front door. But they didn't. They saw this as their home, and saw Wan as family. One thing was certainly clear to her: no matter how he treated them, they were willing to put up with it, just to be around him. Nothing could be worse for them than not having Wan around.

Getting to the top of the stairs, Franny felt the familiar sense of anger rush through her. She walked down the corridor, carrying a bag full of designer clothes. She'd decided if Wan or his men caught her here, then at least she could say she was dropping off some bits for the girls.

Though she suspected no one else *was* around. That was the thing. Wan didn't have anyone patrolling the place or keeping the girls under lock and key, they were *free* to do what they wanted – at least on the face of it they were.

To her though, it was obvious Wan was an expert in playing these girls, giving them just enough attention mixed in with fear to get them to want him. After all, he was rich, handsome, strong, possessive and controlling. A toxic combination for the girls who were clearly vulnerable. And she knew only too well that although they may not see it and they might think staying here was their choice, it was clear Wan had them under lock and key with psychological chains.

She sighed and continued quietly up the landing, hoping that her instinct would be right and no one would be around, because although it wasn't out of the question that she'd pop in to see the girls, she could tell that Wan was starting to not trust her. She had to be very, very careful, otherwise she'd be in big trouble. And having any kind of trouble with Wan meant being put in a shallow grave on the far side of Epping Forest.

'Franny, what you doing here?' A voice behind her made her *literally* jump with fright.

She spun around and saw it was Ellie. She hadn't realised that Ellie lived here along with Sasha, who she'd actually come to see.

Recovering from the fright, Franny smiled. She kept her voice down as she talked. 'Oh hey, Ellie, how are you? I thought I'd just come and see Sash and bring her a few things. You know, cheer her up a bit.'

Ellie scowled. 'I don't know why you'd bother with that stupid bitch. You should've seen her earlier, like she was Queen fucking Bee. I hate her.'

'I thought you were friends?' Franny said, surprised at Ellie's venom.

Ellie crossed her arms and walked to the first room off the corridor, which turned out to be her bedroom.

Dressed in red pyjamas, she sat on her unmade bed and stared at Franny as she followed her in. 'Who told you that?' Ellie replied, still scowling.

Sitting down on the large, pink velvet chair, which was in the shape of a throne, Franny shrugged. 'I just assumed.'

'Why?'

Franny watched Ellie take a drink from the bottle of peach water by her bed. She was so defensive and it was obvious by her manner that she didn't trust what she was hearing. Not that it offended her. Ellie was just a kid and no doubt most of her life she'd had to battle for survival. Franny's heart went out to her. She could see that the kid was messed up and she could also see how Wan was clearly using it to his advantage.

'I don't know why, I thought most of you girls were friends.'

'Not when they're bitches.'

Franny gave a sad smile as she looked around the room and maybe she was overthinking it but although it was nicely decorated, the whole place had a clinical, sinister vibe. 'I don't think Sasha's a bitch, is she? She's always seemed so sweet to me.'

'Well that's you and you don't know her like I do. She goes around mouthing off and talking shit.'

'We can all do that at one time or another. I know I do,' Franny said warmly.

'Yeah, but you don't go around telling everyone that you're Wan's girlfriend, do you?' Ellie said, her eyes filling with tears.

Choosing her words carefully, Franny answered as delicately as possible. 'No, but maybe she thinks she is.'

'Well she fucking ain't – she's just a desperate slag. She's always draping herself over him, she's that desperate to get his attention, but he's only got one girlfriend and that's *me*!' And with those words, Ellie burst into tears.

As Franny went to comfort her, putting her arm around her, it occurred to her that Wan was either stupid or it was part of his plan that he put both Sasha and Ellie in the same house. No doubt it was the latter: play the girls off against each other. That way they're even more ready to please. She sighed. 'Maybe Wan told her he was.'

Ellie pulled away from Franny's embrace and she looked

125

like she was going to explode with hurt and anger as she blurted out her words. 'And why would he do that? He wouldn't, he wouldn't! She's just a fucking liar! I told her that much. I told her that if she said it again and carried on talking shit, I'd sort her out.'

'And what did she say to that?'

Ellie shrugged as a scowl appeared on her forehead. 'She didn't say much. What could she say? She knew I meant it.'

'Well I saw her earlier this afternoon and she looked upset,' Franny said calmly, deliberately leaving out the fact that she'd seen Sasha with Wan, who'd been in the process of talking boyfriend, girlfriend.

'She was fine when I saw her this evening, not that I care how she was.'

Knowing that Ellie would run back and tell Wan if she said the wrong thing to her and knowing Ellie was like a cat, ready to pounce in Wan's defence, Franny kept it as casual and light as possible even though she wanted to ask about the bruises on Ellie's thighs, wanting to know if she remembered how she got them. But she also wasn't stupid. She knew that it would be a big mistake to do so.

'Oh well it's good to know she's okay. I just thought I'd mention it that's all.'

Feeding off Franny's relaxed vibe, Ellie started to relax herself, speaking quieter this time. 'I couldn't care less about her.'

'No, I'd probably be the same if someone was after my boyfriend,' Franny said as she played the game with Ellie. 'Maybe I should go and see her. Take her these things.'

'She's not here.'

Franny stood up and picked up the bag. 'Do you know where she is?'

'Nope.'

Franny gave her a smile. 'Okay, well, I'll just put these things in her room if you tell me where it is.'

Picking up her phone and staring down at it, Ellie answered, uninterested, 'Last one down on the left.'

21

Franny opened the door of Sasha's room and switched on the light. Looking around, her heart felt like it skipped a beat as she saw a photo on the wall with fairy lights around it of Sasha and Sophie, looking happy, looking relaxed and more importantly, with Sophie looking *alive*.

She sighed as she placed the bag of dresses on the bed, which was made to perfection; pretty flowered sheets and a soft, grey velvet throw along with matching cushions and a teddy bear sat on the top. The white wooden furniture, smart and expensive, and the shelf of trinkets and books made it look like any other teenager's bedroom.

She walked across to the wardrobe and opened it, seeing an array of designer clothes mixed with high-street skirts and dresses. Closing it, she moved across to the chest of drawers and paused for a moment, listening out to make sure no one was coming. Certain there was nobody around, for some reason she couldn't quite understand Franny found herself opening Sasha's top drawer.

Knickers and socks, bras and tights folded neatly with a packet of cigarettes tucked in the corner. She closed it, then opened the second drawer, where everything was folded just as neatly. She did the same with the next but she stopped as she caught sight of something shiny, which was tucked underneath the various colourful vest tops.

Realising it was a book, Franny – making sure it didn't look like someone had riffled through Sasha's things – carefully moved the clothes out of the way. Curious, she took the book out but as she flicked through it, she was surprised to see it was actually a diary. Sasha's diary.

Going across to the door and opening it slightly, Franny looked down the corridor, wanting to be doubly certain that she was still on her own. Then, sitting down on the edge of the bed, Franny began to read . . .

Tuesday 16th

Feeling totally down today. Can't believe that I have to go and see Wan's mate this evening. Wan promised that I didn't have to see him no more. Last time I went, he gave me the biggest black eye and I had to have sex with three old men. MADE ME FEEL SICK. Told Wan but he didn't seem to care what happened and when I told Wan today that I wasn't going to go, he got really nasty with me. Sometimes I really hate him. Just feel like ditching it all and going. Not sure where I'd go though. Can't go home. At least I've got Louise. It's funny how I've only known her

*for a couple of months but she already feels like my
sister. She says she doesn't want to go to the party
tonight either. Can hear Wan coming back. Will
write more later . . .*

Thursday 18th
*Want to die. I don't know what to say. Wan forced
me to go to the party with Louise. It was horrible.
There were about twenty guys there. We had to sleep
with them all. They just put us in a room on a dirty
mattress and they came in one by one. One big guy
got really rough and Louise got scared and started
screaming. Then some other guy came in and took
her out of the room. I haven't seen her since. I'm
worried.*

Friday 19th
*In a lot of pain since the other night – think I might
have got an infection. It hurts when I wee. Saw Wan
and asked him about Louise. He nearly killed me
when I did. Got really angry, pushed me about.
Thought he was going to snap my arm in two. Won't
ask him again about Louise but I'm scared for her.
Still haven't heard anything. Even her phone is still in
her room. Really worried now but don't know what
to do.*

Saturday 20th
*Told Wan I was pregnant. Don't know who the father
is. It could be anybody's, but it don't matter. Wan says*

he's going to take me for an abortion. He gave me a slap. He gives me that many it doesn't even hurt now. At least he apologised this time. Kissed me and told me that I was special. Made me feel good. I like it that he still cares. Still nothing from Louise though. One of Wan's men came in today and took all her things out of her room. I have a really bad feeling something terrible has happened. Can't stop crying.

Sunday 21st
As usual Ellie is being a complete cow. She's nasty to anyone that goes near Wan. She's crazy. Last night found one of my nail varnishes poured all over my tops in my drawer. I just know Ellie did it. She's mean like that. I wanted to be friends with her at first – now I wish she wasn't here. She doesn't seem to care Louise is missing. So worried.

Franny suddenly closed the diary and looked up. She could hear voices coming from the hallway. Even though she wanted to keep on reading, she rushed over to the chest of drawers and placed it back exactly how she'd found it.

Her mind was racing from what she'd just read; she felt shocked, saddened and angry and although she'd originally come to see Sasha, she'd probably found out more than she would ever have done if Sasha had *actually* been here. But she could think about everything later. For now she knew she had to get out of the house as soon as she could without being seen or at least she needed to look like there was nothing suspicious about her visit.

Quietly she switched off the light in the room before she slowly cracked open the door and peered out into the corridor, watching and listening to Wan bundling Ellie out of her room.

'Stop fucking whining, Ellie. And move it. I told you to be ready. Have you seen the time?'

'Do I have to go? It's late. I'm tired.'

'Just shut it, and come on. You owe me after earlier. You were like a sulky little spoilt cow. You're lucky I'm still bothering with you. Now come on.'

'I don't want to. I don't feel well.'

'You'll be back before you know it and anyway, I've got some stuff that will make you feel better. Help you relax. You can't go around being so uptight. You embarrassed me in front of my friend. Is that what you want to do?'

'No of course not.'

'Well then, this time, to stop you being so frigging moody, I want you to take some powder.'

'I dunno, Wan. It made me feel rotten.'

'I thought you loved me, Ellie. I thought you cared about me.'

'I do, but—'

'But nothing then. If you love me you'll do what I ask you to, but like I say, if you'd rather we just be mates, Ellie, that's fine . . . I can ask Sasha to help me out.'

'No! No! No, don't! Don't ask her, I'll do it.'

'That's my girl. Now come on, let's go.'

Franny listened to them go and the house fell silent. She sighed and shook her head, fighting the urge to run after them because right now she knew that it'd do more harm than good. And even though she wanted to shake Ellie, tell her to open her eyes to see how Wan was playing her, she knew it would be pointless – Ellie just wouldn't listen.

Girls like Ellie were prime targets for creeps like Wan. Their vulnerability made them easy to manipulate, easy to make them into anything Wan wanted them to be. And that was the worst part; Ellie was doing all this because she was desperate for someone to love her and it made Franny sick to her stomach.

As she made her way out of the house and into the darkness of the night, as she hurried along the dimly lit street, she knew that although she couldn't stop Ellie wanting to be around Wan, somehow she would stop Wan being around Ellie.

From the blacked-out car, Alfie Jennings watched Franny come out of the house and walk down the street. Every part of his being wanted to let her know he was here, only a few feet away from her. Every part of him wanted to hold her, to touch her. She looked so beautiful and he wanted her so badly, but he'd made a promise to himself that he wasn't going to step in until, and only *if*, he was really needed.

She'd nearly destroyed him before and he wasn't going to let her do that again. There was no doubt about it that Franny was dangerous. And there was no doubt about it either that he was addicted to her, no matter how much he tried not to be. So, as much as it was difficult, the longer he could keep his distance, the better.

What he *was* going to do was follow Wan, who he'd

known since Wan had been a kid. Because he might want to keep Franny at bay for now, but that didn't mean he wasn't going to find out all that he could about Wan; which started with knowing where the piece of scum was going with the young girl.

Alfie put the car in drive and set off, watching Franny disappear in his rear-view mirror.

22

It was getting on for one in the morning and Tia was exhausted. She locked herself in the bathroom, closing her eyes as she leant her head against the door. She needed to think. Her mind was a mess, and in fact, *everything* so far had been a mess. *Was* a mess. And although she could try to tell herself she was back at home with her children where she belonged, it was of little comfort as Harry had made sure she'd hardly seen them.

Sighing, she dropped her pink silk polka dot dressing gown on the floor and stepped into the bath, the heat of the bubbled water stinging her skin, making her wince, distracting her for a moment from her thoughts that were filled with Harry and Alan and Vaughn . . . and Wan. *Especially* Wan.

A knock on the door interrupted her thoughts. 'Tia? Tia?' It was her sister Tammy.

135

Sighing, Tia shouted through the door. 'What is it, Tam?'

'I just wanted to know if you were planning to stay this time. It seems a shame to mess the kids around again. I mean if you're going to leave again, why don't you do it sooner rather than later? I can tell them their Auntie Tammy is going to look after them from now on.'

Shaking her head, Tia snapped. She wasn't going to let her sister wind her up. She wouldn't let that happen, though it was certainly hard.

At times over the years she'd been tempted to turn her back on her sister. Not because she was here with Harry; she couldn't care less what and who Harry slept with *especially* if it distracted him from wanting to be with her. No, Tammy wound her up because it hurt. It hurt her because her sister, her *twin* sister seemed to be on a mission to destroy her any way she could.

But as much as she wanted to throw Tammy out, deep down she knew she wouldn't because, despite everything, she loved her.

They'd both had it rough as kids but Tammy even more so than her. They'd been moved around, going from one care home to another. They'd been separated, which had been painful and Tammy's screams and cries as they'd dragged her away still haunted Tia.

They'd been close up until that point but when they'd been reunited, Tammy had been aloof. Cold. Hard. It was only later that she'd learnt that Tammy had been abused both physically and sexually whilst in the care of her foster parents.

She felt guilty for that, guilty she hadn't been able to

look after her twin sister the way she'd wanted to, the way most people looked out for their siblings. Guilty that Tammy had been traumatised and hurt. And so she'd vowed always to be there for Tammy, no matter what.

So, as hard as this was and as much as she wanted to grab Tammy right now by the hair and throw her out, she wouldn't because, for a start, she knew that Tammy didn't really have anywhere to go. She'd drifted all her life, not being able to put down roots, no doubt from the chaos of their childhood. At least here Tammy had a roof over her head and this way Tia could keep an eye on her, because there was no doubt Harry would hurt her. And if, or rather *when* he did, she wanted to be there to pick up the pieces.

'I ain't going anywhere, Tammy, whether you like it or not and don't forget that this is my home, not yours.'

'I'm just not sure if it's big enough for all of us.'

Not in the mood for her sister on top of everything else, Tia stepped back out of the bath, wrapping her towel around her before opening the door wide. She stared at her sister, looking at her mirror image. 'What are you on about?'

As usual Tammy's face curled up in scorn as she touched Tia's hair. 'Are you surprised that Harry's got bored of you if you're always looking so dowdy? You should get yourself to the hairdresser's, fix up, do something with yourself. You're an embarrassment, Tia.'

Pushing Tammy's hand away, Tia shrugged in dismay. 'Is this why you knocked on the door, just so you could have a dig? Because if it is, I think I'd rather get back to me bath.'

As Tia went to close the door, Tammy put her foot in

the way, stopping it from being shut. 'You should be grateful to me, Tia. I'm giving you some advice. Now if you don't want to take it, then that's down to you.'

Sighing again, Tia said, 'Fine, well if that's everything?'

'No, it's not. Like I say, I was wondering how long you'll be around?'

'Look, Tammy, I ain't going anywhere. You've got what you want by moving in, and I ain't going to bother you, so why don't you keep out of my way and I'll keep out of yours, hey?'

Tammy chuckled nastily. 'I wish it was that simple.'

'Why are you being like this? What did I ever do to you, Tammy? I loved you. I do love you but you make it so hard.'

Tammy sniffed and stared at her perfectly done manicure. 'I'm not asking you to love me. I'm asking you to move out.'

'You're crazy. My kids live here, so that ain't ever going to happen,' Tia said angrily.

'Then we'll all have to just squash up, won't we? Otherwise we won't have enough room when my baby comes.'

Tia's face paled. 'Your baby? What are you saying?'

'Oh come on, Tia, you know what I'm saying. I'm pregnant.'

Tia felt sick. 'Oh my God, you can't be . . . No, Tammy, you can't be. *Please* tell me it ain't Harry's.'

'Well who else's would it be?' Tammy smirked nastily.

'What have you done, Tam? You stupid, stupid cow.'

Tammy glared at her. 'I knew you wouldn't be happy, but that don't mean you need to be nasty, Tia. Jealousy ain't a good look you know.'

Tia lunged at Tammy, grabbing her arm. Tears filled her eyes. 'I ain't jealous, you stupid mare. I ain't anything like that. What I am, is worried for you. You really don't get it, do you? You may be sleeping with my husband, but that don't mean you know him like I do . . . I take it you ain't told him yet.'

Tammy shrugged as a slight look of unease passed through her eyes. 'Not yet, I'm just waiting for the right time.'

'But that's the point; there won't *be* any right time. Not with him. Tammy, listen to me. Harry won't want you having his kid, cos he's just using you to get at me.'

With her face turning red, Tammy snarled, 'Keep on telling yourself that, Tia. That's what you like to think, but you and I both know that it ain't true. You just can't stand the thought he wants me and not you. You can't stand it that I'm carrying his baby and that I'm going to be happy.'

Tears streamed down Tia's face. 'What I can't stand is you thinking that it'll be all right. Tammy, *please*, just don't tell him. Get rid of it or move out if you want to keep it. Do whatever you have to do and I'll support you. Whatever you choose, I'll be there for you, but just don't tell him, cos if you do, he won't want you around anymore and that will mean I won't be able to see you.'

The slap from Tammy was hard and loud and Tia's cheek immediately welled up. 'You want me to get an abortion? You make me sick, Tia. I'm going to keep this baby and Harry and I are going to be happy and if I've got anything to do with it, it'll be *you* who's moving out and besides, who says I even want to see you?'

139

Tammy stomped away down the corridor leaving Tia terrified for her sister.

Scrubbing her skin in the bath, Tia's head was filled with anxiety. Not only was she filled with panic over her sister's pregnancy but she wanted to remove all traces of the afternoon.

Her skin was red and sore from where she'd scrubbed it too hard. It was always the same thing, no matter how much she cleaned herself, she still felt dirty.

Usually she would've had a shower at Lydia's but she'd seen all the calls from Harry and Vaughn and so she'd decided to leave without washing, wanting to get back as soon as she could. Which had been the other reason why she hadn't let Harry touch her earlier, besides not wanting him to. He would've known, she was certain of it, certain that Harry would sense that she'd been with another man . . . *men*. And whether Vaughn had been there or not, Harry would've happily beaten her to a pulp on the spot. She'd been lucky and slightly surprised that instead of insisting on sex like he usually did, he'd just stomped off out of the house, moody and angry.

Sighing at the thought, she looked up at the built-in digital clock on the wall, wishing she could just lie in the bath and shut out the world, shut out Tammy's bombshell. Instead, Tia finished off washing herself before quickly stepping out of the bath. With a heavy heart she dried herself with the thick, fluffy cream towel, fighting the temptation to talk herself out of what needed to be done. But the problem was, she didn't know how much time she had, if any, and even though she really wanted to go and speak to her sister instead, to try and persuade her to see sense, she knew with Harry being out, this might be the best opportunity she might have of getting out without Harry or Vaughn.

Glancing at her phone and pushing the thought of her sister to one side, Tia saw another text from Wan. Deciding not to read it, she hurriedly dressed in a pair of skinny jeans and a grey marl cashmere sweater. Tying her hair in a ponytail, Tia slipped on her Gucci sneakers before creeping out into the hallway, and making her way silently downstairs.

At the front door, with her heart racing, Tia listened out again, checking for any noise in the house, but all she could hear was the steady hum of the distant London traffic. With her hand shaking, she covered the alarm with her scarf to mute the sound of the beep as she turned it off. Then, glancing one more time up the stairs, she opened the door and stepped out into the cobbled mews, shutting the door behind her before hurriedly running up the street.

What Tia Jacobs didn't see, was her sister Tammy watching her leave from the upstairs bedroom window.

23

Having made her way to the private resident car park located a few streets away in Upper Wimpole Street, Tia drove through London, grateful the traffic was light as she made her way up the Finchley Road and along the Hendon Way.

Getting to Brent Cross and trying to persuade herself what she was doing was the right thing, the *only* thing open to her, she eased her white Range Rover onto the M1, putting her foot down on the accelerator as she headed for the tiny village of Jockey Row in the heart of the Hertfordshire countryside, which was just under an hour's drive from her house.

Glancing at the time and with a sense of foreboding, Tia turned on the radio, trying not to think about anything as she headed up the motorway. The problem was, she couldn't help *but* think about Tammy, about Harry, about Vaughn and moreover, she thought about herself and what a fool she'd been getting herself into her own mess. Now she had no idea *when* or how it was going to end . . .

It was pitch black as Tia turned off her lights and parked along the grass verge of Clements End Road, a country lane just outside Jockey Row and just under a quarter of a mile from the farmhouse that Harry owned.

Never having been afraid of the dark but shaking from the idea of what would happen if she were caught or if Harry even found out she'd left the house, Tia got out of the car.

There was an unsettling silence and it was almost like she could hear the sound of her own heart beating. Using her phone as a torch she made her way up the lane, carefully walking alongside the ditch towards Harry's property, which he'd purchased a few years back.

It was cold and as Tia's eyes adjusted to the dark, she could see her own breath as she hurried along.

At a small copse, she turned off the lane and battled her way through the dense brambles and bushes, feeling them snag on her clothes and hair.

Making it through to the clearing, she found herself standing in one of the fields, which was overgrown with grass and weeds, from where Harry had neglected to care for it. From where she was, she could just make out the outlines of the farmhouse, barn and outhouse on the fifty-acre property.

She took a deep breath and tried to push aside her nerves as she continued to walk, feeling the first drops of rain as she clambered over one of the wooden fences before turning up a hidden gravelled path . . .

Five minutes later and thinking that it hadn't been the smartest of ideas to choose to wear her sneakers, Tia, with her feet cold and now wet, froze as she saw the farmhouse front room light on. *Shit.*

A huge part of her wanted to run back to the car, wanted to get back to the relative safety of her house, but she knew she needed to do what she'd come here for. After all, she wasn't sure when she'd get another opportunity and she'd come this far; it would be stupid to turn back now. But if Harry was here and he spotted her, then it would all be over anyway.

Turning off the light from her phone, and feeling the sweat begin to run down her back as she saw one of Harry's cars parked near the old oak tree, Tia cautiously approached the house, knowing that she needed to keep to the far left side of the rose bushes if she didn't want to be spotted.

Trying not to let her imagination get carried away as images flashed in her mind of what Harry would do to her if he caught her, Tia continued to duck down low as she sneaked towards the outbuildings on the other side of the house, trying not to stand on anything that would make even the slightest of noises.

Suddenly, she stopped as she heard a sound. Voices coming from within the house. Then a scream . . . There it was again, but it didn't sound like whoever it was, was having fun and messing about. They sounded frightened. Scared.

Although Tia knew she shouldn't, knew she should just keep on going – because after all it wasn't anything to do with her – she found herself turning around and going back to the house.

Pushing herself up against the wall Tia, her heart racing, stood in the pouring rain as she tried to work out how many people were inside. And more importantly, *who* was inside.

She could feel herself shaking, and she knew it wasn't just from the cold and wet. But she was glad it was raining – at least it was less likely she would be heard over the sound of it hammering down against the roof.

Listening again, Tia crept along the side of the large, weatherboard house. Getting to the kitchen window, she slowly, *cautiously* peered inside. She could see the kitchen was a mess, as if there'd been a non-stop party. Bottles of wine and beer cans were strewn along the expensive worktop. She could also see neatly cut-up lines of what looked like cocaine and on the marble table there was a large bottle of vodka and overflowing ashtrays. On the floor, in the centre of it all, lay a naked woman; motionless.

Tia gasped, panicked and worried for the woman, and she immediately started to run towards the side door to see if she could help, but almost straight away, she stopped. Frozen. What the hell was she doing? How could she go inside? How could she explain to Harry what she was doing here? But then, how could she just let this woman lie there? She had to do something.

Pulling out her phone, with hands shaking Tia quickly began to dial 999. But no sooner had she started, did she stop once again. She couldn't. She just couldn't. There was no way she could bring the police or the ambulance or anyone for that matter, here.

As she fought back the tears her mind was racing. She had no idea what she was going to do. She had no one she could call, no one she could turn to for help. For a moment, Vaughn came into her mind, but what could he do?

A noise behind her made her break her thoughts. Someone was coming! *Shit! Shit!* She could hear the footsteps in the hallway of the house. Her mind whirled. There was no way she could run back to the trees without being seen if they were on their way outside.

Then, looking at the large-leafed pink rhododendron bush, which reached nearly up to the bedroom window and spread across most of the side of the house, Tia quickly pushed herself into the dense shrub, feeling the scratches of its branches against her skin at the same time as the door was opened.

Through the thick foliage she could just about manage to make out three people. She recognised the smaller one as one of Harry's men, the other she didn't know, and of course she knew the third one only too well. It was Harry himself.

She listened to him speak. 'For fuck's sake, I just don't need this shit.'

'Sorry, boss, I dunno what to say. She just passed out. I was sitting there and she just started freaking out, then the next thing I know she just bleeding well collapsed.'

'Just get her the fuck out of here. The last thing I need is some dumb bitch in my kitchen. She makes it look messy.'

'No problem, boss, I'll sort it.'

'Well make sure you sort it quickly.'

The next moment Tia watched the two men go back inside, leaving Harry with his back to her just a few feet away. She saw him light a cigarette and she listened to him humming like nothing had happened. He was close, so close, and she was frightened to even breathe in case he heard her. If she moved, if she made even a tiny shift to the left or the right, he would know she was there.

Subtly shaking, she closed her eyes, desperate to try to calm herself down. Even that, even her shaking would make the branches move and rustle and if he did see her hiding in the bush, it wasn't as if it would be easy to explain what she was doing sneaking about. The idea of what he might do terrified her.

'Where do you want her, boss?'

Hearing the men come back outside, Tia opened her eyes, shocked to see them dragging the naked woman out. She bit down on her lip as she continued to watch and listen.

'Well not in my fucking car like that,' Harry snarled as he walked towards them. He bent down, roughly slapping the naked woman's face, causing her head to loll to the side. 'For fuck's sake. She's well out of it. Get her away from here. I don't need this shit.'

'You think she needs a hospital, boss?'

Tia saw Harry glare at his paid goon. 'A hospital? You fucking mug! And who's going to take her there? Are you? Cos I ain't playing Florence Nightingale for any stupid little whore, and I certainly ain't going to worry about what happens to her. All I care about is you getting her out of here. Now shut the fuck up for a minute and let me think.'

'Boss, I just think—' The man hadn't finished his sentence before Harry raised his fist and gave him a sharp, quick jab to the mouth. '*I said shut the fuck up* . . . She's still breathing, she's still alive, ain't she? So what's all the fucking panic about?'

With his mouth split and blood trickling down his chin, the man nodded. 'You're right, boss . . . sorry. I don't know what I was thinking.'

'No, none of us fucking do . . . Now look, I'm not responsible for the silly bitch OD'ing and I don't need a fucked-up hooker in my house. So, as long as she don't die on my doorstep, I don't care what you want to do with her – just get her out of here. Now I'm going inside, I got to make a few phone calls and when I come back out, I want her gone.'

'No problem, boss. I'll put her in my car and drive her somewhere, dump her, some other chump can deal with it.'

'Good, well I'm glad we've got that sorted, now fuck off out of my face.'

Harry stormed back inside.

24

With the rain pouring through the rhododendron bush, Tia stood in shock. She had no clue what was going on and had no clue either who that woman was. But one thing she did know was that she needed to get back to London as soon as possible – at least there she would have time to think, get her head around what she'd just seen. For now though, she also knew she needed to get what she'd come for.

Hearing the man's car drive off and certain that Harry was inside the house, Tia sneaked out of her hiding place, dashing across the wide, gravelled path before darting into the shadows.

Trying to push the image of the woman out of her head, she ran through the woods across to a small, agricultural outhouse. She paused only for a moment before quickly punching in the numbers on the rusty padlock. Rusty, not due to neglect but due to the fact that it suited Harry to make it look like it was a disused place of no interest to anyone.

The lock came off easily and Tia moved swiftly inside, edging her way past the old tractor, another ruse of Harry's to make it look like the place had long ago been abandoned. Squeezing past the tractor, she used her phone's torch light, making her way to the end of the building where she bent down and lifted a pile of empty wooden crates out of the way, careful not to make any noise.

Having moved the crates, she lifted the wooden flap, which was cut into the floor, to reveal the way down to the basement. With her heart racing, she stepped onto the ladder and carefully made her way into the darkness.

As quietly and as quickly as possible, Tia stepped off the last rung and shuffled and squeezed past empty wine crates, piles of old boxes and bags. All part of Harry's plan.

Coming to a pile of tarpaulin stacked up in the corner, Tia began to move it and jumped only slightly at the sight of a rat scurrying past. She took a deep breath and steadied herself, crouching down and pulling the tarpaulin away to expose a cupboard which, like the entrance to the building, had a rusty-looking lock.

With her hands still shaking, she leant her phone against the side to give her some light as she undid the lock and pulled open the tiny cupboard.

Inside was a trunk, which she slid out slowly. She flinched at the sound it seemed to make along the concrete floor.

She flicked open the catches of the trunk and pushed up the lid, immediately taking a deep breath as she saw what she was looking for. Cocaine. Three large bags of cocaine. *Harry's* cocaine.

Her hands hovered over them as every part of her wanted to turn back, but it was too late; she knew that. She was already in too deep, and there was no getting out of the mess she'd started. And again, she had to push the thought of Harry out of her head.

Taking one of the bags out of the trunk, she swiftly pushed it in the backpack she was carrying and in its place she put a bag of white powder, a mixture of crushed-up products she'd put together to look identical to the cocaine.

Of course she knew if anyone tasted it, snorted it or smoked it, Harry would know straight away it wasn't coke. But for the time being it was certainly better for it to look like all the bags were there rather than gone.

She wasn't sure when Harry would open the trunk, especially as he'd been out of the drug-dealing game for some time. Forced out by the Russians, he'd been focusing on counterfeiting and money laundering instead. But when he *did* eventually look, and he would, she wanted it to look as normal as possible. Though she wasn't sure how much a single bag of cocaine this size was worth, she knew it would be something towards the two hundred thousand plus mark and therefore she certainly had to make sure that the finger of blame wasn't pointing towards her.

Taking the other two bags of cocaine and exchanging them for the fake bags of powder she'd brought along Tia felt sick, hoping that by some miracle when Harry *did* notice, she would be long gone. She didn't even want to begin to think of what he'd do to her if he knew she was stealing from him.

Closing the trunk and sliding it into the cupboard again, Tia put everything back just as it was. She glanced around and once certain nothing looked different, she hurriedly made her way out of the building and back up into the darkness where she raced along the path and through the woods, all the time checking over her shoulder.

Coming to the fields, Tia paused for a moment to catch her breath. She pulled out her phone and quickly wrote a text.

I've got it.

The moment she saw it was sent, she deleted the text and with the wind and the rain gearing up, Tia Jacobs began to run.

It was dark and it was still raining as Alfie crouched down by his car. He'd parked in the woods quite a bit back from where the grey Audi he'd followed was parked, but it was certainly close enough to get a good view.

He'd been following the car for a good few hours now. In West Hampstead it had pulled over and Wan – but not the girl – had got out, so he'd continued tailing it all the way to a small village in Hertfordshire. Then he'd waited in a lane for a couple of hours and just as he'd decided to head off home, thinking nothing more was going to happen, he'd seen the same Audi speed out of the property. So, keeping a discreet distance, he'd set off again and found himself by a waste ground on the edge of Essex.

Still crouching and well hidden, and feeling the strain in his knees, Alfie watched whoever it was drive off. He stood up and rushed down the steep ditch and up the other side, scrambling through the dying bramble bush to the open wasteland.

Pulling out his gun from his pocket, Alfie hurried across the rubbled grounds. He looked behind him, but all he could see was darkness.

At the spot where the Audi had parked, Alfie looked around.

He'd watched the driver stand by the car's trunk for over ten minutes, and he'd been convinced that he'd seen whoever it was get something out of it. But maybe he'd been mistaken – after all, it was dark and it had only been the Audi's car lights that had given off any illumination. But then, why did they come here? Why drive the car to the middle of nowhere without good reason?

Looking around again, about to put his gun away, Alfie froze as he heard a slight noise to the far side of him. He pointed his gun and slowly crept along, all the time keeping alert, ready to make a move as he stared into the night.

'*Fuck!*' Unintentionally, he shouted loudly as he tripped over something, sending him sprawling face forward onto the cold, wet ground.

Scrambling up, he felt for his gun and grabbing it, he spun around. But there was no one there . . . He couldn't see anyone but he'd definitely heard a noise. He looked again and he thought he could just make out a shape on the ground. Yes, over there, he could see something.

Carefully, he moved forward and as he got closer, he realised what it was. He'd been in this business long enough to recognise that shape anywhere. It was a shape of a body taped up in black bin liners.

Putting his gun back into his jacket, Alfie suddenly jumped back as the shape started to move, then the next moment, he heard a muffled cry . . . A voice . . . And it sounded like a female voice!

Dropping down onto his knees, as quickly as he could Alfie pulled away the wrapping, as whoever it was continued to gasp and cry.

He spoke to them as he pulled away the gaffer tape from their head, tearing a hole in the plastic to let them breathe. 'It's okay. It's okay.' Then with one final tug, the bin liner came off and Alfie immediately saw it was a young girl. The *same* young girl he'd seen Wan bundle into the car.

'Oh fuck. Oh Jesus, it's okay . . . It's okay . . . Can you talk, darlin'? Can you tell me if you're all right?'

The girl didn't answer but continued to cry and Alfie could see she was shaking. Realising she was naked, he quickly took off his jacket and pulled the last of the bin liners off her before covering her with his jacket.

What the fuck Franny had gotten herself into, he didn't know, but he knew whatever it was, it was certainly shady, sinister and not something he'd ever imagine her to be any part of. Right now though, the only thing that mattered was getting the girl to hospital. Not that he could afford to get involved; he needed to keep his distance, so he would just drop her off anonymously. That way, until he was ready, he could still stay in the shadows.

With that thought, Alfie picked the girl up, bringing her into his chest to keep her warm, and ran as fast as he could back to his car.

25

Late Friday evening, Ellie slowly walked along the corridor of the house in Whitechapel that she shared with the other girls. She was tired and she felt ill but at least Wan would be happy with her, or she hoped he would anyway. She hated it when he was cross, hated it when he told her that they should be nothing more than friends. But more than anything she hated Sasha.

Right from the off, Sasha had tried to push her out and tried to be Wan's favourite. Sucking up to him all the time. A lot of the girls did that. Wanting his attention. Well she didn't think it was fair because there was no one who could love him the way she did, so she wasn't about to let a cow like Sasha come between her and the only person who'd ever wanted her.

Suddenly she stopped and stared into one of the

bedrooms, her face curling up into a sneer. 'Look what the cat's dragged in.'

Sasha, wearing a black Azzedine Alaïa open-back stretch-jersey dress, turned around and stared at her. 'What do you want, Ellie?'

'Why do I have to want anything? I can stand here – it's a free country ain't it?'

'Can you just go?'

Folding her arms, Ellie ignored Sasha's request and stepped into her bedroom. 'I'm not going anywhere.'

Sasha sighed and shrugged as she continued to stare at herself in the mirror. 'Suit yourself.'

'I will,' Ellie said as she sat down on the bed. 'Is that the dress Franny gave you?'

'Yeah, it's all right ain't it?'

'Yeah, if you want to look cheap. It looks like it's something you picked up from Whitechapel Market.'

Spinning around, Sasha stared at her. 'Why do you always have to say mean things? You're just jealous.'

Ellie curled her face up again. 'What! Jealous of you! I don't think so.'

'All the girls are right about you. You're so horrible.'

Hurt by Sasha's words but not showing it Ellie smirked instead. 'You talking about girls like Louise or Sophie? Oh no, you can't be can you, cos they're dead.'

Sasha's eyes filled with tears. She shook her head. 'Why would you say that? How could you say something so horrible? There's something wrong with you.'

'I'm only saying what's true.'

Taking a sip of her bottle of peach cola, Sasha wiped

away her tears. 'Just like when Wan told us all that he wanted to get rid of you because he was bored of you and you were too needy. Too desperate.'

Ellie's eyes flashed with anger. 'Why would you say that?'

'*I'm only saying what's true,*' Sasha said mockingly. 'You don't like it when someone tells you stuff you don't want to hear. It's not nice, is it?'

'Take that back.'

Sasha shook her head. 'Why should I? I'm only telling you what he said.'

Ellie stood up slowly. 'I said, *take that back!*'

'No!'

For a split second Ellie didn't move and then she raced across the room to Sasha, pulling at her dress. She shoved her hard, sending her sprawling across the floor. 'You bitch, I hate you!'

Trying to defend herself, Sasha put her arms up, stopping Ellie's fists. 'Stop! Stop! Ellie, stop! Leave me alone!'

'Not until you take that back! He loves me. Wan loves me!'

'You're crazy!' Sasha shouted as Ellie continued to attack her. Then she screamed even louder as Ellie grabbed her hair, dragging her onto the bed with her head feeling like it was on fire. 'Please stop, Ellie, Ellie! Don't! You're hurting me!'

Crying hysterically Ellie yelled into Sasha's face as she slapped her around. 'Then leave him alone. He's mine!'

Blood trickled into Sasha's mouth from her nose. 'What are you talking about?'

'Just leave Wan alone. You hear me? He's mine. You ain't taking him away from me. He's mine!'

With her mouth full of blood, Sasha began to cry. 'Okay, okay.'

'He's my boyfriend, Sasha, mine! Remember that. So, you shut your mouth about him. You're nothing but a slag.'

'I'm sorry, I'm sorry!'

Ellie shook her head as tears rolled down her face as well. 'I don't think you are though, cos that's what you said before, but you keep on talking shit and you need to be taught a lesson . . .'

26

Early Saturday morning Harry sat and stared at Tia over his double bacon and eggs. She looked tired, edgy, and she couldn't even look at him. Last night he'd got into bed with her and it had been like he'd been fucking a corpse. She'd just lain there motionless, and even after he'd got pissed off with her, and given her a slap, she'd still acted like she was on the mortuary slab.

In the end, he'd gone to relieve himself with Tammy, though as usual that had enraged him – staring at the face of Tia but with Tammy's eyes – so he'd got up and gone to the sauna and had a couple of grams of cocaine along with a blow job from some miserable-looking whore.

Of course he would rather have had one of Wan's girls but after the other night, he wasn't sure if that was going to happen again anytime soon. Wan had called him up giving him a bollocking for the way they'd left the girl, tied and strapped up. And in truth Wan's attitude had pissed him off. He'd really thought that the girl might have croaked on his doorstep and there was no way he wanted a dead whore in his house.

So, getting rid of her before it got messy was the most sensible thing to do. How was he supposed to know that not only would she pull through but also start complaining to Wan about the way they treated her? It was a fucking joke. A joke for Wan to give him an earful, *especially* as he knew that when it suited Wan he was just as likely to dispose of the girls himself.

Sighing, he glanced at Tia again. He could see the bags under her eyes, although that didn't deter him from seeing what a sort she was. But there was something wrong, something more than usual. Maybe she was sulking. Yeah, that was probably it. Sulking that it hadn't all gone the way she'd wanted it to.

That didn't mean she had to be a miserable bitch. It wound him up no end. But if he were honest with himself, he supposed in truth what really got under his skin was that she didn't seem to need him and if given the chance, she'd walk out of the door without looking back.

She hadn't even said anything to him properly since she'd come home that day from court and that pissed him off as well. All he'd gotten was cold looks and begrudging conversations.

Sighing, wanting to get her attention and knowing that he might get a rise from her, he said, 'Have you heard from that daughter of yours, Tia? Have you heard from Milly?'

Tia raised her eyes slowly to look at Harry. 'You know

I haven't,' she replied, lying through her teeth but knowing that she couldn't possibly tell Harry that she'd seen Milly, let alone that she was still in regular contact, *let alone* that she was paying for her daughter to be close enough so that she could see her when she had the chance.

Shoving a piece of bacon in his mouth before taking a huge slurp of tea, Harry smirked at her.

'I ain't surprised. Milly was always an ungrateful little bitch. Like mother like daughter, hey?'

Fighting the hurt, Tia ignored Harry, knowing exactly what he wanted her to do. He wanted her to react, to bite at his words, to see her defend her daughter. But she wouldn't, because she didn't have to, because knowing Milly was nearby was enough reason for her to sit here and keep her mouth shut, no matter what Harry threw at her.

She took a sip of her freshly squeezed orange juice, not wanting to look at him longer than she had to. Last night he'd hurt her, forcing her as usual to have sex with him; as usual she'd just lain there but it was even more difficult than usual. Every time she saw his face, she thought about the woman she'd seen being thrown into the car boot and the guilt she felt for not having done anything sat on her like a heavy weight.

She wished she knew what had happened to her. She didn't even know if she was alive. She didn't know if Harry's men had just thrown her into the Thames and the worst part was, maybe she would never find out.

Even though it had been a long shot, she'd looked at the newspaper and listened to the radio in case anything had been reported. But of course, there hadn't been anything there. It wasn't Harry's style or his men's style. Harry liked to hide his dirty laundry, which probably meant she was buried in some shallow grave.

'Hi, guys, now ain't this a lovely picture of domestic bliss?' Laughing as she walked into the kitchen, dressed in skin-tight white jeans along with a skin-tight top, Tammy smiled as she sat down.

She reached for the coffee pot and stared at Tia who looked pale and drawn.

'How was your little trip the other night, Tia? I haven't had the opportunity to ask you until now.'

To Tia it felt like her blood had just run cold. She could almost hear the sound of her panic. The sound of the silence in the room. She stared back at her sister, feeling Harry's sudden renewed interest as his glare burnt into her.

Taking a deep breath, she tried to laugh it off, tried to stay calm but even to Tia she knew it sounded put on. She could hear her voice trembling. 'What are you talking about now, Tammy?'

Tammy took a sip of coffee, enjoying making her sister squirm and giving an even bigger smile. 'Oh I'm talking about the other night. You went out, didn't you? Surely, you can't have forgotten already?'

Tia was sure that it wasn't just her imagination that her face had turned red. 'Don't be stupid, of course I didn't. You like to talk rubbish sometimes.'

Tammy cocked her head and smiled. Since she'd seen Tia sneaking out, she'd begun to follow her, wanting to know what she was up to. So far, nothing had come of it. She'd drawn a blank, but sooner or later her sister would trip up, she just knew it. In the meantime, she was going to have some fun. 'Do I? That's odd, because unless we're actually triplets not twins, it was *you* I saw going out and not coming back in until well after three in the morning.'

The loud crunch from Harry biting on a piece of toast, made Tia jump. She shook, wondering why Tammy hated her so much. She glanced at Harry who was still staring at her.

'Go on, Tia, I want to know what you have to say. I'm interested in this,' Harry said in a voice that spelt danger.

Trying as hard as she could to keep her tone light, Tia shrugged. 'I don't know what she's talking about.'

Suddenly, Harry, driven by anger along with an all-consuming jealousy, leapt across the table, crashing the breakfast dishes on the floor. He grabbed hold of Tia's pink shirt, pulling her towards him, bringing her up off her chair and onto the table. 'Who were you with? Who were you fucking, Tia? Is that what you do when I'm not here? You go behind my back? Is it?'

Trembling, Tia looked at Harry, desperate to appease him. She whispered as she spoke, her face inches away from his. 'Harry, please, she's making it up. I never went anywhere. Where would I be going, anyway?'

Harry's eyes bulged with rage. He shook her hard. 'I have no idea but I do know you're lying to me.'

'I'm not, I'm not, Harry! I swear I don't know what she's talking about. You know what she's like; she's always wanting to cause trouble between you and me. Come on, Harry, I wouldn't be so stupid as to try to sneak out. I've got too much to lose.'

Harry looked between Tia and Tammy. Then he brought Tia so close her nose was touching his. 'You better not know what she's talking about. Because trust me, Tia, it will be the last thing you ever do.'

He turned to Tammy and said, 'You sure you saw her go out?'

It was Tammy's turn to look from Harry to Tia and then back to Harry. She shrugged. 'Maybe I got it wrong. Maybe it was someone else wearing those plain clothes she likes to wear.'

With tears pricking at her eyes, from relief, Tia pushed Harry off her. 'See, I told you. I told you I never went anywhere. Next time, trust me.'

Nodding more to himself, Harry wiped off the crumbs from the baby blue Ralph Lauren shirt he was wearing. 'Well just let that be a warning to you, Tia. Cos if you ever go behind my back and I do find out, your life won't be worth living. Understand? And as for you, Tammy, don't be a fucking wind-up, otherwise you'll find yourself out on the fucking streets.'

Harry turned and marched out of the kitchen, leaving Tia and Tammy alone.

The moment he had gone, Tia turned to Tammy and smiled warmly. 'Thank you. Thank you for saying it wasn't me.'

But Tammy didn't return the smile. She scowled, and her eyes darkened as she stared at her twin sister. 'Oh don't thank me, Tia, because I didn't do that for free. You owe me now.'

'What are you talking about?'

'I want you to leave.'

'Tammy, are you crazy? Harry will *never* let me go.'

'Find a way, otherwise I'm going to tell him that you went out. Your choice, Tia. Do it the easy way or the hard way.'

Tia shook her head. 'And then what? You and Harry can play happy families?'

'Basically, yes, because like I told you, whether you like it or not, I'm going to tell Harry about the baby.'

'And like I told *you*,' Tia said, 'if you do, Harry is going to kill you.'

27

Later that day, Vaughn – having once again been instructed by Harry to keep an eye on Tia – looked in the rear-view mirror. She was sitting in the back looking tense, looking like there was something on her mind. A huge part of him wanted to ask her, to find out what was wrong. But the other part of him knew to get involved was stupid. He had enough shit on his doorstep without embracing someone else's.

Turning in to Mount Street, Vaughn drove slowly, passing the restaurants and Catholic church as he made his way towards Park Lane in Mayfair. Then, unable to stop himself and having never been any good at uncomfortable atmospheres, he spoke. 'You all right, Tia?'

'I'm fine.'

'You don't look it.'

Tia gave a rueful smile. 'Oh thanks.'

Vaughn shrugged as he slowed down enough to wave an old man across the road. 'You know what I mean.'

Tia glanced out the window as they continued down Mount Street, passing the various clothes shops. 'I need to ask you something.'

'Go on. Ask away.'

Taking a deep breath, Tia said, 'First, you got to promise me not to say anything to Harry.'

Pulling over in front of a large block of flats, Vaughn spun around in the cream leather front seat. 'That depends what it is.'

'Please, Vaughn. Just promise me.'

Once again reminded of how much he hated being in this situation, Vaughn nodded. 'Fine. Fuck's sake, Tia. Fine. I promise I won't tell him anything you say, but Jesus, girl, you're putting me in a position that I ain't comfortable with.'

'Oh and I am?'

Sighing, and not wanting this to escalate, Vaughn began to drive again. 'I'm not saying that . . .' He trailed off, waiting for Tia to speak.

'I need you to drop me off and pick me up in a couple of hours.'

'You know I can't do that.'

'Vaughn, *please*. I just need to do something.'

'And I need to look after you.'

Tia shook her head, biting down on her lip, trying to stop herself from crying. 'It's too late for that now, don't you think?'

Looking in the driver's mirror again, Vaughn rubbed his

head, now wishing he'd just kept his mouth shut and driven to Harrods as arranged. Give him a department store over women's emotions any day, and that was saying something.

'Vaughn, you just don't get it – this is a matter of literally life or death. *Please.*'

Vaughn sighed. 'I think you're being a bit dramatic, darlin'. Buying a new Prada handbag might be up there with your life emergencies, but it ain't up there with mine. I reckon you'll live,' he said as he indicated to pull over.

'Don't you dare, don't you dare condescend to me! You have no idea what's going on,' Tia screamed as she hit the back of Vaughn's seat.

He swivelled around and stared at her. A look of shock on his face. 'What is your problem?'

'Just, let me go,' Tia hissed slowly through her teeth.

He shook his head. 'I don't know what's going on, but you're asking too much of me, darlin'. I got Harry to think of.'

Clearly agitated, Tia pressed on. 'Come on, Vaughn, don't do this to me.'

The pressure of the situation making him angry, Vaughn raised his voice. 'I ain't doing anything to you. Don't you get it, Tia? If Harry finds out that I'm letting you go for walkabouts then not only do I have to put up with the crap he's bound to send my way, but there'd be a good possibility that he'd drop me. Then I'd have to deal with Wan. Because if Harry decides to wash his hands then Wan and his men will come after me.'

Angrily, Tia snapped, 'If Harry decided to wash his hands?'

'Am I speaking double Dutch? I really don't think you get it.'

'You have no idea how much I get it, Vaughn.'

Pissed off he growled, 'What's that supposed to mean?'

Not wanting to say any more, Tia stared at Vaughn. 'It means, Harry ain't all that he makes out to you. What you think you're getting isn't always the case.'

'Tia, I hate it when people talk in riddles; it reminds me of Alfie. He always liked to do that and the last thing I want to do is think about him. So talk straight and if you need to say anything, just spit it out, for fuck's sake.'

Seething but resisting blurting out the truth, Tia said, 'Just let me out. I'll meet you here in a couple of hours. I swear I'll come back on time. It won't be like the last time.'

'Sorry, babe, no can do.'

'Don't do this to me, I'm begging you.' As she said it, Tia suddenly saw two police officers walking along. She banged hard on the window, causing them to look her way.

'What the fuck do you think you're doing, Tia?'

'What I have to . . . If you don't let me out I *will* tell them that you're keeping me in here without my consent – not only that, but also that you've got a gun in the back of the car.'

Red-faced, Vaughn snarled, 'You wouldn't dare.'

'Try me.'

They held each other's stare for a moment, but it was Tia who said, 'I'm sorry, I wouldn't do this if I didn't have to, but I have to do what I have to do. I'll meet you here in a couple of hours . . . No hard feelings, hey?'

'You bitch.'

And with those words Vaughn, watching the two officers walking closer, immediately pressed the unlock button to let Tia out while thinking he wasn't about to let her get away with this.

28

Franny sat slumped at the table of Marco's Italian restaurant in Wardour Street. It was just gone 5pm – the place was getting busy – and although she'd walked in over twenty minutes ago, she still hadn't decided what she was going to eat. In fact, sitting here now, she just didn't feel very hungry at all. All she could think of was the diary. The diary and Sasha and Louise. Especially Louise.

Who was she? *Where* was she? The diary entries had only been from a couple of months before Wan had agreed to protect her. But she'd never heard any of the girls mention her name. Perhaps she was just letting her imagination run away with her. Perhaps if she'd continued reading on, then she would've found out that Louise was safe and well.

Yeah, maybe that was just it. Louise was now doing what teenagers do . . . So why then, no matter how much she tried to convince herself, did she have a terrible feeling in her stomach, a feeling that something very, very bad might have happened?

She'd wanted to go back and read the diary again but she'd thought it was too risky, so she'd gone to speak to Sasha, ask if she'd got the dress she'd left on the bed for her and then from there see if she could get Sasha to talk. But according to the other girls, Sasha hadn't been about. And no matter how much she tried to tell herself she was being paranoid, she couldn't help thinking that like Louise, Sasha might be in trouble. Everything about this whole situation spelt trouble.

She pulled out her phone and with a sinking feeling before she'd even pressed dial, she called Alfie's phone, knowing that within a couple of rings it would go straight to voicemail.

Trying not to sound too despondent, she began to leave a message. 'Hey, Alf, it's me . . . *again*. You know the drill, just call me when . . .' She paused and just as she was working up to say that she was sorry and that she missed him so badly, she heard the words, *'Mind if I join you?'*

She looked up, cutting off the phone message as Detective Carter sat opposite her. She glared at him. 'What do you want?'

He grinned, his velvet black skin shining from an excess amount of moisturiser, his brown eyes twinkling. 'What is it with you guys? Anyone would think you're not happy to see me. First Vaughn, now you.'

'Vaughn?'

'Yeah, your mate.'

Franny's face flashed with anger. She pushed a stray bit of her long chestnut hair behind her ear. 'I seem to

173

remember that he was your mate. Anyway, I don't want to talk about Vaughn.'

Carter smiled. 'That's funny because that's exactly what *he* said about you. No love lost there, is there?'

Franny said nothing and continued to stare. She knew Carter well, or as well as she could ever get to know a copper. He'd started off in vice and then in the serious crime agency and she'd first come across him when he had dealings with her father, who was a face in Soho, and then she'd had her own dealings with him . . . more than she'd care to remember.

She was also aware that Vaughn and Carter had once been friends. Once. A long time ago. Though obviously now they'd moved on in different directions. But for all she hated the police and certainly it was a question of *them and us*, Carter was at least honest. Straight. And she would even go as far as saying he cared about people. Cared about the community and the streets of London. No matter how much they had different trains of thought, Carter, if there was such a thing, was one of the good ones.

Sighing, Franny said, 'Listen, Carter, there's no love lost between me and anyone else, and that includes you.'

He laughed. 'Always hard-faced, aren't we? But I don't believe that's all there is to you. I know there's a heart in there somewhere, Franny Doyle.'

'Well that's what the doctors tell me, but I'm not so sure,' Franny said coolly.

'Come on, Franny, all of us have our soft spots. What is it for you? Cute, fluffy puppies? Christmas movies? A night in by the fire?'

Franny regarded him evenly. 'Dogs make me sneeze, I don't watch TV and I've got central heating.'

Carter reached for a toothpick from the small pot on the table and stuck it at the side of his mouth. 'I don't buy it. I don't buy the tough act, Franny. Oh yes, you've got balls. You've had to fight your way to the top, I know that. But that doesn't mean you don't have any feelings. I don't believe you don't know how to let down that guard . . . to care . . . to love . . .'

Franny shook her head. 'Do me a favour. I think it's you who sounds in need of a little bit of TLC, Carter. Sounds like you're projecting.'

Not to be put off, Carter continued. 'I hear that Alfie's gone. That must be difficult for you,' he said not unkindly.

Trying not to show any kind of emotion but for some reason suddenly feeling slightly overwhelmed by everything, Franny shrugged. 'Carter, what are you doing? I thought you were a copper, not a doctor. And sorry to disappoint but for your information, you're wrong. What you see is what I am. There's nothing warm and cuddly about me, so save the psychobabble for someone else.'

She got up to go, but he stopped her, pulling her back down gently onto her chair. 'Franny, I need your help.'

'What are you talking about?'

Chewing the toothpick, Carter brought his voice down to almost a whisper. 'I know that you're working with Wan, but I also know that it wasn't your choice.'

Again, Franny shrugged. 'Whoever you've been talking to has got it wrong.'

He leant forward, his strong, handsome face full of concern. 'I don't think so. We both know what's happened. Soho has a way of talking; word spreads easily. The point is, I need you to help me and you know why I think you will, no matter what you say? I know you care. You're not like the others in this game, Franny. Funny thing is, you remind me of Vaughn.'

'Now you're really taking the piss,' Franny said firmly.

'No, I'm not. You and Vaughn and even Alfie, you might have your differences, you might see life differently to the way I see it even, and yes, you guys might do bad things, but ultimately I don't think you're bad people. And there's a difference. Sometimes good people do bad things, but from my experience, bad people rarely do good things. And that includes Wan Huang. He's bad, Franny, and I want you to help me get him off the streets.'

'Not a chance.'

Carter sat in silence for a moment, then nodded to himself before he continued. 'What do you know about Sophie?'

'I don't know a Sophie,' said Franny, lying as visions of the young girl convulsing on the floor the other day came into her mind.

Carter's stare was piercing. 'Really? Are you sure about that?'

'I've just said haven't I?'

'Okay, what about this girl?' Carter placed a photo on the table of a smiling young girl looking carefree. 'Her name was Louise.'

'I don't know any Louise. I don't know many teenagers

so I reckon you're wasting your time. You need to ask someone else.'

'But I'm asking *you* because we have reason to believe that Louise came and worked for Wan for a short time. So of course we're keen to clarify this with anyone who might've known her.'

Franny felt sick, and although she didn't know it for sure, she was certain that the Louise Carter was talking about was the same Louise Sasha had written about in her diary. 'You said *was*. This *was* Louise. What do you mean?'

'She was fourteen years old and she was found beaten to death, wrapped up in bin liners. Toxicology reports show that she had a high level of cocaine in her system. Fourteen years old. Oh and if that wasn't enough, the pathology report showed that there was some internal vaginal damage from something sharp being inserted inside her. So come on, Franny, are you still trying to tell me you won't help me? Are you still trying to tell me, after hearing about Louise, that you haven't got a heart?'

Having to grip on to the edge of her seat to make sure her voice didn't show a hint of emotion, Franny spoke evenly. 'Like I say, I don't know anything.'

Carter thumped his fist down on the table, causing the other diners to turn around. 'I still don't buy it. I don't buy it that you're this cold.'

'And like I said before, I'm sorry to disappoint you.'

With his usual calm demeanour ruffled, Carter slammed another photo of a young girl down on the table. 'What about her? You know her?'

Unintentionally, Franny flinched.

'You know her, don't you?' Carter said as he watched Franny intently.

'No.'

His brown eyes darkened as he waved away the waiter who was hovering with a menu. 'Don't lie to me.'

'I'm not. I ain't ever seen her before,' Franny replied as she stared at the photo of Ellie. Because it was definitely her. Without the red hair, in her school uniform looking fresh-faced and very young.

'Why is it that I know you're lying to me?'

Franny sneered. 'Maybe cos you're a copper.'

'I think you know who she is . . . Look at her. Look at her again. She's fifteen. She's a runaway and she's vulnerable, Franny. She had a bad start and spent a lot of her life in and out of care. You don't want vultures preying on her do you? Is that what you want for her? Come on, Franny, you might even pretend to yourself that you're some cold bitch but you can't pretend you'd want a young girl to get into Wan's clutches. I know that's not what you'd want.'

Not glancing at the photo again, Franny pushed it away. 'I told you, Carter, I don't know anything. Besides, what makes you so sure that she came to Soho?'

'She told some people that she had a boyfriend here. He owned some clubs and restaurants. She also told them he was an older man. South East Asian. I reckon Wan fits the bill, don't you? After all, you and I both know what he does. It's just a question of proving it.'

'Look, I hope you find her, I really do, but I can't help you.' She stood up and was about to say something but she thought better of it and made her way out of the restaurant and into the chill of the London evening air.

She might not have told Carter who Ellie was, but that didn't mean that she was going to do nothing. Just that she was going to do it *her* way. And with that thought, Franny pulled up her jacket collar and headed down Wardour Street. She was going to find her and then, whether Ellie liked it or not, they were going to have a very long talk.

29

On the other side of Soho, Milly Jacobs sighed and stared at her large stomach in the mirror.

'You look well fat!'

'Thanks a lot,' Milly said as she turned to look at Ellie, a girl she'd met in the arcade in Wardour Street three months or so ago. She liked Ellie. She made Milly laugh, something she hadn't done for a long time, though she knew if her mother found out she'd go mad, because she'd promised her she'd lie low. But she couldn't just sit here doing nothing.

And it wasn't as if she wasn't careful. She was. Because aside from what her mum had told her, she had her own reasons she wanted to lie low. So when she did go out, she made sure that she tucked up her hair and wore her beanie hat and pink Ray-Bans, so it wasn't as if anyone would recognise her.

And anyway, it felt good to have someone her own age

about. She felt old and as Ellie had said, she felt fat as well. Old and fat and she was only sixteen.

'I've got stretch marks! Oh my God! Look! Look!'

Ellie jumped up and stared at her stomach just as Milly let out a breath of exclamation. 'He's kicking! Feel it!'

She took Ellie's hand and placed it on her stomach. 'Can you feel it, El?'

Ellie grinned and nodded, throwing herself back down on the bed. 'I'm going to have a baby with my boyfriend.'

'You're too young.'

Scowling, Ellie shrugged. 'I'm not and anyway, look at you.'

Milly suddenly looked subdued. 'That's different.'

'How?'

'It just is, and anyway, what have I got? I'm stuck here on my own.'

Ellie looked around the bedsit. She didn't see the grimness – Milly had tried to make the place cheery – the dripping water, the mould in the corner of the room and she didn't see the window that was smashed and held together with gaffer tape, all she saw was a place Milly could call her own. 'You're lucky to have this.'

Milly pushed back her hair and looked around as she lay down on the bed next to Ellie. She giggled. 'This place? It's a dive.'

'At least it's your place. I'd love to have somewhere. Just me and my boyfriend and no one else around, no bitches around.'

'You can have it! Take the place!' Milly laughed, which made Ellie laugh as well.

'So who's the dad?' Ellie said as she watched a very dishevelled pigeon sitting on the ledge outside the window.

Milly's face became serious. It was the same question her mum had been asking her from the moment she'd found out that she was pregnant so, like she'd told her mum, she said, 'Just some guy, Ellie. Stupid mistake.'

'Did you love him?'

'Are you kidding?'

'Well I love my boyfriend. He's dead handsome and I reckon he loves me too,' Ellie answered, swooning at the thought of Wan.

'Did he tell you that? Did he say he loves you?'

'No, but I get the feeling he does. You know, I think he trusts me. He asks me to do things that he wouldn't ask anyone else. We have secrets, me and him.'

Piquing Milly's interest, she asked, 'Like what?'

'Stuff.' Ellie turned her head to the side, which made Milly quickly sit up, staring at her new friend. She reached over and touched Ellie's neck. 'What's that?' Milly asked, shocked as she stared at some red and purple bruises.

Having forgotten they were there, Ellie's hand quickly shot up and covered them. 'They're nothing.'

Milly leant on her elbow, resting her stomach on a large, pink fluffy pillow. 'You got a scratch on your face as well.'

'Like I say, it's nothing.'

'Well those bruises don't look like nothing. Did he do that to you? Did your boyfriend do it?'

It was a moment before Ellie answered. 'I don't think so.'

'What are you talking about? He either did it or he didn't.'

Ellie's face crumpled. 'I can't remember.'

'Ellie!'

Shrugging, Ellie tried to downplay it. 'It's fine, it's no big deal and I don't mind, if it makes him happy.'

'Ellie, have you heard what you're saying? That's crazy! You've got to dump him.'

'I can't and anyway, I don't want to. Like I say, I can't remember if he did it or not.'

Milly stared at Ellie. Even though they were almost the same age, to her, Ellie seemed so much younger. 'You ain't making sense, El. What do you mean?'

Playing with her dyed red hair, Ellie took a deep breath as she figured out whether to trust Milly or not. 'You swear you won't say anything to anyone?'

'Like who? It's not like I get any visitors is it?'

'Okay, but swear on your baby's life.'

Feeling silly for not being entirely comfortable in doing so, Milly nodded and said, 'I swear.'

'Okay, well a few nights ago – Thursday night, I think – he took me to this place. The place was in the middle of nowhere and there were these guys, three of them and well, I did things with them.'

With her eyes wide open, Milly spoke in almost a whisper. 'Like what, Ellie?'

Looking awkward, Ellie shrugged. 'You know, sex stuff.'

'Oh my God, Ellie! Where was your boyfriend?'

'He'd gone.'

Shaking her head, in all innocence Milly asked, 'Why would he just leave you there with them? I don't get it, why?'

'Cos that's what he does, okay . . . Do you want to hear this or not?'

'Yeah of course,' Milly answered, wondering how Ellie could sound so calm.

'This one man was horrible, though he was well handsome but he was loud and rough. I'd seen him before, done stuff with him before, but it didn't make me feel any better, cos I knew what was coming. So I took a lot of coke and I must have passed out because the next thing I know . . .' She trailed off and Milly could see the tears in her eyes.

'What, Ellie? What happened?'

'I . . . I woke up and this guy was helping me. He took off . . .' She stopped, not fully knowing herself what had actually happened. 'I'd been tied up, wrapped up in black bags.'

Milly's hands shot over her mouth. 'Oh my God, Ellie! Oh my God. Then what?'

'Then the guy who found me, he took me to the hospital, left me there, and that was it really.'

Ellie shook her head, speaking vehemently. 'That's not it, Ellie. You've got to call the police. You've got to tell them. You could've been killed.'

'I can't.'

'Why not? What did your boyfriend say? He must want you to go to the police, right?'

'I told him, but he never said anything, apart from he wanted to make sure that I hadn't said anything to the nurses.' Ellie sighed, sadness exuding from her. 'Anyway, he said he'll take me out to cheer me up, so I can get my nails done and he reckoned he was going to get me a designer bag as well.'

Angry for Ellie, Milly took hold of her hands. 'Ellie, listen to me. This ain't normal. Has this stuff happened before?'

'Not as bad as this but . . .' She stopped and shrugged, not really knowing what else to say.

'You've got to get away. He doesn't care about you and it's obvious he's going to get you to do it again, and next time you could be killed. He sounds a right wanker.'

'He ain't! Don't call him names. I thought you were my friend,' Ellie shouted angrily.

'I am, I am!'

'If you were, you wouldn't talk about my boyfriend like that. I love him and he loves me. You're just as bad as the rest of them. He looks after me and I help him out. That's what you do in a relationship, but maybe you wouldn't know that, cos your fella ain't even around, is he? And no matter what you think, he does care! I know it.'

Milly began to cry along with Ellie. 'But he doesn't, El. Can't you see that? He can't do if he makes you do stuff like that with other guys.'

'He doesn't make me, I *want* to do it!'

'I don't believe that, Ellie. I don't believe you want to do that.'

Her eyes flashing with anger, Ellie screamed at Milly as tears ran down her face. 'What do you know? What do you fucking know about anything? You don't know him; you don't know what he's like.'

'I know scummy men. I saw the way my dad treated my

mum and she never got away and she's miserable and her life's ruined because of him, and so is everybody else's.'

'Then your mum's stupid, cos I can leave whenever I like, but I don't want to. What part of that don't you get? We're not all losers like your mum.' Ellie stood up and Milly staggered up too.

'Please don't go, El.'

'And what? Stay and have you bad-mouth my boyfriend? I don't think so.'

'Look, I promise I won't say anything else. I just want to help cos you're my friend. And . . . and if you want, you can stay here with me.'

'I'd rather die.'

At that moment, Ellie's phone pinged. She looked at the text, then headed for the door. 'I have to go anyway. Unlike yours, my boyfriend wants to see me.'

She slammed out of the bedsit, leaving Milly standing alone in the middle of the room, listening to the noise of Soho rising up from the street.

She sighed and a feeling of anxiousness came over her but then, she supposed she didn't have to leave it like this, did she? Maybe she could do something about it after all. With that thought in her mind, Milly grabbed her coat and rushed down the stairs. She was going to find out *exactly* who Ellie's boyfriend was . . .

30

Back in Tower Bridge, Alfie sat in his black, silk boxer shorts on the bed with a half-drunk bottle of whiskey and a couple of grams of cocaine on the night table. He sighed as the hooker, Rachel, attempted to bring him to climax, but he wasn't in the mood. All he could think of was the young girl and how she'd ended up in Wan's clutches.

'Jesus, Rachel, watch your teeth. You're supposed to be giving me a blow job not peeling the skin off me dick. If I wanted my penis to be shredded, I would've used a frigging cheese grater.'

With her mouth full, Rachel looked up and winked at Alfie, then gave up and sat back. 'It ain't my fault you're sailing at half-mast. The last time I saw something drooping this much was me auntie's potted Christmas geranium. Anyway, what's going on? This isn't like you. I reckon you need to knock that shit you're snorting on the head. I thought you were giving it up. That's what Jan said, anyway.'

The idea of Jan, the prostitute he'd been with the other day, talking about him irritated the hell out of Alfie. 'Then Jan's a mouthy fucker, ain't she? And besides, when I need drugs advice from a whore, I'll let you know . . .' He stopped and then looked rather sheepish as he pulled on his blue Abercrombie & Fitch T-shirt. 'I'm sorry, Rach, ignore me. I've just got a lot on my mind.'

'Care to share?' Rachel asked as she got up from her knees and sat next to Alfie on the super-king-size bed.

He stared at Rachel, taking in her warm face and her dark green eyes. Although she was still attractive, she looked older than her thirty years, but he guessed the life she led still took its toll, even if she didn't have to stand on street corners anymore.

He'd known Rachel for over fifteen years, if not longer, and there'd been loads of times she'd lent a listening ear. 'What do you know about Wan Huang?'

A look of disgust crossed over Rachel's face. 'I know I wouldn't go near him with a barge pole, no matter how much you were paying me, and you know how much I like my readies.'

'Why not? Why wouldn't you go near him?'

Reaching across to her jacket, Rachel pulled out a cigarette from the pocket and quickly lit it. 'Where do you want me to start? He ain't right in the head. I know his brother was bad, well moody and proper violent too, but Wan, he's got a screw loose. None of the girls I know will work for

him; they've got too much sense, and anyway, we're probably too old for his liking.'

Alfie shrugged as he allowed himself to succumb to
temptation and snort up a line of cocaine. It hit the back
of his nostrils and throat and he swallowed hard, pinching
his nose as it continued to feel like it was burning his
sinuses. 'What are you on about?'

'Oh come on, Alfie, everyone knows that he's into young
girls. Or rather, that's what his business runs on. Even the
Old Bill know it – they just don't do anything about it.'

Alfie slowly turned and looked at her. 'How young are
we talking about?'

'Well it depends on the clients, but we ain't talking about
young young, not like a nonce, not pre-puberty, but you're
still looking at thirteen, fourteen years old. Vulnerable ones,
like runaways and stuff. He's just scum, Alf. He's bad news.'

'But if they're that young, how come the Old Bill ain't
doing anything?'

'Problem is proving it. I think they've given up trying.'

Alfie shook his head. 'I don't get that. How hard must
it be?'

'It's the girls. They won't say anything; they keep their
mouths shut. They wouldn't dream of ratting him out.'

Snorting another line, Alfie lay back on the bed. 'They're
that fearful?'

'Oh no, ain't nothing like that, darlin' – well not in the
sense of fisticuffs,' Rachel said as she took a deep drag of
her cigarette. 'They love him. That's what they're fearful
about, they're scared he'll just walk away.'

'That's messed up.'

'Of course it is, but so are these girls, and that's why he recruits them. He picks them very carefully. He knows exactly which ones to groom. Wan's attention is probably the most they've ever had in their life. And he plays the game well. He's a jack-in-a-box.'

Alfie frowned, feeling his tongue becoming numb from the cocaine. 'What you on about?'

'That's what we call it when a pimp keeps giving and taking his so-called "love", or attention, away. Like he'll give it to you on the Monday, taking you out, buying you stuff, giving you loads of affection, but then the next day, for no reason he'll take it away. Call you names even, make you feel like that unwanted kid again. You end up feeling shit, like you've done something wrong or even worse, like there's something wrong with you. Like you're unlovable. And cos you're so desperate to feel special and cared for again, because the way he made you feel helped you forget what a shit life you've had so far and how bad you feel about yourself, you'll do anything for him to make you feel good again. Then if you decide to walk away for whatever reason, suddenly he's showering you with gifts and love, and you wonder how you could've ever doubted him and you swear to yourself you'll never think of leaving again.'

Even though he was high, Alfie could hear the pain in Rachel's voice. 'You sound like you're talking from experience.'

'Ain't we all, Alf? Ain't we all?'

'I'm sorry, Rach. I don't know what you've been through, but I'm sorry nonetheless.'

'You've got nothing to be sorry about, Alf. I reckon when

it comes down to it, you're one of the good ones. And that's what we're all looking for. Someone that will make us feel good, and if you're desperate, you'll take a whole heap of crap just to get a tiny bit of good. And Wan knows that. He uses that with those girls of his. Wan's tactics are less about being handy with his fists – but of course there's still a bit of that – so the girls aren't terrified of him in the violence sense, but they're terrified of losing him. They're free to come and go as they like, free to walk away, but they won't. They can't. They need him. He's like an addiction. Your coke is nothing compared to him.'

Rubbing his head, Alfie thought about what Rachel was saying. 'How do you know all this about him?'

Rachel looked out towards Tower Bridge. She stayed silent for a moment and then let out a long sigh. 'My sister. She was twelve when she ran away from my bitch of a mother. Thirteen when she went to work with Wan. And fourteen when they found her beaten to death, wrapped up in bin liners. Her name was Louise.'

31

It was almost 6pm as Tia ran through the streets, barging into people and feeling the cold cut into her face. She didn't want to think what Vaughn would say to her when she came back. If only he knew that she didn't have a choice perhaps he wouldn't . . . Tia's thoughts were broken as she heard the screeching of brakes and stepped back onto the pavement just as a Range Rover mounted it, blocking her way, very nearly knocking her over.

'Tia!' It was Vaughn.

She closed her eyes and suddenly felt the tears run down her face as he ran up to her, pushing her against the side wall.

'What the fuck do you think you're doing? Are you getting off on this? Running away all the time and playing games?'

'I ain't a kid, Vaughn.'

'No, so don't act like one. And you know something, I'm not covering for you anymore. Fuck that, I ain't putting my neck on the line for you.'

Furious, Tia snapped her eyes open, her face twisted in rage. 'No, but that doesn't surprise me. You just leave everyone else to put their necks on the line for you.'

'That ain't true.'

Tia's cheeks were flushed. She raised her voice, her face inches away from Vaughn's. 'Oh but it is – you don't even see what's going on around you, do you? You really think that Harry has your best interests at heart? You think Harry can just click his fingers and make everything all right, do you? Is that what you think he did?'

'I've lost you now. What are you even talking about?'

Wishing she could stop herself but with her emotions getting the better of her, Tia's words tumbled out. 'I'm talking about *you*, about Harry, about Wan. If only you knew the truth.'

Vaughn blinked, shaking his head in bemusement. 'You're not making sense.'

'You're just as bad as they are, thinking that it's all about you. Letting people pick up the pieces, poor old Vaughn.'

Trapping her against the wall with one arm on either side of her, Vaughn's handsome face loomed down over her. 'I don't think so and what are you talking about? At least have the fucking decency to finish what you started.'

His words seemed to enrage Tia, and her eyes flashed in fury. 'Finish what *I* started. Me? Are you serious? You can seriously stand there and say that to me! You fucking bastard.'

Vaughn shook his head. 'Tia, *please*. Just stop this.'

Crying harder, Tia's voice cracked. 'Don't. Don't you dare tell me what I need to stop! Now just get out of my way, I've got places to go.'

'You know I can't let you.'

'Just move.'

Vaughn stared at her, locking on to her gaze, then without warning, he leant forwards and kissed her. Passionately, urgently. Long and hard. Then suddenly he drew away. 'I'm sorry . . . I'm sorry, Tia . . . *Fuck*.'

The slap to Vaughn's face stung, leaving a welt on his cheek as Tia glared at him.

'Why? Why would you do that?'

'Tia . . .'

She shook her head, wiping her tears on the back of her grey Chanel coat. 'You bastard . . . you bastard.' At which point Tia ran off, leaving Vaughn standing, kicking himself in the street.

Through the veil of tears, Tia stumbled through the back streets of the West End, turning left along old Clifford Street before cutting through to Savile Row. She darted across Regent Street, not caring about the bus hurtling towards her, sounding its horn. She ran down Glasshouse Street then suddenly stopped, unable to go any further. She leant against the wall outside Prezzo and burst into uncontrollable tears, covering her face with her hands; sobbing and shaking whilst ignoring the strange looks of the passers-by.

If she thought her head was a mess before, well now it was a wreck. First Harry with that girl she couldn't get out of her head and now this. What the hell did Vaughn think he was playing at? But that was the point, she guessed. That was what she was to Harry and Vaughn: a game, a joke.

And who did Vaughn think he was? After everything, he thought that he could just lean in and kiss her. Like she was nothing. Like her feelings didn't mean anything. She wanted to scream. She wanted to tell him everything. But then, what good would that do? She needed to let sleeping dogs lie . . .

It took another few minutes before Tia was able to recover herself enough to continue to walk through the streets of Soho. She felt exhausted but she had a feeling that the worst hadn't even begun.

Turning into Brewer Street, she walked past the vintage magazine shop and just as she was doing so, her thoughts were cut short as she saw Wan standing in front of her. She walked slowly towards him and he smiled as he pulled her into the entrance of the small, gated archway by the side of his restaurant.

She stared at him and tried not to show how uncomfortable she felt.

'You're late, Tia.'

'I know and I'm sorry,' Tia said as she glanced along the street.

'Are you sure no one followed you?'

With her anger giving her confidence, Tia spat out her words. 'Oh, I don't want anyone to know I'm here either. The last thing I want is to be seen with you.'

Wan leant in to her. 'Don't forget, Tia, this was what you wanted. You begged for it. Remember?'

Shaking her head, Tia glared at Wan, who she'd known longer than she'd known Harry. In fact, it had been her who'd introduced Wan's older brother to Harry and it was her who'd regretted it ever since.

Overwhelmed by everything, Tia snapped, 'I never wanted this, I just didn't have a choice.'

Wan put his hand under Tia's chin, lifting her head up. He wrapped his other arm around her shoulder and brought her in for an embrace, kissing her passionately. He pulled away and smiled. 'Yes you did, Tia, you had a choice, but you decided you wanted it this way. You've got too much heart, girl.'

Not reacting outwardly to the embrace or the kiss, but detesting every moment she had to spend with him and feeling too exposed standing there, Tia said, 'Can we get on with this? I have to get back.'

Slipping his hand around her shoulders, Wan led her through the archway into the private courtyard, nodding his head towards a large, yellow steel door at the back of a building. 'Yeah cos you wouldn't want Harry to see you, would you? If he found out, he'd think you were being a very naughty girl.'

Bristling at his name, Tia tried to play it down. 'Just leave Harry to me.'

'Whatever you say, but you know if you ever need me to have a little word in his ear, let him know that there's bigger fish than him, just call me,' Wan said as he played with Tia's long blonde hair.

'I don't think so, Wan, do you?'

'I saw him the other day. He wasn't happy with you then,

either; just think what he'd do to you if he knew you were with me. It would be worth telling him just so I could see his face.' Wan laughed.

'Don't you dare. You hear me! Don't you dare!'

Wan stared at her and grinned. 'Calm down, Tia, I'm only saying.'

'Then don't, cos it ain't funny.'

As they walked into the restaurant, which was closed to the public until later that evening, Wan turned to Tia, his jet-black hair perfectly waxed in place. 'Have you got it?'

Taking her silver Alexander McQueen backpack off her back, Tia took out the three large bags of cocaine. Her hands were shaking as she placed them on the table. 'This is what you wanted.'

'I take it this is the quality stuff me and Harry were talking about the other day.'

'I wouldn't know.'

Wan winked at her. 'Well he wasn't going to sell it, so he might as well give it away.'

Hearing Wan talk about Harry again made Tia even more uncomfortable. The only thing she wanted to do was get out of there. 'And now we're even.'

Wan chuckled as he stroked her face. He took her hand and pushed it down his trousers. 'You know, I always liked you, Tia. My brother always said you were a good worker. Have you ever thought about coming to work for me?'

Tia's face twisted with disgust. 'Not in a thousand life-times.'

Hiding his irritation, Wan shrugged. 'Shame, we could make a good team.'

Tia pulled her hand away and stepped back. 'I ain't one of those girls you play with, not *anymore* anyway. Those days of pitting us and playing us against each other. Those days of making us think that your brother loved us, that he cared, when all he wanted to do was farm us out. Those days that your brother could get me to jump just by asking me are long gone . . . So if that's all, I'll see you around, Wan.'

Again Wan laughed, but this time his laugh was meaner, nastier. 'So you'll bring the rest next week then?'

A look of panic crossed Tia's face. 'You said that was it.'

'I did and it can be, if you want Harry to know, that is. I mean, what would he say if he knew you were robbing from him right under his nose and not only that, what would he say if he knew what the reason was? How would he feel if I told him *why* you were bringing coke to me in the first place?'

'You wouldn't. You promised. Wan, you promised this was all it would take.'

Wan burst into laughter. 'I know, I know. I know I did. And I bet you're thinking "what a bastard" now, hey?' said Wan mockingly.

Tia's eyes filled with tears. 'Don't do this to me. I can't get any more.'

'Not my problem.'

'You wouldn't turn over one of your business acquaintances, not really, so don't do this to me.'

'You're right, I wouldn't, but you're nothing but a little whore.'

Panic rushed over Tia and she could feel her heart racing.

'Wan . . . look . . . look . . .' She trailed off, not really knowing what to say.

'I want another bag of cocaine and then we'll call it evens. I can't say fairer than that, can I?'

'I won't be able to. I can't!'

Wan grinned, showing off his perfect teeth. 'I was always taught that there's no such thing as *I can't.*'

Tia shook her head, her tone full of scorn. 'I know you and even if I could get it, how do I know that that would be it? How do I know if I got some more for you that you won't just keep asking for another bag?'

He leant in and kissed her passionately on the lips again, closing his eyes as she shuddered in disgust. 'You don't, but that's part of the fun, Tia. I just hope it was all worth it . . . I'll be in contact.'

As Tia ran out of the small private courtyard into Brewer Street her mind was racing and whirling, her thoughts on what she was going to do distracted her so much she didn't see her daughter Milly watching in horror from the other side of the street.

And Milly had seen everything, *everything* including Ellie going inside the building earlier . . . though what was much more shocking, what had made her stomach turn, was seeing her own mother wrapped up in a passionate embrace with a man who was not Harry Jacobs.

32

Shaking, Milly stumbled along Brewer Street, back towards her bedsit. She couldn't believe it. She couldn't believe what was happening. Originally she was going to wait for Ellie to come back out again and confront her, talk to her, make her see sense. Tell her how much she needed to get away from Wan, no matter how much she thought she loved him. But once she'd seen her mother whispering and kissing, she didn't want to hang around any longer. She felt sick and it was all her mum's fault.

She couldn't get her head around it. Of all the things she'd thought her mother would do, it certainly wasn't that.

She'd watched Ellie throw her arms around *him*, kissing her so-called boyfriend and looking totally loved up then only a short while later she'd seen her mum kissing him too. It was crazy, disgusting, especially after everything they'd gone through, and it just didn't make sense. Why? Why would she do it?

How long had she been seeing him? Was that why her mum seemed so distracted at the moment? Was her mind on him? Maybe that's why she hadn't come around as often as she said she would, and it wasn't actually anything to do with Milly's dad at all. Even today her mum had said she was going to come around but at the last minute had changed her mind. And this was why. So maybe right from the start she'd been using Milly's dad as an excuse not to be able to come around and visit her because all along she was going out to be with *him*.

She shook as anger and betrayal rushed through her. She turned into St Anne's Court, and like her mother had done a few days earlier, she curled up her nose at the smell of urine, jumping over the pool of vomit at the entrance to her block of flats.

She touched her bump, protecting it from the large group of sightseers pushing past her, and she sighed. Not for the first time she wondered if she'd done the right thing by going ahead with the pregnancy especially the way she was feeling now. Everything was a complete mess.

Though it was too late now for regrets, the more her baby grew in her stomach, the more reality hit her. The truth was, she was scared and now after seeing her mum like that, she was also confused and felt more alone than ever.

She wished things could go back to how they were, well maybe not how they were with her dad, definitely not that – she hated him – but back before . . . She stopped, refusing to let her mind go there. She didn't want to think too much about things because when she did that, *that* was when the regrets really hit her hard.

Not wanting to focus on herself, with her hands still shaking, Milly reached for the bar of chocolate in her pocket as she let herself into the block of flats. She took a big bite out of the Galaxy bar as she thought about Ellie again, about the bruises.

She needed Ellie to see that she didn't need to put up with any crap. She could see exactly how someone like Ellie would fall for *him*, but to put up with what he'd asked her to do, to have to sleep with other men – no, that was so wrong. She *had* to make Ellie somehow see sense.

Suddenly Milly stopped and leant against the broken railings of the stairs as the baby gave her a hard kick. She gasped and closed her eyes, squeezing them shut at the memory that had just shot into her mind. Memories she'd never shared with anyone.

She stood for another moment, wiping her tears on the back of her Love Moschino denim jacket before continuing up the rubbish-strewn stairs, hating as she always did how much of an absolute dump the place was.

Not that she had anywhere else to go. This was it because there was no way she could go home with *him* still there. And now her mum was back at the house with her mind clearly on other things, she didn't know when or *if* she'd ever have a real place she could call home again. Which meant only one thing: this pigsty of a place with the junkies' discarded bloody needles in the stairwell and empty beer cans and rubbish everywhere was where her baby would be calling home.

Getting to the top floor and feeling not only out of breath and slightly dizzy but also unhappier than she had done for a long while, Milly put her key in the door with a heavy heart, wiggling the faulty lock before wearily stepping into her bedsit.

She froze and gasped. 'Who the hell are you?'

A woman stood in the middle of the room. 'I'm looking for Ellie.'

'And what, you thought you'd just break in to some random place and see if she was here?'

The woman smiled and shook her head. 'Not exactly, the door wasn't locked properly and when I knocked it swung open.'

Milly glanced at the door then turned back to the woman. 'Yeah, it doesn't really work properly. I got to get it fixed, but that still don't mean you should just come into someone's flat.'

'Sorry.'

Milly stared in bemusement. '*Sorry?* Are you having a laugh? You barge into my place like it's nothing and that's all you've got to say?'

Franny regarded the heavily pregnant girl. She was a pretty thing, beautiful even, and the funny thing was she reminded her of someone. Her features looked so familiar. 'Like I say, I thought I might find Ellie here . . . When are you due?'

Automatically, the girl's hands went to her bump. She shrugged. 'April . . . anyway, can you just leave please?'

But instead of leaving, Franny sat down on the bed. She looked around the small bedsit again.

She could tell the girl was trying to make an effort with this place, trying to *literally* paper over the cracks with silver and pink wrapping paper and hanging belts and beads but there was no disguising what a dump it was.

'So where's Ellie?' Franny said firmly.

'Are you a copper?'

At this point, Franny burst into laughter. 'Do I look like one?'

'Kind of.'

'Trust me when I say, I couldn't be further from being one if I tried,' said Franny, still smiling at the thought.

'Well if you ain't, who are you?'

'I'm a friend of Ellie's and I wanted to make sure she was okay; you know, catch up with her and have a chat. I saw her coming into the block and I asked the woman on the landing below if she'd seen anyone matching her description and she said she often saw her here,' Franny replied, telling only half the truth.

In fact, after speaking to Detective Carter she'd looked for Ellie and seen her going into the block of flats, but rather than follow her straight in, she'd actually waited for her to come out again before knocking on the various doors, wanting to garner any information she could. Unsurprisingly, most of the residents had told her to piss off in one form or another, but then a woman on the sixth floor, who clearly enjoyed a gossip, had directed her to the bedsit, where she had found the door slightly ajar and, taking the opportunity to see what she could find, she'd had a quick snoop around.

The girl, eating the last of the Galaxy bar, stared at Franny.

'You might not look like a copper but you certainly sound like one.'

Again Franny laughed. 'This is my polite voice, and look, I know it's out of order me coming in like this but I really did want to see Ellie.'

'What's your name?'

'Franny. What's yours?'

'Milly, and she ain't ever mentioned you.'

'No, but then she's never mentioned you either,' Franny said warmly. 'Listen, will you get her to call me? I'll leave you my number.' Milly took the piece of paper that Franny quickly scribbled her number down on. 'Nice meeting you, Milly. Maybe I'll see you again. If I don't, good luck for April.'

'Wait!'

Franny turned back and looked at Milly who was chewing on her lip nervously. 'What is it?'

'Are you really Ellie's friend?'

'I like to think I am – that's why I'm here.'

Milly nodded, her forehead scrunched up in deep thought. Then her eyes filled with tears again and her words began to tumble out. 'I don't know you, and I ain't even sure if I should trust you, but I don't know what else I should do, and I can't tell my mum, not now anyway, and you know if I didn't think it was serious, I wouldn't normally do this but I wouldn't be able to live with meself if anything happened, you see, and Ellie well, I think she's . . .'

'Think she's what, sweetheart?' Franny encouraged.

'I think . . . I think . . . I think Ellie's in big trouble . . .'

* * *

205

An hour later, Franny solemnly walked out of the block of flats after hearing all that Milly had to say about Ellie and the bruises and what had happened the other night. But like Tia earlier, what she didn't see was Detective Carter following her and what *he* didn't see was Alfie Jennings trailing him.

33

Vaughn could wait. He could frigging well wait. Tia didn't care, not anymore; not about Harry, not about Vaughn and certainly not about Wan. She hated them all and she wasn't going to play their game. Not anymore.

Right from the beginning all she was trying to do was make things right, make things better, not for herself though, for others, but where did it get her? Bob, that's where.

She sighed as she gave a sideward glance to Bob, the large, hairy-backed punter who'd been grunting and groaning on top of her for the past five minutes. Her skin felt like it was crawling, and as for the noise he was making, well she wanted to shove his shoes down his throat, just so he would shut the hell up.

Trying to take her mind off Bob, Tia stared at the ceiling hoping that the anger she felt for Vaughn would make this more bearable. She had to keep on thinking she was doing this for Milly. To keep her safe and near until she was able to leave Harry.

'Tell me I'm the best. Go on, tell me I'm the best, Brenda.' Bob grunted breathlessly as he stared down at Tia.

Replying with no interest at all, and wondering how long he was going to last, Tia muttered, 'Yeah, you're the best, Bob, you're the best.'

'Ask me to fuck you harder. Say it . . . go on, Brenda, say it!'

'Fuck me harder, Bob,' Tia repeated with a tone mixed with complete indifference and disdain.

Delighted, Bob screamed with pleasure as he climaxed, the thick, curly hairs on his shoulder full of sweat that dripped down onto Tia's face. She shivered in disgust as Bob broke wind on top of her, then without warning, he suddenly plunged his teeth into her neck, sucking it as she screamed and tried to fight him off, but he was too heavy and strong.

'Get off me! Get off me! What the fuck are you doing? What are you doing?'

At that moment, Lydia, hearing the commotion, ran into the room and hit the naked Bob hard with a large baseball bat. He screamed out as she slammed it down on his spine.

'What the hell are you doing? Get off her!'

'You cunt! Fucking bitch!' Bob screamed out as pain shot through his body. 'I only wanted to leave something special for her.'

As Tia got up from the bed, wrapping her dressing gown around her, Lydia stared in horror at her.

'What's the matter, Lyds? Why you looking like that at me?'

Without saying anything, Lydia shook her head, causing Tia to run to the mirror. And she gaped aghast at the large love bite that Bob had sucked onto her neck.

Panic rushed through her followed by anger. She screamed at the top of her voice. 'What the fuck have you done? What the fuck have you done to me?'

With his penis now partially limp, Bob stared at Tia, a look of puzzlement on his face. 'I thought you'd like it, I thought it would remind you of me.'

Tia exploded, her voice loud and verging on the hysterical. 'I don't want to be reminded of you! I *never* want to be reminded of you, Bob. I want to forget all about you, and let me tell you something shall I, Bob? Every time you touch me, I feel sick. Every grunt and groan makes me feel ill. And do you know what I do when you've gone? I wash myself. Yeah, that's right, *Bob*. I wash myself with bleach. Scrub you off me cos you make me sick. You make me sick to my stomach. Oh come on, Bob, don't look like that, don't look shocked. What, don't you believe me? Shall I show you?' With tears rushing down her face, Tia rushed to the small white cupboards in the bedroom, pulling out bottles of bleach. She threw them at Bob as she continued to scream at the top of her voice. 'See? See? Bottles and bottles of the stuff, just so I can get your smell off me. Just so I can try to feel clean.'

'That's enough,' Lydia said.

Distraught, Tia shook her head as she hissed through her teeth. 'It ain't though, is it? Because it's not enough for Bob to pay me to do anything he wants, he thinks it's all right to leave a mark on me as well . . . I tell you what, how about I leave a mark on you, Bob?' Tia grabbed the baseball bat from Lydia and ran towards Bob swinging it wildly at him.

Trying to protect himself with his arms, he cowered, shouting, as Tia steamed towards him. 'You're fucking crazy, you know that! Fucking crazy bitch!'

'That's right, Bob! And I'll show you how fucking crazy I am, *shall I?*'

She went to slam the bat down on Bob's head, but as she did so, Lydia pushed her to one side and spoke firmly to Tia. 'Enough! Enough, darlin'.' Then she turned to look at Bob. 'And as for you, go on, piss off and don't bother coming back. *Get out, now!*' Lydia yelled angrily.

A few minutes later, with Bob having hurriedly picked up his stuff and left, Lydia gave Tia a sad smile. 'Sweetheart, I'm so sorry.'

Sitting on the floor with her legs tucked up, Tia wept quietly. Her eyes full of pain. 'What am I going to do, Lydia? If Harry sees it, and he will, he'll kill me.'

Knowing what Harry was like, Lydia nodded. 'I can't even pretend otherwise. Look, the best thing you can do is go and get some of that make-up – you know the stuff that disguises blemishes and birthmarks. It's the only thing I can think of.'

'And if that doesn't work?'

With her face full of worry, Lydia shrugged. 'I ain't a religious woman, darlin', but I reckon the only other thing you can do is pray.'

34

Tammy, dressed in a short, black leather Versace skirt and white top, lolled on the end of her bed. She smiled to herself at what she'd seen. Then she laughed out loud, feeling very pleased with herself. Because she'd seen enough for her to know she'd been absolutely *right* about her sister; sly and devious and not so innocent after all.

Earlier she'd followed Tia and Vaughn and just when she'd thought there was nothing to see, her patience had paid off and she'd watched Vaughn kiss Tia.

Perfect little Tia. Well not so perfect now.

She'd contemplated phoning Harry straight away and letting him know what she'd seen but then she thought she'd wait, savour the moment and pick the perfect time. After all, it was the perfect bit of gossip. The perfect bit of ammunition.

Suddenly hearing footsteps she jumped up and rushed to the bedroom door, opening it wide.

'Hey, I've been waiting for you to come back.'

Harry scowled and without saying a word he continued to stalk along the wooden hallway.

'Wait, Harry! *Please*. I need to talk to you.'

He spun around, already annoyed that yet again he couldn't get through to Vaughn or Tia on the phone. Taking his frustration out on Tammy, he barked, 'Well whatever it is, I ain't in the mood for it, *especially* if it's anything to do with your petty jealousy over Tia. So if I were you, Tammy, I'd think twice about chewing me ear off.'

Hurt but refusing to show it, Tammy took a step forward. She wasn't stupid; she knew that Harry still wanted Tia and not her. Right from the beginning that had been true. He'd never been kind, not really. Okay, he'd bought her things, given her money occasionally, but kind and warm? Never.

Not that she was used to anything different. She'd never had anyone who looked at her like she'd seen in the movies. She'd never had anyone tell her he loved her, aside from Tia, that was. And what good was Tia's love? When she'd needed Tia the most, when they'd been kids, where was Tia's love then?

To her way of thinking, Tia had been the lucky one, because whilst Tia hadn't had it perfect by no means, it hadn't been Tia who'd been abused night after night by her foster father. So why should Tia have it all now? What did Tia have that she didn't? After all, they looked alike, they looked identical so by rights Harry should be falling all over her, but he wasn't. He hadn't ever done that, though she had thought that one day he would love her the way he loved Tia.

But as he hadn't, she could only put it down to Tia still being about. Therefore, if she could get rid of her, if Tia would only go, then she would have a chance. A chance to finally have someone who loved her. Because that's all she'd ever really wanted, was to have someone care for and protect her.

She ran her fingers across Harry's chest. She purred as she spoke quietly. 'Come on, baby, let me help you unwind.'

He pushed her hands off and he spoke sharply, punctuating his words. 'Don't fucking wind me up.'

'Harry, don't be like that.'

Angrily, Harry grabbed her wrists. 'What is it about you? You just want to keep on pushing and pushing.'

'I just want to talk. I've got something to tell you, something that might bring a smile to that grumpy face of yours . . . Well?'

Dropping her wrists and deciding it might help him get his mind off Tia, Harry nodded. 'Fine, go on, what is it? But make it quick.'

'Not out here, come on in.' She gently took his hand and pulled her into her bedroom, which was decorated in pink and pale yellows with furniture to match. Looking around, Harry absentmindedly played with one of the several silver trinkets on the dresser and, not one to have patience at the best of times, snapped, his handsome face a picture of irritation.

'Tammy, are you going to spit this out or not? I've got stuff to do.'

'I'm pregnant.'

The room fell silent for a moment and neither of them

moved until Harry turned his head to one side, his expression drawn in a harsh line. 'You what?'

Tammy smiled. 'I'm pregnant, Harry, *pregnant.*'

He stared at her and blinked, then blinked again. 'Tell me I'm hearing that wrong.'

Looking less confident this time, Tammy shook her head. 'I'm having your baby.'

'That's what I thought you said.' And with that, Harry lunged for Tammy, grabbing hold of her chin and squeezing it hard. She squealed in fright as he snarled, 'Is this some kind of joke?'

She shook her head as tears came into her eyes. 'No.'

'How far gone are you?'

'A couple of months.'

Harry nodded. 'A couple of months and you thought you'd only tell me now?'

'I'm sorry, I just . . .'

He cut her off. 'Who else knows? Have you told Tia? Does Tia know?'

Tammy stayed silent and didn't move as Harry bellowed into her face, 'I said, does Tia know?'

Tammy gave the tiniest of nods and immediately Harry drew his hand back and smacked her hard across the face, splitting her lip. 'And I bet you enjoyed telling her didn't you? I bet you thought it was a joke. You're a bitch, Tammy, and I want you gone.'

Panicked and with blood running down her chin, Tammy shook her head. This wasn't how it was supposed to go. 'I know it's a shock right now – it was for me too.'

It was Harry's turn to shake his head this time. 'No,

214

darlin', this ain't a shock, this is a fucking mess. Now get out.'

'Harry . . .'

'I said, *out!*'

Again Tammy shook her head. 'No, Harry, I ain't Tia and you're *not* going to treat me like that.'

Harry moved nearer to her as rage rushed through him. 'You're right, you're not Tia. You don't even come close. You're nothing but a nasty little bitch. Right from the beginning you handed it to me on a plate just so you could have a dig at your sister.'

'No, that's not true.'

'Oh but it is, darlin'. You can't stand it that Tia is loved and you're not.'

'Don't say that,' Tammy cried.

Harry laughed again. 'Why not? Because it's true. You couldn't even come close to Tia and you know the sad thing about it is that you're too stupid to see that your sister loves you. You're too full of bitterness.'

Tammy's face twisted in pain. 'She don't love anyone but herself.'

'Are you kidding? You stupid cow. She'll probably be the only person who ever loves you yet you want to throw it away? For what? For some petty revenge.'

'You can talk; you're no better. You're just a hypocrite.'

Harry smirked. 'You're right but the difference is, darlin', I don't pretend to be something I'm not. So, as I like to say to people, you can do this the hard way or the easier way, Tammy, but either way, you're going to get out of my fucking house.'

Flushing red, Tammy stared at Harry angrily. 'I ain't something that you can just throw aside. You ain't going to do that to me.'

'Ain't I?' Harry said as he grabbed her arm, pulling her towards the door.

'Let go of me! I said, let go of me . . . You're going to pay for this.'

At those words, Harry spun around and glared at her, his face contorted with hatred. 'Are you threatening me, Tammy?'

'Too right I am.' The minute she'd said it, Tammy knew she'd made a mistake and before she was able to backtrack Harry flew at her, causing her to try to make a run for the door. But being too quick for her, Harry grabbed hold of Tammy's hair, dragging her backwards, yanking it as hard as he could.

She screamed, trying to pull his hands away whilst he tugged her back onto the bed. He raised his hand and slapped her across her face as tears came into her eyes. He roared, bending down to pick her up by the collar of her shirt as anger ran through him. 'Are you for fucking real?'

'I'm sorry, I'm sorry, I shouldn't have said it – I didn't mean it.'

'Yeah, but you meant to get pregnant, didn't you? You meant to fuck me over like you fucked your sister over.'

'No, it wasn't like that.'

Harry's eyes bulged in anger. 'Did you really think that I'd want *you* to have my baby? *Did you?*'

'I just thought that . . . that . . .'

'That what?' screamed Harry. 'That I'd want a little bitch like you carrying my kid?'

Terrified, Tammy nodded. 'Yeah, I thought that you and me . . .'

Harry roared with laughter. 'There is no *you and me*. There was never a *you and me*.'

'But . . . but . . .'

He lifted her up by her hair to face him then tapped her forehead hard with his finger. 'But nothing, darlin'.'

'I don't get it. You were the one who brought me here. You were the one who asked me to come.'

'You can't be that stupid. Are you really that hard of hearing? How many times do I have to tell you this? You mean nothing to me. You must have a screw loose to ever think that. Like I just said, I was just using you, Tammy, using you. You were just a cheap fuck. Something to wind your sister up with.'

Tammy's face crumpled up, pain etched across it. 'No, no, I don't believe that. I mean, maybe that's how it started, but I know eventually I will be something to you. I know I will.'

'Sweetheart, desperate is an unattractive look,' Harry said nastily.

Panicking, Tammy spoke quicker. 'You're just angry right now – that's why you're doing this. That's why you're saying this. I don't believe that there's nothing between us.'

'Trust me, *believe* it. Now I want you to pack your bags and get the fuck out of here and I never want to see you around here again *but* before that, you are going to go down to the clinic and get that *thing* terminated.'

Crying hard, Tammy shook her head and covered her stomach. 'I can't do that, I can't.'

Snarling, Harry bent down to her. 'Then if you can't, I will. I'll take you. You ain't destroying my family.'

Tammy screamed. 'You think the sun shines out of Tia's arse, well you're wrong! You're wrong, cos I've seen her!'

He stopped and turned to look at her. 'What the fuck are you talking about?'

'I saw her with him. I saw her with Vaughn. I saw them kissing!'

But the minute she said it, Tammy Owens knew she'd said the wrong thing once again.

35

'I'm worried about some of the girls.'

Wan stared at Franny, noticing as usual how beautiful she was but her beauty certainly didn't make her less irritating, nor did it make him think – and not for the first time – that he hadn't made a big mistake in having anything to do with her.

With annoyance riding high, he said, 'How many times do we have to go over this, Franny? It isn't your job to worry, it's your job to look after them, keep them happy, keep them sweet and after that, you look after my clubs. Earn me money, keep the punters coming in. That's it. That's all. Surely that's not fucking hard to do, is it?'

Sitting down on the other side of Wan's desk, Franny rolled her tongue in her mouth as she glared at him. 'How can they be happy when they do what they have to do?'

'Firstly, they don't have to do anything. I'm not forcing

them. They know where the door is and I'm happy for them to use it. No skin off my nose. And secondly, there's other ways of keeping them happy. Pills? Powder? Come off it, Franny, wherever those girls were they'd need a little pep from something or somewhere. Make them forget who they are. Where they come from. Look at it like we're doing them a favour.'

Franny shook her head. 'The scary thing is, part of you really believes that.'

'Not part of me – all of me. I do believe it. These girls have a roof over their heads, they have clothes, they have their hair and nails done, they have good fun and they have their freedom to come and go. No bills to pay, nothing to worry about. No responsibility. Now, if I suddenly turned them out, turned them away, where would they go? Do you really think that they'd have it so good? Do you think they'd have a warm bed to sleep in each night? No. You know they wouldn't. So get off your fucking high horse and see it for what it is.'

Franny fumed. 'Oh I see it for what is it, that's the problem. Those girls are vulnerable, Wan.'

'And like I say, wherever they went they'd be vulnerable. I didn't break them.'

Franny laughed bitterly as she swept her long chestnut hair behind her ears. 'You've got all the answers, ain't you? Problem is you're talking shit.'

Wan pointed at Franny, anger beginning to wash all over him. 'I'd watch it if I were you, Franny. That mouth of yours will get you in serious trouble.'

'So many people have told me that, yet I'm still here.'

'Now who's got all the answers? Let me tell you something for nothing. Those girls, they love me. I give them the attention that they've never had. They'd do anything for me and in return I look after them. What's wrong with that?'

'Everything, Wan. Just listen to what you're saying. They're desperate to the point where they're willing to be raped by several men at a time just to please you. Just so that you don't take the tiny bit of attention that you give them away.'

Wan stood up and walked around the desk to where Franny was sitting. He leant against the desk as he spoke. 'Rape is a very strong word, Franny.'

'It is and that's what happens to them night after night because of you. Is that what happened to Louise?'

'What do you know about Louise?'

'I know she was murdered.'

Wan's face darkened and he clenched his jaw. 'Who told you that? Who the fuck has been telling you shit? What's Sasha been saying, cos if she's been spouting shit, she'll be in trouble.'

Franny stared at him curiously. 'Sasha? She ain't said anything. It's common knowledge, Wan, but what isn't common knowledge is *who* did it. Did some of your friends' games go too far? Did they get worried and then need to dump her somewhere? But of course, that was after she'd been abused and had internal damage from something sharp being inserted inside her. Or was it you, Wan?' she said, full of hatred.

Without warning, Wan used the back of his hand to slap

Franny hard across the face. Her head was knocked to one side and her lip slit open but immediately she stood up and slapped him back just as hard. 'We may have a deal, Wan, but that don't mean you ever can put your hands on me,' she said, tasting the blood on her lip. 'If you ever do that again, Vaughn or no Vaughn, Harry or no Harry, you will regret it.'

Wan's hand shot out and grabbed Franny by the throat. 'A fool knows no fear.'

Pushing Wan's hand away, Franny glared at him. 'Then that makes us both foolish.' And with that, Franny Doyle marched out of Wan's office.

It was over an hour later by the time Franny got to the house in Whitechapel. The traffic had been worse than normal and she'd had to ditch the car by the Blind Beggar pub – made famous by the Krays – just so she hadn't been sitting in a traffic jam for another half hour.

Walking into the house, Franny was pleased that the place seemed like it was empty and she suspected that all the girls had gone to the club or were still out having their nails done, which they always did on Saturdays.

Going up the stairs quietly, Franny stopped at Ellie's door. She knocked but there was no reply so instead she walked along the corridor to Sasha's room, as she still hadn't caught up with her yet. Again she knocked, but again there wasn't a reply. Instead of walking away, Franny opened the door.

She walked across to the chest of drawers and stopped, listening again, checking to make sure she was still on her own. Certain there was still no one in the house, Franny opened the drawer and saw that Sasha's diary was still tucked away, hidden under her vest tops.

Pulling it out, Franny sat on the edge of the bed and started to read, hoping that there'd be something in there that would help her better understand what was going on . . .

Thursday 1st
Louise is dead. Thought it was just a joke at first from that nasty cow Ellie. She was going around saying mean stuff, so when she said Louise was dead, thought it was a lie. Asked Wan about it and he got real mad with both me and Ellie. He slapped Ellie really hard, burst one of her eardrums – well that's what she said later. Don't know if it's true or if it's another lie. Wish it was a lie about Louise but eventually Wan told us it was true. Don't know what I'm going to do without her. Can't believe it. At least I've got Sophie but I'm gutted about Louise. Keep crying. Wan told me I was being a baby and Ellie thought that was funny. I hate her. She's such a nasty cow.

Sunday 4th
Worried about Sophie. She takes a lot of that gear that Wan gives her. I think it must be cut with something cos she keeps on blacking out. I told her to stop but she told me that I sounded like her mum. Just scared for her. Think Ellie is jealous of Sophie. None of the girls like Ellie.

Franny stopped and reread the line . . . *I think it must be cut with something.*

She thought about the way Sophie had been convulsing but then she knew that it was possible to convulse on coke as well. But if Wan was doing that, if Wan was cutting it up with something then that was a dangerous game . . . a dangerous game for the girls.

Looking back down at the diary Franny continued to read . . .

Monday 5th
Ellie told us that she wants to marry Wan. Sophie
laughed and Ellie got really nasty. She's such a bitch.
A girl came in, someone I didn't know looking for
Wan today, someone else for Ellie to get jealous
about. Don't know if I hate Ellie because she's nasty
or I hate her because she's so into Wan. Wan told me
that he didn't really like her and that it was me who
he loved. It's hard to know what to believe sometimes
especially as I saw him in bed with Sophie. Can't
hate Sophie cos she's my friend but it made me feel
so bad that I ended up cutting myself. That made me
feel better. Maybe I should leave, go somewhere
else . . . But would miss Wan too much and also
miss Sophie. My head's a mess.

Franny closed her eyes and she shook her head. It made her feel sick, reading about Wan and the girls and how much they thought of him. How much he'd manipulated their feelings. It also made her feel sick that she'd ever come to work for him. She'd have rather taken her chances with Vaughn and Harry than be a part of this, if she'd known what she was getting into. But then, that sounded like an excuse. She wasn't entirely innocent was she? She knew this business and she knew what people did. She also knew that Wan and his brother had a reputation and she'd chosen to ignore it so she was just as much part of it as he was.

She really needed to speak to Ellie and Sasha. He was clearly playing them off against each other, making them hate each other so they were easier to manipulate. They were all vulnerable but it seemed like Ellie was especially vulnerable because behind that hard, bitchy exterior meant to push everyone away, there was a young girl hurting. A girl who was just desperate to hold on to love, or rather hold on to what she thought love was. And it was clear that Wan was going to continue to use and abuse these girls and many more like them.

He was so good at it. So good at making them think it was all *their* choice when in fact he had groomed them, making them believe they couldn't live without him. And it was for that reason he didn't need to lock any of the girls up or watch or follow them because like the pied piper, Wan knew when he whistled, they would follow.

Unlike all the other things in her life she'd been involved in, this was different. *This* had to stop and maybe, just maybe she needed help outside her usual world after all.

Never ever did she think she'd even contemplate that, but never ever would she stand by and not do something about this.

Angry with herself, she stood up and slipped the diary

into her pocket, then pulled out her phone and began to text.

She hit send and let out a sigh because she knew now there was no going back.

36

At the top of Oxford Street, Tia jumped out of a black cab, hurriedly paying the driver, and without waiting for her change she rushed across to Selfridges.

Getting to the glass doors of the store, she saw a tall security guard stopping people entering. He glanced at her and in an uninterested tone said, 'Sorry, love, we're shut.'

Glancing down at her gold Cartier watch, Tia shook her head. 'You can't be. It's only eight forty-five; you close at ten.'

'I know.'

With the security guard not disclosing any more information, Tia pushed on. 'Then if you know, why you saying you're shut?'

Sighing impatiently the security guard regarded Tia. His grey eyes looking watery. 'There's some kind of problem with the fire alarms.'

With panic beginning to run through her, Tia looked distressed. 'What do you mean? You can't just shut the store now.'

'Don't ask me, I'm just doing my job.'

'Look, I just need to get one thing. I'll be back out in less than ten minutes, I promise.'

'Sorry, love, more than my job's worth.'

With her panic turning to anger, Tia snapped, 'I can see people still in there, so what difference does it make if I go in?'

'The difference is, they're in and coming out and you're out wanting to go in.'

Feeling like screaming at the security guard but knowing that it wouldn't help, Tia changed tack and gave him her best smile. 'Please, it's really important. *Really* important. I wouldn't ask otherwise.'

'If I let you in, I'd have to let everyone in.'

'But you wouldn't though, I—'

Cutting in, the security guard sniffed. 'Sorry, sweetheart, no can do.' And with that the guard jangled his keys and strode over to the other set of locked doors.

Closing her eyes, Tia shook. The only other place she knew she could find the sort of make-up that would cover blemishes, moreover cover love bites, was Harrods and that would shut in less than ten minutes and there was no way she could get across to Knightsbridge now.

She had no idea what to do, none whatsoever. She couldn't start wearing a neck scarf, not in the house, not anywhere in fact. That would be ridiculous. She'd never worn one in her life and wearing one now was bound to draw attention. Maybe if the love bite hadn't been so high up on her neck then perhaps a turtle-neck sweater would've covered it, but again, it wasn't as if she could sleep in it, was it?

So the only solution was concealer, which she couldn't get until tomorrow. But the problem with tomorrow was, she had to get through tonight.

Her phone rang in her hand and almost without thinking she answered it. 'Yeah?'

'Tia, it's me. Where are you?'

Tia closed her eyes as she heard Vaughn's voice.

'Tia, are you there? Tia . . . Look, I ain't angry, I just need to know where you are. Harry will be pissed, and you can't keep doing this and well . . . I'm sorry, I don't know what come over me . . . Tia? Just talk to me, darlin'. Tell me where you are.'

'I'm in Oxford Street. I'll meet you in Dunraven Street. I can be there in a few minutes.'

Then without waiting for Vaughn to answer, Tia put the phone down and pulled up her pink shirt collar, hoping that she could get through the next few hours.

It was fifteen minutes later by the time Vaughn was able to get through the traffic on Park Lane to turn left into North Row before doing a sharp right into Dunraven Street where he saw Tia standing on the corner outside an Italian pizzeria.

He beeped his horn and waved but in return he was greeted with a frown.

Taking a deep breath and vowing to keep his patience,

Vaughn pulled up by Tia's side. He pressed one of the buttons on the driver's door, causing the passenger side window to slowly lower. 'All right?'

Tia gave a tight smile and nodded but stayed silent.

'You getting in?'

She nodded again and opened the passenger door and was immediately hit with the blast of warm air from the car heater. She clicked on her seatbelt but turned away from Vaughn, facing the window.

Not quite sure what to say, Vaughn decided saying nothing was probably easiest, after all, look how talking to her last time had turned out. Putting the car into drive, he set off without saying a word.

'For God's sake, what's this geezer doing?' Vaughn spoke out loud as he waited in the traffic queue, which hadn't moved for the last twenty minutes. He could've walked there and back to Tia and Harry's gaff by now but instead, having been diverted, he was not only stuck on the corner of Brick Street just off Piccadilly, but stuck in the car with Tia with the atmosphere getting tenser and tenser by the silent minute.

Unable to keep it up any longer, Vaughn turned to Tia. 'About earlier . . .'

'I don't want to talk about it.'

Somewhat relieved, Vaughn nodded. 'Fair enough.'

To which Tia, irritated by his seemingly casual attitude, retorted, 'But it ain't fair enough, is it?'

Annoyed with himself for not just being able to keep his mouth shut, Vaughn replied, 'I don't mean it like that.

I mean, if you don't want to talk about it, then that's fine with me.'

Tia's face flushed red and even though she'd vowed to herself when she'd stepped inside the car that *she* wasn't going to say a word, she found herself turning to stare at Vaughn.

'Oh I bet it's fine with you, anything to avoid something difficult. Tell me, Vaughn, how does it feel to be able to put a gun to someone's head but not to be able to have a conversation?'

Feeling like he was the one with the gun against his head, Vaughn shrugged, cursing the fact that there was no way he could get out of the car and walk away. 'I've already said that I'm sorry, and I'll say it again if it will help.'

Knowing that she was taking her frustration of the whole day's events out on him but not caring, Tia raised her voice. 'No, it won't help, cos you can't take it back can you? So go on, why did you do it?'

'Do what?'

Tia slammed her hand on the dashboard, her voice filling the Range Rover as she shouted.

'Kiss me! Kiss me! You know what I'm talking about. Why did you kiss me?'

She stared at him, turning her whole body in the seat and he stared back at her. His eyes slowly darkened and his voice suddenly became hostile. 'What's that?'

'What's what?'

'On your neck,' Vaughn said, his voice dangerously quiet. 'What the fuck is that?'

37

Harry grabbed hold of Tammy's arm again and dragged her across the bedroom.

'What the fuck are you on about?'

'Nothing . . . nothing, it don't matter.'

'Oh it does. You best start talking.'

Not looking Harry directly in the eyes and trying to push down the strange, unfamiliar feeling of doing wrong by Tia, Tammy spoke defiantly. 'I saw Tia kissing Vaughn. I saw them.'

Harry shook his head, his face turning red with anger. 'You're lying!'

Terrified by the look in Harry's eyes, Tammy, trembling, shouted back, 'I ain't, I followed them. I saw them, like they didn't have a care in the world. I swear I'm not lying.'

Harry pulled Tammy up off her feet and shook her. 'You've always liked to cause trouble, always wanting to shit-stir, so how do I know if you're telling me the truth?'

'I wouldn't make this up. I *wouldn't.*'

Grabbing Tammy again and slamming her hard against the wall Harry, fuelled by rage and jealousy, bellowed at Tammy as he slammed his fist into the wall, splitting open his knuckles. 'She wouldn't dare though. Tia wouldn't dare . . . I ain't having it. She'd never do that to me, not with him.'

'But she would. She would, *especially* with him! Harry, you got to believe me.'

With his eyes wild with fury, Harry paced about. 'No, this is just you. This is just your way of taking the heat off the fact that you got yourself up the fucking duff. This is just you being a nasty cunt, but it ain't going to work, Tammy. Not this time. You ain't going to get me to fall for the bait. What did you think was going to happen if you told me? Did you think I'd chuck Tia out and then you and me would play happy families? Did you think that I was going to play daddy? You did, didn't you?'

Overwhelmed with emotion, Tammy blurted out, 'And what's so wrong about that? What's so wrong about me wanting to have someone care about me? It ain't a crime, you know, to want someone to love you.'

Still enraged, Harry, with blood running onto the plush cream carpet from his hand, leant into Tammy's face. 'So you admit it, you were lying. You can't help yourself, can you? Now if you don't want me to put you through that wall, I'd get packed, get all your stuff and get yourself down to the clinic.' He turned and walked away but as he got to the door, Tammy called after him, her hurt as usual turning to anger but this time tears streamed down her face.

Hating being rejected, hating feeling so unloved, hating feeling second best to her sister, Tammy screamed after him, 'Don't you walk away from me, Harry! You might not want me, but that don't mean I'm lying about Tia . . . I can prove it.'

He spun around and his face was twisted in anger. 'What?'

'I said, I can prove it.' She ran across to her red Givenchy bag and pulled out her phone, waving it in the air. 'Here, look, if you don't believe me. I've got proof, I've got a photo of them.' She stopped and smirked. 'So you see, Harry, Tia ain't the virgin princess you like to think she is.'

Harry's face paled as he stared at the phone and then at Tammy who was standing there with a mocking sneer on her face, and with a mixture of humiliation and rage running through him, Harry spoke in a dangerous hush. 'Is this a fucking joke to you, Tammy? Are you having a bubble at my expense? Do you think it's funny that your sister is out there screwing around behind my back? That they're making a mug of me? Well, do ya?'

'No, that's why I'm telling you.'

'Oh don't pretend, Tammy. You're telling me cos you're a nasty bitch who's always out for herself, cos you ain't much better. You think that I'm a mug as well, don't ya?'

'I never thought that, Harry,' Tammy said warily and with all the energy having drained from her, she was suddenly left with a feeling of emptiness. Left with a feeling of loss. She realised that it wasn't actually her sister she hated; all along it was herself.

'Oh but I think you did. I think that you thought you'd be sitting pretty with me. You thought you could turn me over by getting pregnant, didn't you? Well no one gets the upper hand of me. Not Tia, not Vaughn and certainly not you.'

Before Tammy had time to say anything else, Harry flew across the room at her, raising his fist and slamming it into her shoulder, sending her flying. She screamed loudly and as he charged at her again she fought back, hitting him with all her strength.

As he pulled her and dragged her and pushed her, she banged into the large chest of drawers, hitting her side hard. She fell to the floor, bending over double, cramping as Harry stood over her and stared, his eyes full of hatred. 'I want you out of here. I want you gone.'

Another shooting pain rushed through Tammy's stomach, tight pains overwhelming her. Breathless, she tried to stand, pulling herself up on the chest of drawers. 'My stomach . . . Harry, please, help me, I think something's wrong.'

Harry glared at her, his head full of thoughts of Vaughn and Tia, then he turned away and stormed out leaving Tammy to stagger to the door. Holding on to the rail, she tried to walk down after him, but suddenly the pain rushed through her again and the next moment Tammy Owens blacked out, falling forward and tumbling down the stairs.

38

Slamming her hand over the mark, Tia reddened and began to shake. 'Nothing. It's nothing.'

Vaughn's face contorted as he pulled down her shirt collar to expose the large love bite. Looking at her with disgust, he shook his head. 'That ain't nothing, sweetheart.'

'It's from Harry. He likes to . . .' Tia trailed off as Vaughn shook his head.

'Don't lie to me, Tia,' Vaughn yelled.

'I'm not lying.'

'That wasn't there this morning.'

Tia swallowed hard as she fought off her tears. 'It was. You don't know what you're talking about . . .'

'I ain't a mug, Tia!'

'How would you know?'

Glaring, Vaughn toyed with the idea of telling Tia the truth: that he knew because he'd watched her this morning.

He'd seen the way she'd tied her long blonde hair up in a ponytail, he'd seen her spray perfume on her neck, he'd watched the way she'd fastened her Messika diamond necklace, and he'd thought not for the first time how beautiful she was. So he did know. He knew that this afternoon when they'd set off from the house she hadn't had it.

Though he thought better of saying all that and instead he just made it simple. 'Cos I fucking do know, Tia . . . And I suppose this was what you were doing this afternoon, *was it*? Was this why you were so desperate to have a couple of hours alone? So you could go and meet your fancy man?'

Suddenly, without warning, Vaughn put the car into drive and mounted the pavement, cutting past the queue of traffic, and to the sound of horns he skidded into Piccadilly, weaving in and out of the bus lane, speeding down it before taking a left into Stratton Street and into Berkeley Square where he turned to Tia and yelled at the top of his voice, 'What the fuck have you been doing? How long have you been going behind Harry's back?'

Upset as well as enraged by Vaughn, Tia yelled back, 'I've been doing nothing, I already told you!'

'That's funny, cos when *I* do nothing, Tia, I don't end up with a fucking love bite on my neck.'

'And I already told *you* that I had it from last night. Harry came into the room like he always does. End of story. And anyway, I don't know why I'm telling you my intimate details.'

Furious, Vaughn leant towards Tia. 'So when I take you home to face Harry – who is already after me fucking nuts for not answering his calls, *yet again* – he'll take one look at that on your neck and just think, end of story, will he?'

Tia blinked, trying to regain her cool. 'Yeah, he will.'

Vaughn held her stare. 'I tell you what, I'll put it to the test, shall I?'

He pulled out his phone from his jeans pocket and scrolled through his contacts.

'Who are you calling?' Tia knew the panic in her voice and in her expression was palpable.

'Harry.'

Without saying a word, Tia, panicking, knocked the phone out of Vaughn's hands. She opened the car door and jumped out, rushing over to the park in the middle of the square.

Under the street lights she leant on the railings trying to get her breath as her chest tightened. Resting her head on the cool, steel bars she began to cry angry tears.

'Who the hell do you think you are? What gives you the right to come into my life and try to mess it up?' she snarled as Vaughn caught up with her.

'I've been asked to.'

Tia turned to look at him. 'And when have you ever done what you've been asked?'

Vaughn licked his lips, trying to keep his already triggered temper from exploding. 'Don't fucking start, Tia.'

'Me?'

'Yeah, you and I want some answers. So you better start to talk cos I've got to report back to Harry,' Vaughn said as he grabbed her.

'To Harry?'

'Am I speaking double Dutch *again*? Cos you seem to have a bee in that bonnet of yours about Harry. If you haven't forgotten, he's got my back and because he has, I've got his, which means when his missus goes and opens her legs for lover boy, I've got a problem.'

For the second time that day, Vaughn's cheek stung with a slap that Tia dished out. She pointed her finger at him. 'How dare you. You don't know anything. You think you've got all the answers. Well let me tell you that you don't know anything. The truth is staring you in the face and you can't even see it.'

Feeling like she was having a panic attack and wanting to get away from Vaughn, Tia, seeing a resident come out of the park, rushed into the gardens of the square.

As the rain began to fall, Vaughn ran after her, catching up with her easily. He grabbed her arm.

'Leave me alone, Vaughn. Just leave me alone.'

He held his phone in his hand and waved it in front of Tia's face, not quite sure why he was so enraged, not quite sure why Tia's cheating was affecting him so much. 'Unless you start talking, I'm calling Harry.'

'Why? Cos you think he's the great hero? Saint Harry, that's what we'll call him, shall we? Harry, rescuer and saviour.'

Vaughn stared at Tia and he sighed, trying to calm himself down. 'Look, Tia, I get it, I get he ain't the best husband in the world. And if I didn't have Wan and Franny right on my arse, I wouldn't be here now, but I am cos Harry is looking out for me.'

Drenched, Tia glared at him, wiping the rain from her

face. Furiously, she hissed her words, spitting anger at him. She pointed to herself. 'No, *I, I* have always looked out for you. *Me*. Right from the start.'

'What are you talking about?'

Crying, Tia looked up at the sky, closing her eyes as she yelled, 'You don't get it do you? You should be thanking me, not Harry. Me, Vaughn, me.'

Vaughn shook her, causing her to look at him. 'What the fuck are you on about, Tia?'

'Wan. You're not dead because of *me*, not Harry.'

39

It was gone 11pm that same Saturday and Milly sat in the late-night greasy spoon café in Beak Street with her beanie hat pulled down low. She sighed as she looked at Ellie who was sitting opposite her, full of hostility. 'Thanks for coming, El. I'm sorry about earlier. I never meant to upset you.'

Ellie shrugged and took a sip of milky tea. 'Well you did. You had no right to talk shit about Wan. I love him and he loves me. Why can't everyone understand that?'

'I know and I'm sorry. I'm just worried, that's all.'

Ellie's eyes seemed to darken. 'There you go again. If you've only asked to see me to talk more shit, then I'm going.'

She went to stand up but Milly pulled her back down. 'Please, don't.'

'Then stop saying all that stuff about Wan. He's the only person who's ever loved me in my life, the only person who's ever taken care of me. My mum treated me like a punching bag and most of the time when she wasn't drunk or sleeping with any bloke who would buy her a double vodka, she was locking me out of the house, so I was always out on the street. But Wan's not like that. He buys me things, he feeds me, he looks out for me, he's given me my own room with all matching furniture – I've never had anything like that in my life. So I know he cares, I know he loves me and if he needs me to do him a favour with his mates now and then, it's worth it to be with him.'

Milly's heart broke for Ellie because even though she knew Ellie could come across as mean and horrible, under-neath all she wanted was to be taken care of. So she nodded at her, though in truth she wanted to scream. She wanted to warn Ellie, tell her that this wasn't love, cos although Milly's dad, Harry, had been a nasty bully, her mum, Tia, had always loved her.

Thinking about her mum made Milly feel sad. After what she'd seen she didn't want to think about her, so she turned back her attention to Ellie. 'Okay, whatever you say.' Milly smiled. 'But I want you to come and stay with me. It'll be fun and we can just hang out together.'

'I got a boyfriend in case it's escaped your notice and I'd rather hang out with him.'

Milly shrugged. It was clear that Ellie wasn't interested in listening to anything that even hinted towards the fact that maybe her so-called boyfriend wasn't Prince Charming after all. 'I know but . . . and don't get me wrong here, but . . . look, promise you won't get mad at me?'

Ellie shrugged. 'It depends what you say.'

242

'Well, what do you know about him? I mean, what do you *really* know about him? What are his family like? What are his friends like? Have you met his mum? Been to his house?'

Dropping three more cubes of sugar into her tea, Ellie yawned. 'What's with all the questions? And anyway, I don't need to meet his bloody mother to know that we're in love.'

Playing with the piece of toast on her plate, which had far too much butter on it, Milly nodded. 'That's true, but you don't want to get locked down with one guy.'

Ellie scowled. 'What are you on about?'

'I just mean that there will be other guys apart from him.'

Ellie's face flashed with anger. 'I don't want other guys, I don't need other guys, cos I've got him, ain't I?'

Milly chewed on her lip. 'Yeah, but—'

'But nothing. You know what, I'm sick of this. Maybe you can't get your head around that fact that I love him and he feels the same. I reckon you're just bitter cos you're going to be one of them sad, single mums . . . Oh shit.'

'What?'

'Don't look now, but the guy who's just come in, he's the one I've been telling you about.'

Instinctively, Milly began to turn around but Ellie hissed at her. 'I said, *don't turn round*! Oh shit, fuck, he's coming over.'

'You like to cause trouble, don't you?'

Milly froze. The minute she heard his voice she knew exactly who it was: Harry. Her dad. Standing directly behind her.

Pulling her beanie further down her head, as well as pulling her hoodie up, Milly kept absolutely still, praying that Harry wouldn't move from where he was. If he did, he would see her. A beanie and a hoodie for a disguise only went so far.

She could feel herself shaking. All the memories of living at home came rushing back. All the times she was terrified of his temper whirled around in her head. The day he'd literally thrown her out into the street came thundering to the forefront of her mind.

He was one of the reasons – no, he was the *only* reason – why the last year of living at home she'd got herself in trouble, partied, hung out with the wrong people.

Looking back she knew it was an act of rebellion to not only get pregnant but also to keep the baby. It was her way of taking back control. Stupid, she knew it was, but when he'd found out that she was pregnant, he had beaten her black and blue and dragged her out of the house.

Of course it was an excuse. She knew that he'd been waiting for one. Waiting to be able to throw her out with what he saw as a valid reason. He was nothing but a hypocrite, a bully and worse still, from what she was picking up from this conversation, he was one of the men Ellie had been sleeping with. And that thought not only made her shiver and feel sick, it made her want to kill him.

'What the fuck are you talking about?' Ellie said as she stared up at Harry.

Harry brought down his voice to a whisper making sure that the large Greek man sitting in the corner eating a plate of chips and onion rings, didn't hear. 'I'm talking about a

244

little whore like you causing trouble. Complaining how we treated you. Well next time, you won't be so lucky. Next time, I'll get them to bury you a-fucking-live.'

And with that Harry stomped out, leaving Ellie and Milly sitting there.

'Who was that?' Milly said, pretending she didn't know.

'One of the guys I sometimes do a favour for.'

Not looking directly at Ellie, Milly frowned. 'What do you mean?'

'Jesus, do I have to spell it out? Wan asks me to sometimes keep his friends happy, that's all.'

Angry for her, Milly shook her head. 'Can you hear what you're saying? That's why he can't love you.'

Ellie stared at Milly across the table. 'What did you say?'

Unable to stop herself, Milly's words rushed out. 'He don't, Ellie, he just don't love you! He can't do if he makes you sleep with my . . . if he makes you sleep with men like that, and I just wish you'd listen to me.'

Ellie stood up scraping her chair back. 'I don't even know why I came to see you. You can't stand it that I'm happy.'

'But I don't think you are. You can't be, not with him anyway. You can't be happy with him! Look at your neck, look at your bruises, and you can't even remember what happened properly but he doesn't even care anyway. You could've died . . . It's sick, Ellie!'

Furious, Ellie picked up her drink and threw it at Milly, drenching her face and coat in cold tea. 'You don't know anything and you're the sick one.'

'But I do! I know more than you think. And I know that your so-called boyfriend wouldn't get you to do those things if he loved you and I know that he wouldn't . . .' Milly trailed off, tears running down her face.

'Wouldn't what?' Ellie screamed as the waitress came over to see what was happening.

Not wanting to say anything more to hurt her friend, Milly shook her head. 'Nothing.'

'Yeah it better be nothing and you need to keep it shut. From now on, don't call me, cos you and me ain't friends anymore and if I ever hear that you've gone round slagging off my boyfriend, you'll be sorry.'

With Ellie gone, Milly attempted to dry off her coat in the café's toilets before leaving. Stepping out into the road to avoid the group of school kids milling on the corner, she crossed to the other side of the pavement and with her heart thumping she continued to rush down the street. Taking a deep breath, she instinctively placed her hand on her stomach, knowing that if Ellie wouldn't help herself, then she would help Ellie . . .

40

It was hot inside the building as Milly walked down the stairs and at the first door she came to she took another deep breath, her hand trembling as she placed it on the door handle. She closed her eyes for a moment before pushing the door wide open.

'Hello, Wan. Long time no see.'

Wan looked up from his desk and smiled, showing no attempt to hide his surprise. 'Milly, what do I owe this pleasure to?' He stopped suddenly as he looked at her large, pregnant stomach. Then he grinned.

'I take it it's mine.'

Milly stared at Wan. She shook her head. 'No.'

Putting out his cigarette in the solid gold ashtray, Wan came around from his desk and laughed, striding over to her. He took her hair into his hands, playing with her gold curls.

'You were never a good liar, Mills.'

'Whereas you were.'

'Touché, darlin'.' He placed his hand on her stomach but immediately she jumped away as if she'd had an electric shock.

'Don't touch me.'

'Oh come on, Milly, don't be like that. After all, by the looks of you, I'll be playing daddy soon, won't I?'

Milly's face turned red. 'I already told you, the baby's not yours.'

'Milly, I know you too well. Why else are you here? Did you miss me? I told you that you would.'

'No, Wan, I didn't miss you . . . not one little bit. I saw you for what you were.'

Wan licked his lips. 'Not before we had our fun.'

Milly stared at him. He was right, they had. But that was *before* she'd known what he was like. *Before* she'd seen what a liar, a creep and worse he was.

She'd first met him when she'd been hanging out at one of the arcades off Tottenham Court Road, wanting to be there, wanting to be anywhere, rather than go home. He'd made her laugh. He'd made her feel special. Safe. Everything she needed to feel.

He'd treated her like a princess. Taking her out, buying her things, being the perfect boyfriend, but then over time she'd seen the way his moods had changed when she didn't do something for him – small things at first, like not drinking when he wanted her to, not wearing the things he'd asked her to, not taking the coke he'd wanted her to take.

And at first, like Ellie, she'd wanted to please him, but then one night everything changed.

Wan turned to look at Milly, smiling and gesturing her inside the room. 'Hey, Milly, good to see you – I'm glad you came, darlin'.' He shut the door then proceeded to lock it.

She frowned. 'You okay? What's going on?'

'Oh I'm fine, I just thought it was time.'

Milly shrugged. 'What you on about?'

'Come on, Mills, you ain't that stupid . . . I just think it's time I got to know you better, don't you?'

Feeling uncomfortable, Milly reached for the door, but Wan stood in front of it. 'It's locked, Milly, and besides, no need to rush out, is there? We've got all night.'

Beginning to panic, Milly shook her head. 'I . . . I . . . I've got to get home. My mum will go mad. She'll go ballistic if I stay out late again.'

He stepped towards her and shrugged. 'That's never bothered you before; in fact, most of the time you didn't want to go home. What's changed?'

Milly could feel her heart racing as Wan stared at her. 'Nothing, I just, you know, I'm tired, that's all.'

'Well how about I give you a massage? Help you relax – or maybe you want a couple of pills or some powder. What do you say?'

'No, it's fine, I'd rather go home, thanks.' She went for the door again but again Wan blocked her.

He laughed. 'Where you trying to go, Mills? What's with the drama?'

'Please, Wan, just let me out.'

He looked at her strangely. 'Milly, you sound like I'm holding you hostage. Come on, stop. Stop being so uptight.' He grabbed her coat and pulled her into him.

'Wan, don't!'

Wan's tone became hostile as he dropped his hold. 'Don't? Don't? Are you being fucking serious? You weren't saying "don't" when I was buying you things, when I was letting you eat in my restaurant or when you were getting your nails done. It wasn't "don't" then, was it? Did you really think that I was just doing all that for nothing? Did you think that I wouldn't want anything in return, Milly? I ain't a fucking saint and I never said I was.'

'I didn't think about it.'

'Oh come on, don't try the innocent act with me. You owe me, sweetheart. It's all about the give and take. Ain't no big deal.'

Milly rushed for the door again but he grabbed her, holding her by her waist, his strength overpowering her. 'Stop playing hard to get, or is that what turns you on? You like a bit of rough?'

'No . . . no, no I don't.'

'Jesus, Milly, lighten up, have some fun, for fuck's sake. You never know, you might enjoy it.'

'I just don't want to.'

He laughed. 'Don't tell me this is your first time?'

Milly nodded, to which Wan said, 'Well ain't I the lucky one?'

She could feel his erection as he pulled her into him and she struggled as he kissed her on her neck, holding her in an embrace she couldn't escape from.

Trembling, fear rushed through her. 'Please, Wan, don't, don't!'

'Sshhhh, Milly, stop struggling.' He ripped at her top, pulling it off, exposing her breasts as tears rolled down her face. Then with one arm still clutched around her waist he undid his trousers, causing Milly to whimper in terror. Then, without warning, Wan slammed her against the wall.

'I said stop. This is what you wanted from the beginning, so don't start pretending it ain't. I ain't doing anything you didn't want.' His fingers caressed her neck as he leant in for a kiss. 'Don't look like that, Milly – you and me are going to have some fun. I'm only doing what boyfriends do . . .'

Suddenly Milly halted her thoughts; she didn't want to think any more about that night. She still blamed herself. She should've known better. And she guessed it was like Wan said: how could she ever think that he wouldn't have wanted anything in return? But that was the point – she hadn't thought.

She'd just been so unhappy at home, so desperate not to feel miserable that it had felt good to hang out with Wan. Felt good to get his attention. So she knew. She knew exactly what Ellie was going through. She knew how Wan had made her feel. Loved, special, but most of all wanted, just when she'd needed it the most.

That's why she hated Wan so much – he was a wolf disguised in sheep's clothing. He had known how to give her and girls like Ellie enough attention, enough care to make them think that they meant something to him.

But unlike Ellie, she *did* have someone who loved her.

Her mum. No matter how difficult it was at home, she'd always known that her mum had cared, and it was that love that had eventually let her see what Wan was giving her was as far from love as a punch in the face.

That's why seeing her mum with Wan had been so difficult. It had messed up her head. Why would her mum want to see some scummy guy like Wan? Her dad was bad enough. Maybe that was her mum's taste. Guys who treated her like shit. She hoped it wasn't but why else would she be hanging out with him? She still had no idea how long her mum had been seeing him or how she knew him for that matter . . . Suddenly she stopped her thoughts again, not wanting to go there. It hurt too much.

And of course when it came to her and Wan, she hadn't told her parents about what had happened with him and especially what had happened that night. And she certainly wouldn't be doing that now. As far as they were concerned, it was just some boy she'd slept with at a party.

And as for the baby, well, she'd kept it for many reasons. At first it had been to spite her dad. He'd told her to abort it and by keeping it she felt like she was defying him, sticking two fingers up at him; whereas in fact, she'd actually hurt herself more than she'd hurt him. And by the time she'd realised what she was doing and *why* she was doing it, she was too far gone in her pregnancy to do anything about it.

So she'd decided to change the way she thought. She'd decided that even though Wan was the father of her baby, he or she was the good that came out of something bad, something evil, something painful. So instead of thinking of Wan when she thought of her baby, she thought of the love she'd give it, just like the love her mum had showered on her.

'Come on, Milly, you intrigue me, darlin'. If you're not here to whisper sweet nothings, what are you here for?'

Milly's gaze flicked around the leather-walled room, looking at the expensive ornaments and furniture. Then she stared back at Wan. Yes, he was handsome, strong, charismatic, but she was no longer blinded by those traits. She could see him for who he was.

'I want you to leave Ellie alone.'

Wan stared back at her and then slowly a grin appeared on his face before it turned into a snort and then loud laughter, though there was a dawning puzzlement on his face. 'Ellie? I didn't even know you two knew each other. She wasn't about when you were here.'

'Yeah well, I do know her and the point is, I want you to leave her alone. Just stop hurting her.'

'You sure you're not jealous because you think she's taken your place?' He winked and amusement played on his voice. 'Don't worry, Milly, she'll never take your place. There'll always be room for you.'

'I would rather die than come back. But like I say, leave her alone.'

'Or what, Milly? You'll stamp your feet and throw your dummy out? Is that what you'll do?' He chuckled then added, 'No, darlin', I won't be leaving Ellie alone anytime soon, not even for you, not even for the mother of my child.'

And it was that part of the conversation Ellie heard on the other side of the door . . .

41

'What are you doing here?'

Milly jumped as she walked along the hallway of Wan's club. She shrugged as Franny, who had appeared in the hallway in front of her, stared at her suspiciously.

'I'm . . . I'm looking for you.'

Franny gave her a wry smile. 'I never told you that I worked here.'

Milly, hiding her surprise that Franny was part of Wan's set-up, looked worried. 'You must have done, otherwise I wouldn't know . . . Anyway, I have to go.'

'Milly, wait!' Franny said as she grabbed her. 'I haven't told anyone what you said about Ellie, if that's what you're worried about. I ain't here to cause trouble. I genuinely wanted to help.'

'Yeah but you work for Wan.'

'It's not like you think. Trust me. And anyway, you still haven't explained what you're doing here.'

Looking sheepish Milly shrugged again. 'I already told you, I was looking for you.' She turned to walk away but Franny held on to her arm and dragged her out towards the exit.

'I may not be a copper, Milly, but I ain't stupid and it don't take detective work to know you ain't telling me the truth, so you need to start talking, *now*.'

Shaking Franny's arm off, Milly stood in the street as it began to rain. She burst into tears, feeling overwhelmed by everything that had happened and the box of memories she had opened up inside her head. 'Look, Franny, it was actually Ellie I was looking for. I just didn't want to say. Me and her had a falling-out.'

'Why is it that I don't believe you?'

'I dunno.'

Franny stepped towards her and brought down her voice. She spoke quietly but not unkindly. 'Well I do; it's cos you ain't telling me the truth. Look at me, Milly. What's going on?'

With a long sigh, Milly said, 'Not here.'

Franny looked over her shoulder as she pulled Milly towards her Range Rover, which was parked a few metres from the club in Greek Street. 'Fine, then we talk in here. You can tell me all about what's going on.'

Giving a small nod, Milly stepped in the car and for some reason she felt good that Franny was on her side. What neither of them realised was Wan was watching them on the CCTV.

An hour later, Milly sat on her bed in the dingy bedsit in St Anne's Court. She felt shell-shocked and tired but at the same time she felt relieved. She had told Franny everything. About her dad, about her mum, about Wan and about the baby and of course, she had also told her of her concerns for Ellie.

Franny had just sat and listened and then she'd given her a hug before she'd driven her home. They'd arranged to meet tomorrow to chat some more but for now she was tired and needed to sleep.

About to get changed, Milly jumped at a knock at the door. Before she could get up, the door was kicked open. 'Hello, Milly, I want a word with you.'

She trembled as she stared at Harry. 'What do you want, Dad? What are you doing here? How did you find me?'

'Oh come on, Milly, did you really think that beanie you were wearing in the café was any sort of disguise? I knew it was you straight away. You and that little whore friend of yours.' Harry grinned nastily then he stared at her belly. 'You've got some fucking front. I thought I told you to get rid of that.'

'You told me a lot of things that I don't want to hear and anyway, it ain't nothing to do with you.'

Harry looked around the room, seeing the damp wallpaper covered with beads and bright sparkling drapes. He took it all in: the bed, the sofa, fluffy pink and white cushions hiding the tattered brown couch. 'Does your mum know you're here?'

Milly shook her head. She could feel her face going red. It was like Wan and Franny had said: she was no good at lying. 'No, I ain't spoken to her, not since you chucked me out. I ain't interested in her and I ain't interested in you.'

Harry nodded. 'So how are you paying for this place and more to the point, darlin', if you ain't seen her, why the fuck is your mum's cashmere scarf over there when I saw her wearing it only last week? I think you and I better have a little chat, don't you? And I'm warning you, Milly, don't fucking lie to me cos today of all days, I ain't in the mood. I found out a few home truths about your mum today, which I don't like. So do yourself a favour and don't mug me off, otherwise, you'll be sorry.'

Outside the optician's in Poland Street, Franny leant on her blacked-out Range Rover, taking in the night air of Soho. Her head was full of what Milly had told her and now more than ever she needed to speak to Ellie and to Sasha, because if it was the last thing she did, which she hoped it wasn't, she was going to stop Wan in his tracks.

'Hello, Franny, thanks for texting me. I must say I was surprised, but I'm also grateful.' Franny whipped around and saw Detective Carter standing there. His handsome face lighting up. 'What happened there?' he said as he gently touched her lip, torn from where Wan had slapped her.

'It's fine, it's nothing.'

'You all right?' Carter cocked his head to one side. 'And I don't mean your lip,' he said quietly.

'Not really and well, doing this, it ain't exactly me.'

Carter smiled, a genuine warm smile. 'But it is, Franny, because as I said before, you're different. You may want everyone to think you haven't got a heart, but I know you, Franny. I know you would never let Wan continue to do what he's doing. I know you would never stand by and do nothing. And that's what separates you from the others. When it comes down to it, you do care.'

Suddenly, from what felt like nowhere, Franny was overwhelmed with emotion as she fought back the tears that she usually buried far down inside her so that she'd never feel them. 'It is what it is,' she said, trying to sound casual.

'Franny.'

She shook her head and looked down at the ground, breathing the cool night air in deeply as she tried to steady her emotions. 'Leave it, Carter.'

'I know we go back a long way, but you doing this, it isn't nothing and I'll always appreciate it.'

'I said, just leave it.'

He nodded and then from out of her pocket, Franny pulled Sasha's diary. 'Hopefully this will help. I'm not sure how much though. I mean, there's a lot about Wan and the girls and what he makes them do. There's stuff about Louise as well.'

Putting the diary in his jacket, Carter nodded. 'This will go some way I'm sure.'

Just as Carter turned to go, Franny called after him. 'Fancy a walk? I could do with some company.'

'Are you sure that's sensible? You being seen with me? You've got your reputation to think about,' Carter said with a wink.

Franny smiled and the irony wasn't lost on her that needing to feel wanted was something the girls that worked for Wan were so desperate to have and it was something that right now she also craved, even if it was with a member of the Old Bill. She had also always felt intrigued by him.

There was something about him that felt safe yet dangerous. Something strong and attractive.

She sighed and nodded. 'Well, how about a drink at mine? And for tonight only, how about we pretend we're just strangers who happened to bump into each other? I won't be who I am and you won't be who you are. No strings. No regrets. No repercussions. Just you and me. What do you say?'

But Carter didn't say anything. He just smiled and got into Franny's Range Rover.

Alfie watched from across the street and although he couldn't hear what they had been saying, he could see the way Carter had looked at Franny and for some reason a pang of jealousy shot right through him.

42

Nothing had been said for the past couple of hours. Vaughn was still in shock from what he had heard. It didn't make sense why Harry would make out as if it was *him* who'd been the gatekeeper between Wan and a bullet in his head. Not only that, but he felt a mug having been at Harry's beck and call only to find out that it had been Tia all along. But how? Why?

He wanted to ask Tia more about what she'd said but each time he did, it ended up with him losing his temper, so he decided to sit in silence. The combination of what felt uncomfortably like jealousy in regards to the love bite plus the revelation was doing his head in.

So now here they were, sitting in his car, *in silence*, looking out over the River Thames.

'Vaughn, this is stupid. Come on, talk to me.'

He whirled around and stared at her. 'Talk to you? Are you kidding me?'

Bemused, Tia stared at him. 'What is your problem?'

'My problem, Tia, is that both you and Harry have been lying to me.'

Breathing hard through annoyance, Tia snapped, 'Grow up, Vaughn, stop making this all about you. Just listen to yourself. Have you any idea what I've had to put myself through just so I can make sure you're all right? So I could make sure that Wan didn't put a gun to your head?'

'But that's what I don't get. How . . . why . . . and has this got something to do with that love bite on your neck?' Vaughn said, full of hostility.

Absentmindedly, Tia put her hand up to her neck. 'No. That's . . . look, it don't matter what it is.'

Raging again, Vaughn raised his voice. 'Oh but it does matter. It matters to *me*.'

'Why? Why does it matter? You're alive, ain't you? Isn't that enough? So just drop it. I've already told you more than I should've done.'

Furiously, Vaughn shook his head. 'No the problem is, you ain't saying enough, cos I need all my facts straight when I go and talk to Harry. Ask him what the fuck he's been playing at.'

Tia's face paled. 'Don't you dare! Don't you dare! Leave Harry out of it, understand? He don't need to know any of this.'

'But hold on, surely he already knows that it's not him stopping Wan?'

'Of course he doesn't.'

'What?'

'Just leave it!' Stepping out of the car to get some fresh

air, Tia rushed across to the embankment wall. She leant over, breathing in the River Thames air, watching the darkness of the water float by.

From behind her, Vaughn spoke. 'Tia—'

Interrupting, she spun around to look at him. 'I don't know why I bothered. I should've let them kill you, cos you don't seem to give a fuck about anyone else except for yourself. But then you always have, haven't you?'

'Not this again, Tia.'

Hurt and angry, Tia slapped Vaughn right in the middle of his chest repeatedly. 'Yes, yes, yes this *again*! Cos this is the first time I've ever been able to tell you how I feel, cos let's have it right, Vaughn – you never gave me the opportunity to tell you before, did you? But I guess that happens when you walk out on someone and don't look back.'

'Listen, darlin', it was years ago. We don't have to drag it up now.'

Incensed, Tia continued to rant. Her hurt palpable. 'Drag it up? Is that how you see it? I waited for you to come back. Day after day. Night after night. I thought that I'd done something wrong when you left me. That there was something wrong with *me*, that I was too damaged to love.'

'It wasn't like that,' Vaughn said looking ashamed.

Sobbing and angry, Tia was racked with pain. '*It was for me!* You knew that even before I'd left care, before I'd even turned fifteen that Wan's brother groomed me, fielded me out, made me feel like I was nothing, made me feel like the only way for someone to love me was to agree to sleep with any man they wanted me to. And it was only when I met you that it changed. You made me feel special, you made me feel loved and, God, I certainly loved you. But then you left without a word, just a note telling me that you couldn't do it anymore.'

'I was a coward and I was young and I was ambitious but more to the point I was wrong.'

'Yeah you were but stop the excuses – you weren't that young. You weren't a kid, Vaughn, so don't pretend you were some young naïve thing.'

'Okay, I know. I know, I fucked up. I was immature but I was ambitious and I thought that I couldn't become what I wanted to become if there was a you and me . . . I know now how stupid that was, and looking back, it wasn't as if I didn't love you. *I did.* I just didn't know how to handle it. And I thought about you all the time afterwards. I even thought about coming back to you but I thought it would be too late, I thought you wouldn't want to know. So I pushed you out of my head cos it was too painful and I convinced myself it was nothing more than a fling. But when I saw you the day I picked you up from court with Harry, I knew then, like I always had deep down, that I should never have left you . . .' He trailed off knowing that his words couldn't convey how sorry he was not only for hurting her but also for missing out on a life with her.

Tia answered ruefully. 'It's easy to say all that now, but don't you get it? You made me think there was something wrong with me. You made me feel like the only people who could care for me were people like Huang and Harry.'

'For fuck's sake, Tia,' Vaughn said not unkindly.

'What was I supposed to think?' Tia said as she looked

263

out across the Thames to the London Eye, feeling the chill of the wind blowing off the river.

'Not that. You weren't supposed to feel that.'

'Well that's exactly what I felt. And when you left, apart from Lydia, I had no one else around. I had no idea how to put myself back together but then along came Harry, sweeping in, making me feel like I was worth something after all. Jesus, I must've been a proper easy target. What a mug, hey?'

'Did he ever know about us?'

'No, he'd hardly have you looking after me now if he did, would he? I knew you and him became friends later on; it was inevitable in the life you're in. It's a small world, but I prayed I'd never see you again and I made sure that our paths never met, until now of course.'

For some reason Tia's words stung. 'What about Tammy? She must've known.'

'She suspected, but she had it worse than me, remember? She was just trying to survive too. Her head was all over the place. She was so messed up: going in and out of different care homes and chucked out on the streets at sixteen to fend for herself. We weren't in contact again until after you'd left. And by that time, like I say, she was a mess. I think that's why she's so angry with me. She feels like I left her . . .' Tia shook her head, wiping away her tears on her sleeve. Hurting for not only herself but also for Tammy. 'So here I am, still picking up the pieces. *Your* pieces. *Your* mess. Have you any idea what it was like to see you again after all this time? After years of never speaking to you or hearing from you for you to suddenly turn up like this? For you to suddenly be Harry's right-hand man?'

'That wasn't my choice though.'

'No, maybe not, but did you think that walking back into my life after all this time wouldn't bother me?'

'I just shut it away. It seemed easier.'

'Well ain't you the lucky one?'

They fell silent again but eventually Vaughn said, 'So the situation with Wan was really nothing to do with Harry at all? Nothing to do with him looking out for me?'

Tia took a deep breath trying to steady her emotions. 'Not really. I mean he did try, you know, just saying what a top bloke you were. But Wan was having none of it. I heard him tell Harry how he was going to make you pay for what you did to his brother. You were going to be pushing up daisies. I knew I couldn't let that happen. I couldn't let him kill you.'

'How though? How did you get him to listen to you?'

'Well I went to Wan and pleaded for your life. And because me and Wan and his brother went back a long way, he agreed. He agreed to make it look like it was because Harry asked him not to do it.' Tears ran down her face as Vaughn stared at her in amazement.

'Franny was right then,' Vaughn said as he lit a cigarette, inhaling it deeply.

'What are you talking about?' Tia said, puzzled.

'The last time I saw her she said that there was something more to it. She said that there was no way Wan wouldn't look for revenge just because Harry had asked him not to.' He paused and stared at her. 'But why would you do that for me and *why* would Wan do it for you?'

'Oh for fuck's sake, Vaughn. Wan and his men, they were

going to kill you. Chop you up into little pieces. You murdered his brother so what did you expect? You should've never messed with the Triads.'

'Yes, but you still ain't telling me why you did that for me?'

Tia yelled in his face. 'Ain't it obvious? No matter how hurt I was by you walking away that day, no matter how much at times I wanted you to suffer, I couldn't let something happen to you. Cos stupidly, a little part of me has always loved you. I never stopped loving you, Vaughn, not really. You were one of the few good things in my life. But hey, loving you – well that's the easy part. The hard part is owing Wan.'

'What?'

'The price for your head was six kilos of cocaine. I stole it from Harry, from a stash of it in a trunk in his outhouse at the farm, but now Wan wants more, and if I don't get it, we're both dead.'

43

They drove once more in silence with Vaughn mulling over everything Tia had said. As they sped through Holborn towards the West End, Vaughn suddenly pulled over in Drury Lane. The street was dark and quiet with only a few night-time revellers in the distance.

Taking a deep breath he readied himself for the answer, determined he wasn't going to lose his temper. 'Tell me about the love bite, Tia.'

Tia looked down and fidgeted with her fingers. She spoke quietly, exhausted from the night's events as well as the realisation sinking in that somehow she had to explain to Harry why she hadn't been about. 'Please, Vaughn, don't ask me. Just leave it. You don't need to know anything else.'

'Who are you seeing? I mean, I get it . . . I get that we all need someone and if you going behind Harry's back to get a bit of TLC makes you feel better, well that's okay.'

Raising her head to look at him, Tia snapped, 'I don't need your permission, Vaughn.'

It was Vaughn's turn to snap. 'I ain't saying you do. All I'm saying is I understand and I hope whoever he is deserves you . . . Do you love him?'

Tia's laughter was full of bitterness and like so often of late tears fell. 'Love? Is that what you think? That I'm being wined and dined, and swept off me feet? Oh yeah, that's me, long passionate nights in Paris, dinner on the Seine. Or perhaps, a couple of hundred quid round at Lydia's for lying on my back with Bob or Alan or any other geezer who happens to have a spare fifty quid.'

Vaughn's face paled. 'You what?' he said with a dangerous, slow lull in his voice.

Tia's eyes were full of pain, her expression haunted. 'Yeah that's right – anything you want, anything goes as long as you have the readies. Do what you like with me as long as you pay.'

Hardly able to find his words, an array of emotions rushed through Vaughn. Anger. Jealousy. Betrayal. Disgust. Disbelief, all mixing together. 'Are you saying what I think you're saying, Tia?'

'It depends. If you think I'm telling you that I'm a whore earning money behind my husband's back, then yeah, I'm saying exactly that.'

It was too much for Vaughn and in the darkness and the heat of the Range Rover, he leapt at her, his hand clutched but not squeezing around her throat. His voice shook with emotion as he growled at her and his handsome face was contorted with pain. 'Why, Tia? Why would you do something like that? Why the *fuck* would you do it? I just don't get it . . . Tell me you're just winding me up. Tell me it's just your way of having a dig at me, getting me back for what I did.'

She slapped his hand away and glared at him. 'Why is it still all about you? Look around you, Vaughn, the world ain't revolving around you. What happened to caring about how I feel? What happened to stopping a moment and asking why I would have to go to those lengths to earn a bit of money? But oh no, you can't do that, that would be asking too much, wouldn't it, cos it's all just about Vaughn again.'

Vaughn's eyes flashed with anger. 'What the fuck are you talking about? How the hell do you want me to react? I just hear that my ex is spreading her legs for a few readies and—'

Once again the slap stung but this time it not only stung, it hurt. 'Shut up! Just shut the hell up. Don't you dare start preaching to me about being your ex. For sixteen years you never once thought about that. You never gave me a second thought, and don't look like that, cos you know what I'm saying is true.'

'I just can't get my head around it. Whilst I was driving you about like a mug, all the time you were planning your next move, planning how to get away so you could whore yourself out . . . How could you? How could you do that?' Vaughn hissed through gritted teeth.

'What, you want the step-by-step guide to it? Is that with or without the diagrams?' Tia said sarcastically.

Slamming his palm against the steering wheel, Vaughn

couldn't contain his rage. 'Are you trying to take the fucking piss?'

'No, *you* are.'

'Me? No, darlin', not me. I just want to know why you did it. That ain't too much to ask surely?'

'What possible business is it of yours?'

Enraged, Vaughn, wishing he didn't feel as if he'd just been hit by a sledgehammer, yelled, 'Stop with the clever replies, Tia, and just tell me.'

'No!'

'*I said tell me!*'

Yelling back, Tia blazed with anger. 'Why? Why does it matter to you? It's who I am, ain't it? That's what I did when I met you, so what's the difference now?'

'The difference is, that's what Huang and his men made you do and you got out of it, but for some fucked-up reason you've got back into it and I know for a fact that Harry ain't the one getting you to do it. Fuck me, if he knew you'd be six foot under.'

'I needed the money and it's not like I could get any money off Harry. I've got to account for everything I spend and you know that.'

'Then get a fucking job!' Vaughn screamed. 'That's what other people do. You want a few shillings to buy a frigging bag, then stack some fucking shelves.'

'You ain't even making sense. Like Harry would let me. Why does it even bother you anyway?'

Vaughn's face was flushed red with anger. 'It's you who's not making sense and if you must know why it bothers me . . . it's cos . . . cos I can't stand the thought of it. I can't stand the thought of them touching you. I can't stand the thought of some scuzzy fucker with his hands all over you. I can't even stand the thought of you with Harry, cos I still care. I still want you. That's why I kissed you, cos even after all these years, it's you I want.'

Suddenly he leant towards Tia and kissed her, hard and passionately, and this time Tia responded. She kissed him back just as hard, just as passionately, losing herself in him. But Vaughn suddenly pulled away. 'Are you in trouble? Is that what it is? I mean besides Wan? Whatever it is, let me make it better for you.'

She stared at him then nodded her head, stroking his handsome face. 'The money wasn't for me. It's for Milly. I needed to help her . . . I needed it to pay for *your* daughter.'

44

It was the early hours of Sunday morning and Harry knocked back his fifth double whiskey. He was angry. More than angry. He was ready to do some fucking damage. What Tammy had said about Tia and Vaughn ate at his very soul. All he could think about was the two of them together.

Images of his wife rushed through his head as well as images of what he was going to do to Vaughn. What he was going to do to both of them, but first he needed to see someone.

Sighing, he gestured to the woman behind the bar to refill his glass then, from the corner of his eye, he saw Wan, the person he'd been waiting for.

'You took your fucking time – I called you over a couple of hours ago.' Angrily he stared at Wan as he sauntered into the club.

A small smile spread across Wan's face. 'That can't be me that you're talking to like a cunt? Cos firstly, Harry, this is *my* club you're drinking in and secondly – and most importantly – I'm not here to jump when you say jump. Now if you have a problem, take my advice and don't send any of your shit my way.'

As much as Harry wanted to rage and punch the daylights out of Wan, he knew that if he did anything even close to that, he would be heading for an early grave. The Triads were certainly a gang not to be messed with.

Harry nodded and looked contrite as he knocked back another double whiskey. He wiped his chin from the stray drop and shrugged. 'You're right, mate, I shouldn't have chewed your ear off like that. No hard feelings?'

Wan nodded back. 'Appreciate that, but what's with the ag?'

Harry looked around. The club was full to heaving so he certainly didn't want to start talking business in front of people. There were too many ears and eyes watching for his liking. 'Can we go somewhere quieter?'

Without bothering to answer, Wan turned and walked towards his large private office on the other side of the club.

He opened the door and they both walked in. Immediately the noise of the place was drowned out, leaving only a small hum in the background.

Going to the box of expensive cigars, Wan took one and threw it to Harry who lit it eagerly. 'Come on then. Spill.'

Letting out a cloud of thick smoke from his mouth, Harry stared at Wan. 'I just wanted to let you know that I'm going to revoke my protection of Vaughn. I'm no longer

273

going to be looking out for him. He's on his own now, which means you're welcome to him . . . but, if you don't mind, I'd like to be the one who kills him.'

There was a long pause before Wan said with a frown, 'I don't follow you. *You* want to kill Vaughn? Jesus Christ, the man's got a queue of people lining up to put him in the ground. Soon I won't have enough fingers to count how many. So go on then, what's happened? What did he do to piss you off? What did he do? Drive too slowly? Pick up the wrong dry-cleaning for you?' Wan said, not taking Harry seriously.

Sitting on the couch, Harry, irritated by Wan's amusement towards the situation, looked down at the floor whilst trying to hold his temper. 'This ain't a piss-take. I'm deadly serious.'

Realising how sincere Harry was being, Wan whistled and raised his eyebrows. 'Go on, I'm listening.'

'Let's just put it this way, he's crossed the line and I thought it only respectful to come and speak to you. You know, I didn't just want to go ahead and do something without letting you know. Though I also get it that it was me who pulled you back from doing anything to Vaughn in the first place.'

As Sasha walked into the room carrying a tray of drinks, Wan burst into laughter but there was a nasty tone to it. 'You really think that, don't you? It always amazes me that you'd think that.'

Harry looked up and stared at Wan as he took the drink Sasha was offering him. 'What the fuck are you on about?'

Leaning back in his chair, Wan winked at Sasha as he

pulled her onto his knee before putting his feet up on his walnut and leather trimmed desk. He pulled deeply on his cigar and grinned. His dark brown eyes twinkling with amusement. 'You. I'm talking about how *you* thought you had enough sway with me to say a few words and suddenly I'd back off from going after my brother's killer.'

Harry looked confused. 'You've lost me.'

Playing with Sasha's hair, Wan shook his head. 'You must think a lot about yourself to think that I'd just roll over and agree.'

Angrily, Harry spoke, not liking one bit the sense of being made fun of. 'I don't get it.'

'You want to kill Vaughn, then you need to get permission from your wife.'

'Excuse me?'

Again, a huge smile spread across Wan's face. 'Your wife. If you want to kill Vaughn you need to go and ask her; after all she's the one who's holding the price on his head.'

Harry stood up and glared at Wan as he walked slowly across to him, leaning on the desk. His eyes bulged with rage as he snarled, 'You better start talking, cos right now I don't care who you are. I'd be happy to get chopped up just so I can have this out with you.'

Wan pulled on his cigar. He winked. 'I'll remember that when I'm wondering what to do with you.'

With Harry's temper having gotten the better of him he slammed his fist down on the desk, causing the ashtray to go flying across the room. 'Tell me what the fuck you're on about. How is my missus anything to do with this?'

Chuckling nastily, Wan shrugged as he spoke mockingly.

'That's what I thought when she came to me begging for Vaughn's life, but then I thought whatever the sentiment behind it, that don't matter, it's currency that talks.' He burst into laughter again.

'I don't get it still. Why though? Why the fuck would she do that?'

'Women are strange creatures,' Wan said in amusement.

Harry bit down on his lip so hard he drew blood. It was all he could do to not rip off Wan's head. 'Why the fuck didn't you tell me? Why the fuck did you let Tia go behind my back?'

'She's your wife, mate. You control her, not me.'

At which Harry raged. He picked up one of the chairs and threw it against the wall. He kicked the gold vase in the corner of the room, smashing it up into thousands of pieces, then with his face red he turned back to Wan.

'I ain't anyone's mug.'

Wan regarded the room and a cold expression crossed his face as he glared at Harry. His cockney accent strong as he pushed Sasha off his knee roughly, he said, 'I hope you'll be getting the hoover and cleaning this up.'

Harry pointed at Wan. 'Do not take the piss.'

Wan stood up and walked across to Harry. He stepped in close, inches away, speaking in a hush. 'It's you who's taking the piss and if I wasn't feeling so charitable, I would get that machete over there and cut your fucking balls off before I shoved them down your throat. But seeing as I'm in a good mood, I tell you what, if you want to kill Vaughn, you can, be my guest. I give you permission . . . as long as you're prepared to top her offer.'

'In what way?'

'You give me five hundred thousand big ones and his head's all yours.'

Breathing hard, Harry didn't say anything for a moment and then he nodded. 'Okay, you've got a deal. I'll have your money by the morning.' He turned to go but Wan called him back.

'Wait . . . you didn't hear the second part of the deal . . . seeing as you're clearing house, I reckon my house could do with tidying too . . . As I say, you can kill Vaughn, but before you do, I want you to get rid of Franny Doyle. Kill Franny then you can have Vaughn.'

45

Another person who was drinking heavily that night was Alfie. He sat at the bar of his friend's club in Covent Garden, knocking back whiskey. He'd had a few lines of coke on top just to get rid of the edge, just to get the way Detective Carter looked at Franny from out of his head.

Why he should care, he didn't know. Well, he did, it was because Carter was a copper. Yeah, that was it. Franny Doyle talking to the Old Bill . . . *Fuck, no*. Who was he kidding? That wasn't it at all. It was the way Carter had looked at Franny and the way he'd looked at her only meant one thing.

He'd followed them to her large Georgian townhouse where he'd watched them walk through the front door, the same front door he'd walked through thousands of times. But he wasn't going to sit there and wind himself up. Why should he? After all, not only had he basically upped and left her, but also he'd probably got through every single prostitute in London.

'You all right, Alfie?' Rachel smiled as she leant on the bar, looking at him.

He nodded. 'Give me another one.'

Raising her eyebrows, Rachel took his hands. 'Alf, tell me what's wrong. You've had a face on you since you came in here.'

Alfie glared at Rachel. 'Just cos you're serving drinks behind the bar tonight instead of lying on your back, that don't mean you've suddenly changed into some therapist and that bar certainly ain't a couch.'

'You can be a jerk sometimes, Alfie Jennings.' And with that, Rachel turned away to go and serve another customer at the bar.

Alfie sighed. 'Rach, Rach, I'm sorry. Ignore me!'

Rachel looked over her shoulder at him. 'Oh that's exactly what I'm planning on doing.'

Deciding not to say anything else, Alfie walked around the bar and helped himself to some more whiskey. He knocked it back but as he did so, the thought of Franny and Carter came rushing into his head as he tried to convince himself they were just back at her place having a chat and a coffee. Yes, that's all it would be. A chat and a coffee . . .

Carter got up and walked over to Franny. He took the glass of Chardonnay out of her hand, then gently kneeled down in front of her as she sat on the bed. 'You fascinate me, Franny Doyle.'

She smiled and shrugged. 'Carter, you've known me long enough to know that what you see is what you get. There's nothing to be fascinated about.'

'I just wonder what it's like when you crack, when that hard exterior of yours is put down. Did you put it down for Alfie?'

Hearing Alfie's name made Franny bristle. He was the last person she wanted to think about. It hurt when she did. He had basically ghosted her. Ignored her calls, turned his back on her even though she needed him. Not that she'd told him that. It was too hard, too difficult to make herself vulnerable.

Maybe the reason she'd never actually said anything was the fear of rejection, which certainly would cut through the armoured exterior that Carter kept talking about. He was right: she knew she could be hard. She knew that most people saw her as cold, but Alfie had been able to make her feel something other than steely. He had made her feel like a woman.

No doubt he was sunning himself in Marbella, having women fall at his feet. So why did she care when she heard his name? Why did she feel like she'd had a body punch each time anyone mentioned him?

She sighed, trying to push the images of Alfie out of her mind. This wasn't what tonight was about. Tonight was about forgetting. 'I thought I said we should act like strangers. No talking. No questions.'

'It's not that easy, Franny. I can't help wanting to know.'

'Yes you can and besides it's pointless knowing anything more, cos when tomorrow comes, tonight never happened.'

Carter shook his head and laughed warmly. He'd always liked Franny, been intrigued by her. There'd always been something about her but he'd always known she was off limits, and not just because he was the police and she was a face in Soho. 'You know how to make a guy feel special.'

'I ain't here to make you feel special, I'm here for me.'

'Fine, have it your way,' he said, nodding as he looked up at her with his warm brown eyes.

'I always do, Carter, I always do.'

Without saying another word, Carter leant up and kissed Franny so softly on her lips it felt electric. He pushed her back on the bed and she could feel his hard body against hers as he gently caressed her, undoing her shirt. Then he bent over her and carefully took off the rest of her clothes.

He smiled, not saying anything as he took off his jeans and shirt, watching her as she closed her eyes. In the silence of the bedroom save the sound of the distant traffic, Carter kissed her again as he pressed his naked body against hers.

'Are you all right?' he suddenly said as he saw a tear running down her cheek.

She opened her eyes to look at him and smiled. 'I'm fine.'

'Franny . . .'

But she shook her head and put her finger over his mouth. 'Shush, don't talk, Carter.'

'But—'

She touched his face. 'Don't worry about me. Strangers, remember?'

He sighed, leaning his head down onto her shoulder. 'Okay. If it's really what you want.'

She smiled again, stroking the back of his head as she whispered her words. 'It is, it's what I need right now.'

He pulled himself up slightly and smiled back though it held a slight trace of sadness. 'You really are different to anyone I've ever known.'

'I'm going to take that as a compliment.'

Without saying anything else, Carter pushed her long chestnut hair behind her ears.

'Kiss me,' Franny said.

'Yeah?'

'Yeah, I'd like that . . .'

And as Carter kissed Franny again, his strong, muscular body hard on top of hers, she closed her eyes, trying to shut Alfie out of her head at the same time as wishing it was him and not Carter she was with . . .

Back at the bar in Covent Garden, Alfie had his head in his hands. Having been unable to convince himself that Carter had gone round to Franny's house purely for a coffee, he'd decided that getting wasted was as good a policy as any; it was a way of making him not think. Something over the past year he'd got particularly good at. So he'd resorted to another few fat lines of cocaine as well as several more shots of whiskey.

'Alf? Alf, I need a word.'

With his head pounding, and the room spinning, Alfie looked up at Rachel in a blur. 'Listen, Rach, I'm sorry okay, I shouldn't have—'

'It ain't nothing to do with that,' Rachel said, interrupting. 'I want you to meet someone.' A young girl stood next to

Rachel. 'This is Sasha, Alfie. She was a good friend of my sister Louise. She's got some information you might be interested in. It's about Franny. She knows her and she thinks she might be in danger.'

46

In shock, Vaughn paced up and down outside the Aldwych Theatre in Drury Lane. He pointed his finger at Tia, his face and his voice full of rage. 'This is like *The Twilight Zone*. How much more fucking news can one man take in a night? You see, this shit happens to people like Alfie, not people like me. Other people have daughters they don't know about.'

Having tried to calm him down for the past half hour, Tia spoke quietly. 'I'm so sorry. I wasn't ever going to tell you.'

He stopped in his tracks and spun around to look at her. 'You see, that's what makes it worse. You were happy not to tell me that I had a kid out there.'

Tia shrugged. 'Well, there was no need.'

Vaughn opened his eyes even wider. 'No need? No need for fucking who, Tia?'

Getting irritated herself now, Tia barked back, 'Stop the victim routine, Vaughn. You were the one who left me in the first place, remember? You walked out without even having the bottle to say goodbye, so when I found out I was pregnant, I was hardly going to start tracking you down, was I?'

'So she's sixteen? You're saying she's sixteen?'

'Bleedin' hell, Vaughn, I know how old she is,' Tia snapped.

'Are you sure?'

'What? Am I sure that my own daughter is sixteen? Don't be stupid, of course I'm bloody sure.'

'No, I don't mean that. I mean, are you sure she's mine?'

Tia said nothing for a moment. She just stared at Vaughn as her eyes narrowed. 'What did you say?'

Vaughn shrugged. 'Is she mine? I mean it's a question I need to ask, ain't it?'

Tia pushed him hard, causing him to have to step back to keep his balance. 'No! No! No, you don't get to ask me that! How dare you! Who do you think you are?'

'Oh come on, Tia, back then . . .'

'Back then, what?'

'Well you put it around a bit, didn't you?' Vaughn said but immediately he regretted speaking those words. Hearing them they sounded harsher, meaner than he'd intended but by the look on Tia's face it was too late to take it back.

'*You bastard! You bastard!* If you mean, did I get palmed out by Wan's brother to lots of different men before I met you, yes I did. But if you mean was I loyal, faithful and totally head over heels in love with you from the start, yes

I was. And if you need to tell yourself an excuse why you didn't know, why you didn't stick around, why you can't possibly be the father, don't bother cos we don't need you and I won't be asking for anything, so don't worry about that, Vaughn. Now why don't you just piss off and leave me alone.'

Ashamed, Vaughn lowered his voice to a whisper. 'Sweetheart, I never meant it like that.'

Tia's eyes blazed. 'Yes, you did though. We both know it.'

'I'm sorry, I'm a jerk. I'm lashing out, okay. I'm a prime arsehole.'

'At least we agree on something.' She turned to go but he ran in front of her, blocking her way.

'Tia, please. I am sorry. Look, it's just a shock. Tonight has been like someone's taken me fucking balls and just hammered nails in them.'

'Oh grow up,' Tia said wearily. 'I ain't got time for this. Somehow I have to go back home to Harry, who so far doesn't seem to know anything but that doesn't mean he ain't suspicious. Oh and if you want another nail in your balls, I forgot to tell you, Milly's pregnant.'

Vaughn fell silent. His head was spinning and just for a moment he suspected that this is what Alfie's life felt like on a continual basis: a car crash. A life that seemed to be constantly out of control. A life that just had shit flying at you from all angles and that was even before he added Franny to the mix.

Taking a deep breath, Vaughn frowned. 'But she's . . .'

'Only sixteen? Is that what you were going to say?'

He shook his head. 'No, no of course not, I was just wondering where she was. I mean Harry ain't said a lot about her, but he told me she was trouble.'

Bitterly, Tia nodded. 'And you believe that? She wasn't trouble; she was always a good kid. The trouble was with Harry. That was the problem. She couldn't stand the way he treated me. It cut her up to see Harry being handy with his fists and words.'

Vaughn recoiled at the same time as instinctively clenching his fists. He felt like killing Harry but then, he'd always known what Harry was like and he'd chosen to turn a blind eye to it, just so he could save his neck. Though, ironically, it turned out that it was Tia who'd been saving his neck, which made him feel not only a coward but a right cunt too.

'I can't even say I didn't know but I'm sorry,' Vaughn said, genuinely remorseful.

'The point is, Milly stayed out rather than coming back home. She stayed away from him cos he not only was a bastard to me but he was to Milly as well.'

'But that's his daughter . . . well . . .' He trailed off again feeling uncomfortable at what he was hearing.

'He knew she wasn't. He's always known. I was honest with him from the beginning. Okay I didn't tell him it had anything to do with you, but he knew I was pregnant from the off. He just thought it was some random bloke's . . . A bit like you did.'

Vaughn squirmed. 'I shouldn't have said that.'

'No, you shouldn't. I thought he'd take her on as his own – that's what he said anyway. It couldn't have been further

287

from the truth. So when he found out she was pregnant he just used it as an excuse to throw her out, but like Milly says, he was always going to throw her out.'

'Who's the father, I mean who's the father of Milly's baby?'

Tia shrugged. 'She's never told me, and I ain't pushing her, not after everything that's happened. All I can do is be there for her . . . Anyway, now you know and now I've got to face Harry. So I'll catch you later.'

Once again she turned to go and once again Vaughn stopped her. 'Wait! Tia, wait! We'll face him together. Yeah? You and me, not that I'm saying there's a you and me, not that I wouldn't want there to be a you and me and . . . Oh fuck . . .' He trailed off then added, 'What do you say?'

Tia just nodded.

It turned four in the morning as they drove home in silence and Vaughn turned into the cobbled mews just off Harley Street. He pulled the Range Rover up outside Tia's front door and turning off the engine he spoke to her quietly. 'I'll do the talking and if it gets nasty, then I want you to come back to the car. Understand?'

'Are you sure? You know what Harry can be like.'

'I do, but I know what I can be like as well.'

Getting out of the car, Tia put her key in the front door and took a deep breath but as she turned the lock and pushed the door open, she screamed in horror. 'Vaughn, quick! Help!' There, lying in the pool of her own blood, was her sister.

47

Tia ran to her sister. In shock she knelt down, cradling Tammy's head as blood seeped onto her hand. 'Tammy? Tammy can you hear me?'

There was no response and Tia turned to look at Vaughn who stood above her, his face drawn with worry. 'She must have fallen. Is she still breathing?'

Tia put her head against her sister's chest and nodded. 'Call an ambulance. Quick, call an ambulance!' As Vaughn went to call, Tia continued to speak to her sister. 'Tammy, it's me, darlin'. Can you try to say something? Just let me know that you're all right?'

Suddenly Tia heard a groan and she looked up at Vaughn who was busy talking to the emergency operator on the phone. 'She's breathing, tell them she's breathing but only just. And tell them to hurry!'

Not stopping his conversation, Vaughn nodded as Tia

stared at her sister. She could see where Tammy had fallen down the stairs, banging her head on the black marble floor of the hallway, cracking her head open, her face bruised and bloody as well.

Just looking at her sister caused Tia to fight back the tears. How long she'd been lying at the bottom of the stairs on her own was something she didn't even want to contemplate.

She turned again to Vaughn, who was in the process of repeating the address to the operator. 'How long?' she said urgently.

'They're coming as soon as they can but they won't give me a specific time. If it wasn't for the head injury maybe we could take her ourselves but they're saying don't move her.'

'Tell them she's pregnant. Tell them she's just a couple of months pregnant.'

Finishing his call, Vaughn looked surprised. 'Tammy's pregnant?'

Tia nodded as she held her sister's hand. 'Yeah, she told me a few days ago.'

'Jesus, I had no idea.'

'Well why would you?' Tia shot back but immediately added, 'I'm sorry, I ain't meaning to bite your head off.'

He smiled kindly. 'Don't worry about it.'

'It's Harry's,' Tia said matter-of-factly.

Vaughn walked up to where she was kneeling and crouched down himself. 'Tammy is pregnant with Harry's baby? Christ, Tia, what a fucking mess.'

Tears came to Tia's eyes though she didn't say anything.

'I'm so sorry, babe. This must be so difficult for you.'

She turned to look at Vaughn and shook her head. 'Oh, don't be sorry. I ain't bothered who Harry sleeps with – it ain't that. I'm gutted cos I just know that Tammy thought that Harry might be her happy ever after. I guess that's why she got herself pregnant but I know it ain't going to end well.'

'How could she think that Harry would be her knight in shining armour? More like the prince of fucking darkness.'

Tia shrugged, checking the clock on the wall to see how long the ambulance had been so far. 'We all need to feel love.'

'But with Harry? She wouldn't have got anything from him. The way he talked about her, he made her out like she was just some little scrubber. That's hardly whispering sweet nothings is it?' Vaughn said, his eyes full of warmth for Tia.

'Sometimes you'll just take whatever's on offer to feel loved, even though the truth is staring at you right in the face. I know I did with Wan's brother. I'm just worried about when she tells Harry. I warned her not to. I told her if she wanted to keep the baby I'd support her or if she wanted to get rid of it, I'd be there for her either way.'

'And what did she say?'

'She wasn't having any of it but I know what he's like. He'll go mad, he'll think that she's trying to corner him, make a fool of him, turn him over. But Tammy, well she wouldn't believe me, she just thinks that I'm saying it cos I'm jealous.'

291

Vaughn turned to look at Tammy who let out a slight moan. He stared at her face and frowned and then looked at where she had fallen from the top of the stairs. 'Maybe she's already told him.'

Tia frowned back. 'Why would you think that?'

In the quiet of the hallway he stared at Tia. 'I don't know for sure, and this might only be a guess, so I don't want you getting upset, but look at her face. See those bruises on her cheeks and the way her lip is split? Well, that ain't from being knocked about by the stairs; that's from being knocked about by someone's fist.'

Tia continued to stare at Vaughn, letting his words sink in. She looked down at her sister, seeing exactly what he was saying. 'Oh my God. Do you really think Harry was responsible for this?'

Not wanting to upset Tia any more but believing it was true, Vaughn just shrugged and simply said, 'I dunno. Who knows?'

'Oh, come on, Vaughn, just be straight with me. This ain't the time for keeping anything from me.'

He rubbed his face, tired from the day's revelations, tired from the mountain of trouble that was bound to be coming their way. He sighed. 'Well I know I ain't a doctor, but I've seen enough fat lips and busted faces to know that someone's been handy with their fists. And if I was a betting man, I'd say Harry was at the top of the suspect list.'

It was another ten minutes before help arrived and Tia watched the ambulance men load Tammy onto a stretcher. She could see her sister was stirring, which was good, and although they placed an oxygen mask on Tammy's face, it didn't seem like she was struggling for air.

Walking by her sister's side towards the ambulance, Tia squeezed Tammy's hand and she smiled as Tammy squeezed back.

'One of you can come with her if you like,' the ambulance man said as he smiled sympathetically.

Tia turned to look at Vaughn, the worry in her voice clear as she said, 'Look, I'll go in the ambulance and I'll meet you there. Is that okay?'

Vaughn nodded and although it was very clear the shit was about to hit the fan and he had to somehow work out what the hell he was going to do about Wan – which, in turn, also meant he had to figure out what the hell he was going to do about Franny – the idea of having a daughter was beginning to grow on him. 'No problem. I'll come and find you.'

Tia turned away and jogged back to catch up with Tammy, watching as they loaded her up in the back of the ambulance, the idea of Harry being the cause of her injuries making her feel ill.

'That's it,' she said. 'You'll be right in no time and then I'm going to look after you.'

'I need to tell you something,' Tammy muttered from behind her mask, though it was barely audible.

Tia shook her head. 'Tammy, don't talk, darlin' – that can wait until later. You need to keep your strength. You hear me?'

'But I just need to . . .' Tammy's voice was weak and her breathing turned into staggered gasping.

'Tammy, please, we can talk later. I love you, I always have and there's nothing ever going to come between us. I'll always be here for you.'

'Harry knows . . . Harry knows about you and Vaughn . . . He's going to kill you.' But with the oxygen mask on and the sound of the traffic, Tia didn't hear her sister's warning.

48

It was almost eight in the morning and outside the ICU of University College Hospital on the Euston Road. Vaughn brought Tia a cup of coffee. 'Here, get this down you. You need to keep your strength up.'

She gave him a small smile. 'That's exactly what I said to Tammy but I ain't sure that a watery cup of coffee from the machine is going to do the trick.'

He smiled back, seeing the worry on her face and the tiredness around her eyes. 'Listen, Tia, tonight has been a whirlwind. It's been extreme. But throughout it all, and I should've said it earlier, it hasn't been lost on me that you've . . . well, you've had some shit to deal with. I know that I was part of it, a huge part of it. I was the great big fucking avalanche that started it all. The whole snowball effect. If I hadn't walked out, none of this would have happened. You and Harry wouldn't have happened. Milly,

Tammy and . . . well you know, the stuff you had to do . . .'
He swallowed hard, trying to find the words, hating the
image of Tia with countless men, being used and . . . Jesus,
he couldn't even go there. He felt a combination of jealousy
and rage that she'd sold herself for sex, even if she'd sold
herself to help her daughter . . . their daughter. 'What I'm
trying to say, is I'm sorry. I know it's too late for that but
I am, and whatever I can do to help sort this shit out, I
will.'

Sadness oozed from her eyes. 'Thank you, that means a
lot,' Tia said quietly.

'We'll get it sorted with Wan. God knows how, but we
will . . . and I'm going to kill Harry. Properly kill him. I
just need you to know that. I just needed to tell you.'

Tia stared at him, thoughts rushing through her head.
She opened her mouth to say something but she felt the
buzz of her phone in her pocket. She pulled it out and
stared at it. There was a text from Milly, several texts. She
frowned and then remembered that she'd turned her phone
off yesterday because of Harry; she hadn't wanted his
constant calls coming through. She was pleased to hear
from her daughter because for some reason it seemed like
Milly had been ignoring her. Every time she'd called, she'd
been ignored and the texts she'd sent hadn't been replied
to, which was not like Milly. As she scrolled through the
texts they seemed a bit incoherent. The last couple were
even just letters. Just the odd letter.

'Everything all right?' Vaughn said.

'I don't know. They're from Milly. They just seem a bit
random, maybe her phone isn't working.' She pulled a

puzzled face as she dialled Milly's number, but it went straight to voicemail.

'You worried?'

Tia shook her head. 'Not really . . . well, a bit. I just hope everything's all right with the baby.'

'Why don't you go around to see her? I'll wait here for any news.'

Tia's gaze flitted to the door of the ICU and then back to Vaughn. 'I don't like to leave Tammy. I need to be here in case she needs me.'

'Well why don't I go around to see Milly?'

'Vaughn, I don't think that's a good idea, do you?'

'I don't mean to confess I'm her father, I mean to just check on her. I can just say you sent me, that's all.'

Tia, not looking convinced, said, 'I don't know.'

He stepped forward, put his hand under her chin, lifted up her head towards him and smiled. 'What harm can it do? I'm not going to say anything, I promise. And to tell you the truth it'll be nice to see her. You know, just see what she looks like.'

'She looks like you.'

Vaughn was surprised and then another smile spread across his face. 'Poor cow,' he said, laughing.

'No, she's beautiful, inside and out. You'll like her and I'm sure once she gets to know you, she'll like you as well . . . Okay, if you would go and see her, just to put my mind at rest that would be great. But if there's anything wrong with the baby or she's not feeling great herself, call me and I'll be there.'

Vaughn leant down and kissed Tia, closing his eyes as

a rush of emotions ran through him. It felt good but more importantly it felt right.

He pulled away and with a frown he asked, 'Will you be all right here on your own though? I mean we don't even know where Harry is and the messages I got from him when I didn't answer the phone yesterday are fit to kill. He's not happy with us and at the moment he doesn't suspect anything and we need to keep it like that. Why don't I call him, keep him sweet or rather take his bollocking and then play his game until we're ready to make our move? If I can get him to think that everything's normal, then we stand a better chance. I just need a bit of time to work things out.'

'Okay, sounds like a plan,' Tia said, though she pushed the sense of unease down inside her.

'And as for Wan, you say he wants some more coke?'

'Yeah he wants another two kilos, but the problem is, even if it *was* safe to go to the farmhouse in Jockey Row to get some, it would be pointless because I—'

'Tia?' Interrupting, a nurse called out to Tia from the door of the ICU. 'Tammy's asking to see you.'

'Okay, I'm coming.' She turned to look at Vaughn. 'You'll let me know straight away what's happening?'

'Of course, now go and see Tammy.'

A few streets away in Endsleigh Gardens, Vaughn cursed the parking warden who'd given him a ticket. He screwed it up, putting it in his pocket before leaning on his Range Rover and lighting a cigarette.

He thought of Tia and smiled. He hadn't felt like this

for a long time, if ever. He hoped that she would give him a chance to try and make up for lost time, to try and make things better. And as for Milly, Christ, it was huge. The idea of fatherhood was both exciting and scary and in truth he was nervous to meet her. Okay, he certainly wasn't going to start introducing himself to her but just going to see her seemed like a massive step. A massive head wreck. An Alfie kind of head wreck.

He sighed, taking the smoke down into his lungs. But he knew before he thought of all that, he had to make a call.

Holding the cigarette in his mouth with the smoke going up into his eyes, he pulled out his phone from his jean pocket and called Harry. It rang twice and then he heard the familiar voice.

'Hello?'

'Harry, it's me!'

'I know who the fuck it is, cos your name comes up, though right now, I wish it didn't.'

Vaughn rolled his eyes. 'I'm sorry, Harry, I can see all the messages you've sent me. I know it feels like the last time we went AWOL, but it ain't.'

'It ain't what? That you're treating me like a muggy cunt *again*? That you and Tia are taking the piss.'

'Harry, look I'm sorry, and you have every right to bollock me but hear me out . . . The only reason that we ain't been in contact is because Tammy's in hospital . . . Hello?'

'I'm here for fuck's sake, I'm just thinking.'

'She's in ICU and obviously Tia's worried about her. That's

299

where she's been, that's where she is, she don't want to leave her side.'

'Has Tammy said anything?'

'Like what?' Vaughn said, knowing exactly what Harry was hinting at. Wanting to play the innocent, he added, 'To tell you the truth, Harry, I've just kept out of it. I just waited in the corridor. The only thing I know is she fell down the stairs. That's it.'

There was a long pause before Harry said, 'Fine, look, I've got some stuff to do on my end. I'll speak to you later.'

As the call was cut off, Vaughn frowned. It was odd because for some reason Harry seemed unusually calm. He'd expected him to be threatening blue murder and worse. Still, he supposed that it was a good thing and maybe it was because Harry was uncomfortable talking about Tammy – seeing as it was blatantly obvious to him that Harry was the cause of her being in hospital – and so it was a case of the less said the better.

Anyway, whatever it was he didn't have time to think about it right now. All that mattered was Harry clearly didn't think anything was amiss so at least now Vaughn could focus on what he was going to do about Wan; but first he needed to get to Milly.

Stepping into his car, Vaughn took a deep breath to steady his nerves as he got ready to drive to see his daughter for the first time . . .

It nearly had fucking killed him. Speaking to Vaughn, pretending everything was all right, had made him feel like he was *literally* going to implode. What a cunt and God, he was going to make him pay. Slowly and painfully.

He breathed deeply, spinning the gun on the desk. Thinking about how he was going to make Vaughn beg for his life and then he'd make Tia pay. Just as slowly, just as painfully.

In truth he wanted to go and do it now. Shove a gun down their throats and make them choke on it. Make them choke on their lies. Oh yes, that day couldn't come too soon. But of course before he was able to do that, he had to go and do that small favour for Wan: putting Franny Doyle in the ground.

Although time-consuming, it would be easy. He'd never been partial to the mouthy bitch who had balls of fucking steel and the way he was feeling he was more than happy to blow that beautiful face of hers right off.

So the only good thing right now in waiting was Tia and Vaughn didn't suspect anything and that's the way he needed to keep it. They were a slippery pair and if they got wind of anything, then it would make his job much harder.

He sighed again and rubbed his head, looking around his mahogany oak office. He had no idea what he'd done to deserve such a fuck-up for a wife. From the moment he'd met her, he'd looked after her. She'd been pregnant with another man's baby, and even that hadn't bothered him. He'd still taken her on, bringing up Milly as if she was part of the family. He'd housed Milly, fed her, clothed her, but like Tia, she'd turned out to be an ungrateful little bitch.

When he'd gone to see her last night as usual she was a spiteful little cow. She hadn't said, but he knew that somehow Tia was behind the fact that she was still in town.

He shook his head and absentmindedly he touched the scratch on his face. Then, picking up the gun and slipping it in his jacket pocket, Harry Jacobs walked out of the room, wondering about the best way to kill Franny.

49

'Here get this down you . . . Alfie? For God's sake wake up . . . Alfie? Alfie? Pass me that glass will you?'

'Fuck! Fuck! Fuck!' Alfie jumped up from the couch as Rachel emptied the glass of water over him.

'What the fuck are you doing, you stupid cow?' He glared at her but she just shrugged.

'I've been standing here trying to wake you up. Now get this coffee down you – we need to talk. Sasha's still here.'

Alfie sat forward on the velvet couch of his friend's club and rubbed his head. He looked around and saw all the punters had gone home. 'What time is it anyway?'

'Just gone nine . . . *in the morning*,' Rachel emphasised.

Taking the milky coffee and grateful that Rachel seemed to have put half a bag of sugar in it, Alfie looked at her. 'I can't even remember what happened.'

'Well that's what you get when you shove the whole of Colombia up your nose.'

He rubbed his head again. 'Don't start chewing me ear off, I got a raging headache.'

'If you're looking for sympathy, jog on, Alf. We've been waiting to talk to you, well Sasha has; she's been here since last night.'

'Who the fuck is Sasha?' Alfie growled, not wanting to talk and simply wanting to be left alone.

Despairing of Alfie, Rachel shook her head. 'She came to see me last night. She was a good friend of my sister's, remember? She works for Wan and she thinks that Franny's in trouble.'

Rachel's words made Alfie sit up. He wiped the water from his face and stared at Rachel. 'Go on, tell me.'

'Well that's what we've been trying to do, since last night! Sasha, come here will you, sweetheart?'

Shyly Sasha walked over. She gave a small smile to Alfie and sat down on one of the leather chairs opposite him, curling her legs underneath her as she did so.

Immediately, Alfie could see how young she was . . . how vulnerable she looked even though her face was caked in make-up. 'Hello, darlin', I'm Alfie,' he said smiling, though he could hear his words were slightly slurred and he wasn't one hundred per cent sure if he was talking too loud or too quiet. He had a buzzing in his head and his eye felt like it was pulsating out of its socket.

'Rach, pour us a whiskey will you, and make it a large one . . . Don't look like that, just do it will you?'

Obediently Rachel went across to the bar leaving Alfie

and Sasha alone. 'What makes you think Franny's in trouble and how do you know her?' he said, lighting a cigarette at the same time as wishing that Rachel would hurry up with his drink.

'I work for Wan. I'm his girlfriend . . . well I was, I think I was, I dunno . . .' She trailed off, looking upset.

Before he could say anything in response, Rachel came back and handed him not only a glass but also the bottle of whiskey. He winked gratefully. 'Thanks, Rach, you know how it is, hair of the dog and all that.'

As Alfie quickly knocked the whiskey back hoping to feel better, he winced, feeling a lurch in his stomach as he suddenly remembered what had put him in this state in the first place: Franny and Carter. *Fuck.* Knowing this wasn't the time to think about them, he pushed the thought to one side, pouring himself another drink. 'Tell me exactly why you're here, darlin'. Why don't we start from there, cos I can see that it's difficult for you.'

Fidgeting with the hem of her jacket, Sasha said, 'I was with Wan and he was talking to this guy. I'd seen him before, in fact . . .' She paused and suddenly became coy.

Alfie gave her a genuine smile again, his striking features lighting up. He pushed back his jet-black hair, which fell over his forehead. 'Listen, sweetheart, I ain't here to judge you – fuck me, I certainly haven't got room to talk. Look at me, I'm pretty much a mess, so whatever you do say, please *don't* feel uncomfortable, cos not only have I probably heard it before, but I've probably done it before as well.'

Appreciating his genuine warmth, Sasha began to talk again. 'Well I'd had sex with this guy before, several times.

I don't like it. He's really rough; he doesn't care if he hurts you or not. Some of the girls, well, Wan's had to call a doctor after they've been with him. Everyone hates him. But Wan just says that if it hurts we should take something, you know like coke, but the stuff he gives us, I think it's cut with something, so I'd rather take the pain. I don't want to end up like Sophie.'

Alfie, shocked, looked at Rachel.

'Sophie overdosed. She's not the first girl apparently,' Rachel said, filling in the gaps.

'But this guy, well he has these parties at his farmhouse. It's really plush but they're horrible parties. No one wants to go cos you never know if you're coming back or not,' Sasha continued.

'Jesus Christ.'

'Well he was the one who was with Louise that night. He was the last person I saw her with.'

Alfie let out a deep sigh. He wasn't sure what to say. From the looks of her, this girl was no more than sixteen, seventeen. Wan was scum and although it was shocking to hear it, it didn't surprise him. After all, finding that girl bagged up on the wasteland in Essex was part of Wan's doing. It was obvious he let his friends and the punters use and abuse the girls as if they were pieces of meat.

'And why now, darlin'? Why come and talk to Rachel now?'

Sasha shrugged. 'I didn't want to before. I was scared, and I love Wan and . . .' She stopped and thought and then, sounding very much confused, she said, 'I dunno, maybe

I don't love him but I can't get Louise out of me head. I miss her.'

Alfie's heart went out to the girl. Over the years he'd met many girls just like her. Soho had a way of attracting them. It was like a honeypot to bees. 'But how's Franny involved in this? Is Wan planning on doing something to her? And why do you even want to help her, anyway?'

'It's all just a mess; too many girls have got hurt, and Franny's nice. I like her. She always tries to make sure we're all right. I heard her arguing with Wan a few times about the way he treats us and she's always really kind to all of us. She bought me a couple of dresses. I dunno, I guess she's like a mum, or rather I guess she's like what a mum should be,' Sasha said sadly.

'She'd probably like you saying that,' Alfie answered warmly.

'Well she stuck up for us.'

Looking at her black eye, Alfie asked, 'Did Wan do that to you?'

'No. I mean it's not that he hasn't done that before, but a girl did this, cos she was jealous of me and Wan . . . Anyway, when I heard Wan saying he wanted to kill her . . .'

Alfie's face paled. 'Kill her? You mean kill Franny?'

'Yeah or rather he wants this guy to kill her . . . It wrecked my head and I came to talk to Rachel. I just want it all to stop. It's horrible.'

'But how did you know that we knew Franny?'

'I didn't. I came to tell Rachel about Louise really, and everything I knew. I thought it was about time but she said that you'd be interested in hearing about Franny.'

'Yeah I am, but can you promise me something, Sash? If you see Franny, don't tell her that you saw me – that's really important.'

Used to keeping secrets Sasha just nodded as Alfie continued. 'So, do you know what this guy's called?'

'Yeah, I mean I didn't until recently but he's called Harry.'

'Harry!' Alfie said. 'What does he look like?'

'He's dead handsome. He's about six foot two and he's got blond hair and I know he's married. I think when he was talking to Wan he said something about her name was Tia? Do you know him?'

'I do, unfortunately . . . Look, can I trust you to keep your mouth shut? I'll give you my number in case you need me and don't worry, I won't mention anything that you've said to me. And, Sasha, thank you, it's really brave you speaking out like this. I'll never forget it and I'm sure Franny won't either. You've probably saved her life.'

Ten minutes later, after Sasha was gone, Rachel turned to Alfie. 'What are we going to do? If Harry was responsible for Louise's death, which I'm sure he was, then I want him to pay. I want them to both pay. I've waited a long time for this, Alf. It's the most evidence I've had to link Wan and now Harry to the murder.'

'I know and don't worry, they won't get away with it . . . But you know it'll be dangerous?'

Rachel shrugged. 'Listen, I've spent all me life ducking and diving with a whole lot of wrong 'uns and at least doing this, at least stopping that scum, well hopefully some good will come out of it all.'

Alfie gave a tight smile. 'Well I'm going to fucking kill Harry for starters, but as for Wan, I've squared up before with the Triads and they ain't an easy bunch to deal with. You can't mess with them, so we have to be a bit cleverer than just going in guns blazing. But I may just have an idea.' At which point, Alfie got out his phone and started to text.

As Sasha walked along Kingsway, a car pulled up by her side. The window came down and she gave a half-smile.

'Hello, Sasha, where've you been?'

'Just out.'

'You want a lift home?'

Tired, she looked at the driver and shrugged. 'I guess . . . thanks.'

As she got into the blacked-out car, she didn't see the people in the back seat until it was too late, until she felt the gag being put over her mouth.

50

In the block of flats just by St Anne's Court, Vaughn made his way slowly up the rubbish-strewn stairs, smelling the stench of alcohol and seeing the all-round dirt. There were discarded bloody needles along with empty bottles of vodka scattered everywhere. A heavy aroma of urine sat in the air and the communal walls were adorned with graffiti.

Making a mental note that he would sort out a nice place for Milly, Vaughn arrived at the top landing, pausing as he heard voices coming from her bedsit. He could see the door was slightly ajar and, wanting to take absolute precaution, he slipped the gun from his pocket and held it close to his body.

He stood by the door for a couple of moments then he kicked it wide open, springing inside. And he froze. Shocked. Staring. There, standing in the middle of the bedsit, were Franny and Detective Carter.

He glared at Franny. 'What the fuck are you doing here?'

Franny grinned. But it was a cold, hard grin. 'I could say the same about you.'

'This is Milly's place,' Vaughn said, staring at her hard.

Franny stared back just as coldly. 'And there's me thinking that this was the Holiday Inn.'

Fuming, Vaughn turned to his one-time friend. 'You're keeping some kind of company these days, ain't you?'

Carter stared at the gun that Vaughn was holding. 'I could say the same for you. I take it you've got a new job in the Flying Squad because why else would you be carrying around a weapon?'

Slipping it back into his jacket, Vaughn held Carter's gaze. 'So what . . . oh wait, you're just about to tell me you're going to nick me?'

Carter shook his head. 'I should do, but no, not today anyway. But I'm curious too. Why are you here?'

'Why wouldn't I be here? I know Harry, and well, Milly's Harry's girl. I'm just checking up on her for him.'

'What?' Franny's expression turned to shock. She sat down on the bed and Vaughn watched as Carter gently put his hand on her back.

'You all right?' Carter said as Vaughn began to shake his head and clap.

'Oh please, oh please don't tell me that you and her have got it on?'

Franny looked up at him, her expression now one of anger.

'You have, haven't you? Seriously, Carter, of all the women you had to choose from, you chose the black widow who eats her prey. Fuck me, she tried to have me killed but there's you, the Old Bill, shagging her like she's some princess. Turns you on, does it, sleeping with a gangster? Though I would've thought you had better taste.'

'Watch your mouth, Vaughn,' Carter snarled.

'Oh save the heroics. Don't let them big long lashes and those fluttering eyes fool you, she don't need a guy standing up for her. She's man enough all by herself, ain't you, darlin'?'

'What is your problem, Vaughn?' Franny said.

He shrugged. 'Does Alfie know?'

It was the first sign of her tough exterior falling, hearing Alfie's name. She flinched and not only did Vaughn see it but Carter did as well. 'What I do or don't do has nothing to do with Alfie. He and I ain't together. Spain's a long way from here.'

Vaughn winked. 'Well that's settled then – you won't mind me telling him the next time I have a chat with him, will you?'

Not rising to it, Franny just held a steady stare. 'Why don't you just piss off back to Harry? You two deserve each other.'

'No more than you and Wan.'

'Enough!' Carter said. 'You sound like a couple of school kids. But she's right, you better turn around and walk away, and if you don't, I will nick you for possession of a firearm. Your choice.'

'All I'm doing is waiting for Milly. That ain't a crime.'

Franny stood up, anger rushing through her, and for the first time in a long while she wasn't able to keep her temper in check. She flew at Vaughn, grabbing him by his jacket, pushing him back against the kitchen units. 'No, that ain't a crime but what Harry's involved in is. But then, you'd know all about that wouldn't you? You'd know that the scum likes to mess about with young girls and I will not let you be Harry's bitch and come here trying to frighten Milly off!'

Vaughn pushed her back, just as angry, just as hostile. 'Get the fuck off me, Franny, cos whether you've got lover boy here or not, I'll kill you if you put your hands on me again.'

Enraged at the comment, Franny swung her fist and made direct contact with Vaughn's lip. Pain and rage ran through him and he went for the gun in his pocket but suddenly he found himself being pushed down, his arm twisting behind his back as Carter slammed his body down onto the floor.

Breathing hard, Carter sat on top of him, keeping Vaughn in a firm arm grapple. 'Listen to me, Vaughn, if you make one more move, I'm taking you down to the station and you'll be looking at a long time behind bars, so if I were you, I wouldn't make a move. Do you understand?'

Feeling like his shoulder was going to pop out of the socket, Vaughn nodded as Carter gestured to Franny to pick up the gun.

'Right, I'm going to let you go now, but don't be stupid. Don't let your ego get the better of you.'

'Okay! Okay!'

Slowly Carter got up off Vaughn who, although looking furious, got up off the floor just as slowly. He rubbed his shoulder and stared at Franny. He growled at her through gritted teeth. 'Whatever our differences are, and we have a fuck of a lot of them, you know me better than to think that I'd come here and try to scare some teenage kid.'

Franny regarded Vaughn, feeling nothing but hatred. But he did have a point: there were some things that she would go to her grave believing and one of those things was that Vaughn would never hurt someone like Milly. 'Firstly, let me get one thing clear. Me and Carter, well there is no me and Carter. Ain't that right?'

Carter nodded. Although he knew that Franny was trouble, inappropriate and downright wrong for him, she held a fascination for him that had always and probably would always get under his skin. He could see why over the years Alfie couldn't let her go. And last night, well, even though he tried to put it in the box of just a one-night stand – which he'd had hundreds of – he couldn't do it, because the stupid thing was, he actually wanted her more now than ever. He actually felt something for her. But that thought would stay locked in his head. Some things were just better left unsaid.

'You mean he ain't now you've chewed him up and spat him out,' Vaughn replied.

'Whatever, Vaughn, think what you like, cos what you think is irrelevant to me . . . The point is, regardless of what I just said, I actually *do* know that you wouldn't do anything to a kid. So that begs the question: why *are* you here? Cos I know how Harry treated Milly, so he wouldn't be sending you around to bring a pot of soup. She was in hiding from him, in fact, so how come you *know* where she is?' Franny said, puzzled.

Vaughn sighed. 'What is this, *The Sweeney*? Anyone tell you that you sound like the Old Bill, and you two playing good cop, bad cop is a bit too fucking surreal for my liking.' He stopped and a thought ran through his head. 'What did you mean by frighten Milly off?'

Franny shrugged. 'She was scared of him – that's all I meant.'

'No. Just like you know me, I know you. There was more to it than that. What's going on?'

'You're not here to question me, Vaughn, not until I know what *you* want with Milly.'

Taking another deep breath, Vaughn said, 'I came for Tia. That's how I know she's here. Tia's been paying for this place behind Harry's back, but she can't get through to her daughter so I said I'd come and see if Milly was okay . . . Where is she anyway?' Vaughn suddenly said.

Franny shook her head. 'I dunno.'

Uncharacteristically, Vaughn began to feel panicked. 'What do you mean?'

'I saw her yesterday and I wanted to bring Carter to speak to her.'

Vaughn looked at Carter and then back at Franny. 'Why? Why would you need Milly to speak to him?' He stopped and turned to look at Carter. 'Has this got something to do with what you spoke to me about? About Wan and the girls?'

'Yes and like I say, I'm determined to bring him down, more so than ever, and if you have something to say about Harry, it won't go any further,' Carter replied.

Wide-eyed, Vaughn stared back at Franny. 'Is Milly in

trouble? I mean do you think something's happened to her?'

'I hope not, but what she told me about Wan was really disturbing and I think she was trying to stop him hurting her friend.'

Vaughn's words tumbled out. 'What, no, no, no, what the fuck? No, tell me you're bullshitting me, tell me that ain't true. Franny *please*, please, don't wind me up, tell me Milly isn't doing that.'

Franny cocked her head to one side looking at Vaughn with sheer puzzlement, not understanding his obvious panic. Not understanding *why* he was so worried about Milly when he didn't even know her. 'Well that's what I caught her doing last night; she was in the club and she'd just gone to see Wan to ask him to leave this girl alone.'

'But why, how, why would she think that she could just go up to a complete stranger and do that? Why would she?'

'Oh Wan wasn't a complete stranger to Milly. Wan is the father of her child. He raped her. Wan raped her.'

The room felt like it was swimming as Vaughn stared at Franny in horror. He whispered his words. 'I'm going to kill him. I'm going to kill Wan for raping my daughter.'

51

It wasn't often that Franny was lost for words but all she could do was stare.

'So help me, I am going to make him pay,' Vaughn yelled.

'We're all going to make him pay. That's why I'm here. Franny found evidence from one of the girls' diaries, which talks a lot about what Wan was up to, but it isn't enough. We need more. That's why it's important to speak to Milly, get a statement,' Carter said.

'Are you fucking kidding me? You want her to go against the Triads? They'll slaughter her.'

'It's the only way to put him away.'

Vaughn pointed at Carter, his rage evident. 'I will not let you do that to her. You might as well put a price on her head now.'

'It's the only way.'

Vaughn stepped forward. 'Then you need to think again,

cos whether it's Milly or any of the other girls you are putting them in danger to ask them to do that.'

'I hate to agree with him, but Vaughn's right – those girls will be sitting targets. Wan will get a powerful barrister, and that makes all the difference . . . I should know, otherwise I'd still be inside, hey Vaughn!' Franny said, making a dig at him.

Once again, Vaughn ignored Franny and directed his question at Carter. 'What about Harry? How much is he involved?'

'He's right up to his eyeballs in it. But again, it's about proof. The most important thing is we stick together on this. Work together.'

'With him?' Franny said in disgust.

'Feeling's mutual darlin', Vaughn retorted.

'Look, you two, I'm not saying that you both haven't got grievances with each other, but are you really telling me that these girls – including Milly – are less important than this war going on between you? Because if it is, you aren't the people I thought you were. You say you both know each other well and that's true but I also know both of you, and neither you, Franny, nor you, Vaughn, would want these kids to suffer because of that. Come on, guys, we need to do this together; after all, a *common danger unites even the bitterest enemies.*'

Franny let Carter's words wash over her. She watched Vaughn watching her then slowly she nodded her head. 'He's right. I'm willing, for *now*, to put the fact that you tried to set me up for a murder I didn't commit to one side to help stop Wan and the likes of Harry once and for all.'

Vaughn nodded as well. 'Then I'm willing to put aside the fact that you paid Wan's brother to put a bullet in my head.'

'Because you set me up. Don't forget to add that part on the end, Vaughn. I might be putting it to one side for *now*, but that don't mean we erase the facts.'

Carter looked at them both and spoke firmly. 'And I, whether I like it or not, am willing to put aside the fact that I've just heard that *you*, Vaughn, committed perjury at the highest level, and *you*, Franny, were part of a plot to have someone murdered. I am going to pretend I didn't hear any of it, so we can work on putting Wan away together. Right?'

Before Franny could answer, Carter's phone buzzed. He pulled it out of his pocket and read it. He raised his eyebrows in surprise and whistled.

'What's that? Anything of interest?' Franny said curiously.

He shook his head and shrugged, slipping the phone back into his pocket. 'Oh nothing. Nothing of interest.' But in fact the text had been more than interesting . . . especially for Franny.

The three of them sat in Carter's blue Volvo 4x4, making their way through the West End traffic with the lull of Radio 2 in the background.

'This seems so strange sitting here with you. Old Bill and us, it don't feel right . . . Where are we going anyway?' Franny said as she leant forward from the back seat.

With Carter not answering her, she sighed and sat back,

trying her best to ignore the fact that Vaughn was sitting right next to her, but with curiosity getting the better of her, she turned to him. 'How long have you known about Milly?'

Vaughn cut his eyes at Franny, wishing he was anywhere but here. 'I shouldn't have said anything.'

'Yeah well you did, so you might as well answer,' Franny snapped irritably.

Angry with himself for allowing his emotions to get the better of him, causing him to blurt it out, Vaughn bit back, 'Look, I know what you're thinking; you're thinking this is Alfie's life, this is what happened with him.'

'No, actually I wasn't. This is what happens to a lot of people, especially if you've put it around.'

'I wasn't putting it around, not then anyway. Me and Tia, back then we were an item, but I was an idiot.'

'That does surprise me,' Franny said sarcastically as she watched the number 10 bus go past.

Rolling his eyes at the dig, Vaughn continued without rising to it. 'I left her before I knew she was pregnant, and I only found out about Milly last night.'

Franny turned back and looked at him, surprise showing on her face. 'Milly's got your eyes. It's funny, when I first saw her, her eyes were so striking, reminded me of someone and now it makes sense . . . Does Harry know?'

'No. He knows that Milly isn't his, but that's as far as it goes.'

'Have you texted Tia that she's missing?'

Vaughn shook his head. 'I don't want to worry her, not yet anyway. For all we know she just went out. I dunno, she could've gone to the shops or something . . .'

They fell silent for a moment, Vaughn's words sounding empty, unconvincing, as if he was trying to deny what was glaringly obvious.

Franny smiled sympathetically and then said, 'She told me she was terrified of Harry and she hated being in Soho because of the fear of bumping into Wan. She wanted to move away. God, it's all such a mess. What Wan has been doing to those girls makes me sick. The sooner we can work out what to do the better and the sooner we find Milly . . .' She stopped talking, not wanting to think of what might have happened.

'You reckon Wan has her?' Vaughn asked.

'The truth is, I'm hoping he hasn't, but my gut is telling me otherwise . . .'

52

Carter, Vaughn and Franny stood by a luxury block of flats but it was Carter who pressed the slim-line buzzer by the glass doors.

A female voice answered. 'Hello?'

'It's Detective Carter.'

'Oh hi, come up to the penthouse apartment.'

Immediately the door was buzzed open and without saying anything to Vaughn and Franny, Carter walked into the plush, marble reception entrance.

He pressed the lift button. 'I want you guys to meet someone.'

Franny shrugged. 'What's with the cloak and dagger routine? You've hardly said a word since we left Milly's place.'

Stepping into the air-conditioned lift and pressing the button for the penthouse floor, Carter gave a sideward glance to Franny. 'No reason, I'm just working out stuff. There's a lot to mull over.'

'Well as long as you're okay,' Franny replied warmly.

As they stepped out into the corridor, Vaughn shook his head and whispered to Franny as they followed Carter towards a black granite door. 'You really are blind, ain't you? Can't you see that this is what you do to people – you fuck them up? Reel them in and then, *boom*, that's the end of the line for them. I know Carter, and believe it or not, I reckon he's hurting.'

Bemused, Franny hissed back, 'Turn it in, Vaughn. There's nothing between us. It was sex, nothing more.'

'Well I hope you told him that.'

Enraged, Franny stopped and snapped, 'I did actually.'

To which Vaughn, without stopping and with his voice dripping with sarcasm said, 'Well that's all right then, ain't it?'

Knocking on the door, Carter smiled at Franny and Vaughn but neither returned the gesture as they stood moodily next to each other, so instead he waited patiently for the door of the apartment to be opened, which it soon was.

'Hi, Carter, thanks for com—' Alfie's unfinished word hung in the air as he stared in shock, surprise, horror and bewilderment at Franny and Vaughn, who stared back at him with equal shock, surprise, horror and bewilderment.

'What the fuck are they . . . are you . . . I mean, Franny, shit . . . hi . . . Vaughn, what the fuck Carter?'

Carter smiled again. 'I think you've all met. Shall we?' He gestured and, without being invited, walked into the apartment where he greeted Rachel with a nod. She stood with her mouth agape.

'This is a fucking wind-up,' Franny growled as she stormed into the apartment.

'Well, it's awkward, I'll say that, hey Franny, hey Carter,' Vaughn said as he winked at them and it certainly didn't go unnoticed by Alfie who inwardly seethed with jealousy.

Franny spun and looked at Vaughn, pointing her finger at him. 'This ain't funny, and as for you, Alfie? What the fuck? You haven't returned one phone call. You've ghosted me and you didn't even have the decency to let me know that you weren't in Spain.'

'I was in Spain.'

Livid, Franny yelled, 'Oh for fuck's sake you know what I mean. And as for you, Carter, is this your idea of a sick fucking joke?'

'Of course not, I just knew that if I didn't do it like this, you probably wouldn't come. I know you're all pissed off with one another.'

'With good reason,' Vaughn interjected.

'Okay, with good reason, but not reason enough not to work together. We all want the same thing. Get Wan and Harry off the street. Harry is the easy one.'

'Oh no, Harry's the dead one,' Alfie said.

'I don't want to hear that, remember? I'm a police officer.'

'How could we forget?' Franny snarled, feeling betrayed.

Alfie, feeling just as betrayed but for other reasons, glared at Carter. 'He's got a hit on Franny's head.'

'What? Harry has?' Franny said, shocked. She turned to Vaughn, 'This is cos of you.'

'Me? Not me, darlin', so I'd stop the accusations if I were you.'

'Don't talk to her like that,' Alfie said. 'She has got a point.'

With his temper at boiling point, Vaughn stepped towards Alfie. 'Don't play the fucking hero. What is it with you lot that you think this woman needs any help from you? And anyway, it's a bit late to play fucking Superman now. You've been in Spain topping up your tan and by the looks of things, topping up your nostrils with that shit again.'

'Fuck me, it's like old times, ain't it? Vaughn the do-gooder, aka the cunt,' Alfie replied. 'But if you must know, I ain't been in Spain . . . Franny, I ain't, well not for a while. I heard you were in trouble and I came back to make sure you're all right. From a distance that is. In the shadows, but I wasn't far away, I would've been there if you needed me.'

Franny's eyes suddenly welled with tears but she turned away, hating the thought of anyone seeing her cry. 'I needed you, Alfie. I just didn't know how to say it,' she whispered but her whisper was too quiet for Alfie to hear.

'What?' he said.

She turned back around and smiled a huge, fake smile. 'I just said, cheers for that.'

He frowned at her, slightly disappointed in her reply, and he glanced at Carter who, unlike Alfie, had noticed Franny's tears. 'Well, point is,' Alfie said, resuming the conversation, 'Sasha came to see Rachel – she really thinks a lot of you, Franny – but she told us amongst other things that Wan's ordered Harry to kill you.'

'You see that's what happens when you trust a snake,' Vaughn said.

Franny nodded. 'You're right, but what was I supposed to do? I'd known you for so long, Vaughn, so I didn't suspect you'd fuck me over like you did.'

Vaughn's face was red with rage. 'I ain't talking about me, and you know damn well I ain't.'

Franny winked at him. 'Sorry, my bad.'

'If you don't get that bitch out of my face, I will kill her,' Vaughn hollered as he stepped towards her but as he did, Alfie stepped in front of her.

'You need to kill me first.'

'And here I thought you'd never ask,' Vaughn said.

'Stop! This will not get us anywhere! Have you forgotten this isn't about any of you?' Carter raged. 'This is about Wan and this is about Milly who no one has seen. So I am going to pull rank here, because unfortunately for you lot, as you keep reminding me, I *am* the Old Bill, which gives me the power to arrest you all and I have enough shit on all of you to put you away. So, if you don't want me to do that, you shut the *fuck* up and help me work out how we are going to bring Wan down.'

53

Franny came out of the bathroom to be greeted by Alfie standing there, tall and handsome, his jet-black hair as usual falling over his forehead and his dazzling blue eyes focused on her.

'Hey,' he said.

'Hey yourself.'

'Fran . . . it's good to see you and I'm sorry, I'm sorry I never got in contact. It just seemed too complicated. You know after you got out of prison, all the stuff with Vaughn and Wan, it got messy. Everyone was setting everyone up. I just needed to get out. I needed to get away from everything and that meant you too. And I know there's a fuck of a lot of things to sort out, but there's always things to sort out when it comes to me and you. Look, I want to put everything behind us, not just for now to get Wan off the streets, but to move forward. And like I say, I'm sorry for not contacting you sooner.'

'Well you're here now, ain't you?' she said tightly and coolly before turning away.

'Stop, Fran! Fuck, just stop with the Ben and Jerry act – you don't need to be so frigging ice cold.'

She sighed wishing he would just take her into his arms, and then she shrugged as she always did when things felt difficult. 'I am who I am, Alf.'

He spoke quietly as he touched her face. 'I missed you. Tell me you missed me too . . . For fuck's sake, Fran, just say it! Cos I may be who I am, but Christ almighty, I need to hear stuff like that as well.'

'Maybe you shouldn't be so needy, then.'

He laughed bitterly but the next moment he leant in for a kiss, long and sensual. He drew away, his gaze wandering over her face. 'You really are a cold bitch, Franny Doyle, but I can't help loving you . . . and underneath that hard exterior of yours, I know you love me too even if you don't say it . . . Look, we can talk later, but why don't we go and see what Morse has to say. Oh and, Fran, you know the other night, I saw you and him, you know Carter, going into your house and . . . I know it ain't—'

'Ain't any of your business?' Franny replied, to which Alfie slammed his fist against the wall and hissed at her. 'You're my woman, Fran, and that's the end of it. There ain't anyone else I want and I know it's the same for you. I love you, girl, and I just want to know, if . . . if . . . if, you know . . .'

'If I just had a chat and a coffee with him?'

Alfie's face lit up. 'That's what I thought. Fuck me, my head was wrecked, I was thinking all sorts, but then I said, no, not with Carter. She wouldn't do that; it's just a coffee and a chat.'

Franny smiled as she walked back into the lounge. 'Yeah, just a coffee and a chat, just like you and Rachel have . . .'

With Alfie furiously ruminating and standing in the corner unable to say anything from the jealousy that was running through his blood, and unable to even look in Carter's direction, Franny sat on the couch next to Rachel with Vaughn and Carter on the large luxury sofa opposite her, the view of Tower Bridge behind her.

She turned to Rachel, who she'd known during Rachel's days as a high-class prostitute when she'd worked for one of her friends. In truth, they'd never been close. They'd only known each other to nod a hello, but she'd always been sweet and polite.

The fact that Alfie was sleeping with her for money, well, Franny certainly wasn't going to let it bother her, because if she did, she knew it would hurt too much and having her heart hurt was something she was terrified of. So, she'd just put it down to a business transaction and when and *if* she got back together properly with Alfie, there'd be no more hookers and no more Carters, it would be just him and her. And that was something she liked the thought of. That was something she could feel. She smiled at Rachel. 'I'm so sorry to hear about Louise. Sasha was obviously a good friend of hers. In the diary I gave Carter, you can tell how much she thought of her.'

Rachel smiled back and took Franny's hands in hers. 'Thank you, Franny, that means a lot. I just hope between us we can help Carter get Wan off the street.'

She nodded. 'Problem is, like me and Vaughn said earlier, it's not safe for the girls to testify and most of them probably won't anyway.'

'And even if they did, it's their word against his. Wan's clever. He's hardly got his hands dirty, or rather, he doesn't get them dirty in public,' Vaughn added.

Carter, having sat in silence so far but feeling Alfie's hostile gaze from the other side of the room, nodded. 'And from what the diary says and what you've told us Sasha said, it points more towards the fact that it was Wan who provided Louise but it was Harry and his friends who killed her, probably not intentionally, but not caring one way or another if he did. Rough sex parties with vulnerable girls they've drugged.'

Rachel looked pained. 'But they're underage a lot of them. That ain't right. A court wouldn't think that was too clever. What about using that?'

Looking genuinely sympathetic, Carter shook his head. 'I've spoken to my colleagues about this several times but it's always the same answer. A good barrister will say they didn't tell him their age, he didn't know. It's not going to put him away. That's why we haven't been able to get him on that, and if you look at the girls they do look like they're in their twenties even though most of them are teenagers.'

Rachel's eyes filled with tears. 'This is crazy.'

'I know,' Carter said. 'I've had many sleepless nights over this and you all know me, you've all known me for a long time and hopefully I've been honest and fair in this job. I have tried against all odds to be impartial and never abuse my position and I've respected the law. But now I'm angry, I'm angry with a system that protects the likes of Wan and Harry but lets young girls suffer. I'm failing them, but I'm in a corner and I don't know what to do. I haven't the power to bring Wan down, but you have . . . You guys have. Together. Working as one, you can do things that I can't, so I'm falling on my sword and I'm begging you to help, to help me help them. Now I don't want to know what you'll do, so in a minute I'm going to get up and walk out of here because I can't know. But what I can do is be here if you need me on the other end of the phone and once whatever is done is done, I will do everything to protect you, to make sure that any indication that you're involved, any evidence that points your way will not see the light of day . . . You have my word.'

With Carter gone, much to the relief of Alfie, the four of them sat on the couch deep in thought.

'Harry's easy.'

'I'll do it,' Franny said matter-of-factly.

'I wouldn't mind meself,' Alfie said.

Vaughn looked at them both. 'Me too, I mean we all want a bite of that cherry, don't we? We can even draw straws who pops him,' Vaughn said.

'Big problem is Wan. We can't have the Triads after us. Jesus Christ, we'll all be face down in a ditch.'

'It would be worth it,' Franny said with a shrug.

'Yeah, but we don't want that. Alfie's got his daughter to

think of and, well, now I've got Milly to think of.' He glanced at Alfie, adding, 'I'll fill you in later on it.'

'Then what we going to do?' Franny wondered out loud.

'We need to get him off the street for a long time without getting those girls involved for all the reasons we've talked about, and we need to do it without Wan and his men thinking it's us.'

'Yeah obviously, but you ain't stating what we need to do, you're just stating what needs to be done,' Alfie countered.

'I might have an idea,' Vaughn replied.

Before they could ask Vaughn what it was, Franny's phone went off. Seeing the number, she frowned and answered it.

'Hi, honey, you all right . . . What? Ellie, calm down! Sweetheart, calm down, what's the matter . . . what? No . . . No . . . Oh my God . . . Look, just tell me where you are. I'll come now. Don't move . . . Hold on, sweetheart, I'm coming.' Franny put the phone down, her face pale as she swayed and held on to the side of the couch. She looked at the others and in barely a whisper she said, 'That was Ellie. She's just told me . . . that Sasha's dead.'

54

That evening, Vaughn stood and smiled at Tia. 'How's Tammy?'

'Not good and they say she's lost the baby.'

Vaughn hugged her, kissing the top of her head. 'I'm so sorry.'

'Thank you. It's good to see you . . . How's Milly?'

Vaughn looked at Tia, not quite knowing what to say.

'*Vaughn*, how's Milly? Is everything all right . . . Vaughn, what's happened?'

In the whitewashed corridor of UCH, Vaughn opened his mouth to say something but he couldn't find the words.

'There's something wrong, isn't there? For God's sake, Vaughn, just tell me!' Her voice echoed around the corridor.

'Tia, I don't want you to panic, but we can't find her.'

'What? What do you mean?'

'She's not at her bedsit . . . and we're worried. We're worried Wan might be behind it.'

'Wan! No, please tell me you've got that wrong.'

'I'm sorry, Tia.'

'Maybe . . . maybe she's gone to the laundrette. Did you think of that? Did you think of *that*, Vaughn?' Tia yelled as tears rolled down her face.

'Yes we did.'

'You keep saying *we*. Who the hell is *we*?'

'Franny, Alfie, Detective Carter.'

Tia covered her face. 'I don't understand.'

He grabbed her and pulled her hands away from her face. 'Tia, look at me baby, look at me. I haven't got the time to tell you everything, not now, but you need to trust me. You trust me, don't you?'

Through her tears she nodded.

'Well I promise you, Tia, I will bring Milly back to you . . . to us.' He paused, hoping against hope the same fate hadn't befallen Milly as it had Sasha and although he didn't know the details, he knew now, without doubt, Milly was in big trouble.

'I have to go,' Vaughn continued.

'No, you can't. You can't just go like this. Look, I'll come with you.'

'Sweetheart, you need to stay here with Tammy; don't leave the hospital, you hear me? And if they chuck you out up here, go down to Casualty; just do not leave the building. I need to know you're safe. Will you do that for me?'

Again Tia nodded without saying anything.

'I don't know how long it's going to take, but I'm going to be under the radar for a couple of days maybe, and I'll bring Milly back home.'

'How can you be so sure? How can you know for certain?'

He kissed her again, knowing that he was far from sure. 'I love you, just remember that, and I am sorry for ever letting you go.'

He turned to walk away but she held on to him, her whole body shaking. 'Vaughn, please, please be careful. I don't want to lose you again. I want to spend the rest of my life with you.'

He smiled and pulled her into an embrace, kissing her as if his life depended on it. 'I'll be back soon, and when I do come back, I ain't ever going to leave your side again.'

Alfie and Franny sat in Alfie's Range Rover, parked in Chalton Street just behind St Pancras Station, with Ellie crying hysterically. So far all that had happened was they'd picked her up. They couldn't get anything out of her.

Franny held her close, hugging her and rocking her gently as Alfie sat in the front.

'Ellie, just breathe, darlin', just breathe. What happened?' Franny said quietly.

'I can't tell you . . . I can't tell you. You'll hate me . . .'

'I'd never hate you, darlin'.'

Red-eyed and hyperventilating, Ellie nodded. 'You would! You would! And I swear, I didn't mean for it to happen. I was just angry.'

'What didn't you mean to happen?' Franny asked gently.

'That Wan would kill her.'

Franny looked at Alfie who raised his eyebrows but said nothing even though he could see the pain in Franny's eyes.

'Ellie, you've lost me. I don't understand. How do you know he killed her? Are you sure?'

'Yeah . . . cos I was there . . . He made me watch . . . He said if I talked, then the same would happen to me . . . I thought he loved me, but he can't, can he? Not if he says that.'

Franny hugged the younger girl and closed her eyes as she took her jacket off to wrap around Ellie who was shaking. The guilt she felt for being any part of it, she could almost taste. 'Can you start from the beginning, so I can understand properly?'

Sniffing and wiping her nose, Ellie nodded. 'I was angry with Sasha cos she kept going around saying she was Wan's girlfriend and she wasn't. I was. And that's why I hated her so much – she kept saying it to wind me up.'

'Ellie, it wasn't her fault. Wan told her that. That's why she said it. She wasn't saying it to be nasty. I heard him myself. So she was only repeating what he said.'

Ellie's face crumpled again. 'Then that makes it worse, that just makes it worse,' she screamed, breaking down once more.

'It's okay . . . Ellie, nothing – and you need to listen to this – nothing is your fault. You hear me? Ellie, I said do you hear me?'

'It is though, because I told Wan that Sasha was talking about him to you. I told him that she was trying to get him into trouble but I only said that because I was mad with her. I didn't know what he'd do. But me and Wan, well we drove around with one of his cousins and then we saw her walking along Kingsway. He pulled over and offered her a lift but the minute she got in the car Wan's cousin gagged her. Anyway, we drove to this warehouse. I don't even know where it was, but then he made Sasha get out and you could see she was so scared. I begged him not to hurt her but he started strangling her, he was so angry, like he kept shouting at her, saying that she'd betrayed him. Her face went all purple and red and she was fighting him, trying to make him stop but he was too strong . . . I'm so sorry, I'm so sorry, Franny. I'm sorry!' Ellie's whole body was racked with sobs as she screamed and cried hysterically as Franny held her.

'It's not your fault. Please don't think it's your fault.'

'But if I hadn't told him, she'd still be alive . . . Oh God, I think I'm going to be sick.' She retched on the floor of the Range Rover and Franny, feeling slightly nauseous herself now, held back Ellie's hair.

'Are you okay? You think you're going to be sick again?' Franny said caringly as she gave her a tissue to wipe her mouth.

Ellie shook her head and sobbed quietly as Franny spoke. 'Ellie, sweetheart, just because you told him, that doesn't mean you're responsible. He was the one who did it. Not you,' Franny said warmly.

Ellie stayed silent for a moment and then quietly muttered, 'They threw her body into the water. It was horrible, Franny, horrible.'

'I'm sorry you had to see that, but it's over now. We'll keep you safe. We'll take you somewhere where they can look after you, okay?'

She gave a small nod. 'I told him about Milly too.'

'Milly!'

'See, I knew you'd hate me.'

'No, no, I don't. I'm just following what you're saying. Go on, tell me. Tell me about Milly.'

'Well I heard Milly talking about her baby to Wan. He said it was his and I got angry. I didn't even know she knew him. She was my friend and she didn't even tell me. I felt stupid and that's why I said about Milly as well, cos I saw her talking to you afterwards. And I was jealous.' Ellie burst into tears again.

'Ellie, you're just a kid who has had a really bad time and met a really, really bad man, and you're really brave to talk to us. Ain't she, Alfie?'

Alfie nodded and smiled at Franny but again he didn't say anything. His heart felt too broken for Sasha.

'Ellie, did he do anything to Milly? Did he kill Milly as well?' Franny asked slowly.

'No, cos we couldn't find her. We went to the bedsit but she wasn't there.'

Franny let out a sigh of relief. She looked at Alfie. 'So Milly's still out there – the question is where. And the problem is, time's running out . . .'

55

It was 2am on Monday morning and having spoken to Carter on the phone and taken Ellie to the safe house Carter had asked them to, Franny sat next to Alfie in the front seat with Vaughn now sitting in the back of the cleaned car, though the stench of Ellie's vomit still sat in the air mixing with the car deodorant the all-night car valet had used.

They drove in silence, all in their own thoughts, all shocked and hurting for the girls.

Alfie, driving in the fast lane, gave a quick sideward glance to Franny. 'You all right, Fran? You did really well with Ellie back there. I hope she'll be all right.'

'Yeah, so do I. No doubt in a couple of days she'll be begging to go back to Wan. Underneath everything it's clear she still loves him, or rather, what she thinks love is. It's so sad and messed up, but at least where she is, they'll look after her *and* they won't let her go and see him. I don't think she'll like that, but it's for the best. Hopefully she'll have a chance to turn her life around.'

'It was tough, wasn't it though, listening to what she was saying, cos I know she's only a kid and has had a fucking rotten time of it, but part of me does think, if only she *hadn't* said anything, Sasha *would* be alive.'

Franny looked out of the window, watching the passing countryside rush by. 'Yeah, but she had no idea. She was just desperate that no one took Wan away from her. She didn't know that was going to happen and not only will she have to live with the images of Sasha being murdered in her head for the rest of her life, she'll have to live with the guilt as well.'

'Do you think Wan will wonder where she's gone?'

'Not at first – he won't get suspicious probably for a day, maybe two days. They come and go as they please, the girls; Ellie's always out and about.'

'So that just gives us forty-eight hours to turn this around and find Milly. I'm just hoping that she went into hiding, you know? Maybe she got wind of Wan looking for her. That's possible, ain't it?' Vaughn said from the back.

'Yeah maybe that's what happened, mate,' Alfie replied warmly but convincing no one.

They fell silent again and it was a good five minutes later before Alfie pulled up on a country lane, parking up behind some trees. He swivelled around to the back to look at Vaughn. 'You sure this is going to work?'

Vaughn shrugged. 'No, but unless you can think of a better idea to get that scum off the streets without pulling those girls into it, then what other choice do we have?'

'What did Tia say?' Franny asked.

'I haven't said anything to her. I thought it best in the circumstances she don't know anything. What's the point? She's got enough shit going on without me adding to it and the less she knows the better. We don't need her anyway. I know where it is. Harry apparently keeps his stash of cocaine in a trunk in the outhouse.'

In the darkness as the wind began to get up, the three of them battled their way through the dense trees and bushes, making their way towards the farmhouse.

'You sure it's this way?' Franny whispered but she got no reply from the others who continued up the steep slope of the rugged fields and hedges. They hurried through the overgrown fields and nettle-strewn ditches until finally getting to a clearing where Alfie nodded towards the horizon. From where they were standing, he could see the outline of the main house as well as a barn and an outhouse.

'Over there, that's where we need to be,' he said.

Franny's eyes flitted towards the farmhouse. There were no lights on but she knew they still had to be careful. 'Come on then, the sooner we get out of here the better. For all we know Harry is about.'

Pulling his gun out of his pocket, Vaughn said, 'Then let's go. We ain't got time to waste.'

With the ground a little easier to run on, they dashed along the potted track, clambering over one of the wooden fences before dashing through a small wood and across to the outhouse.

Getting to the door of it, Vaughn stared at the thick, rusty padlock. 'Fuck, how we going to get in?'

'We can always shoot it off,' Alfie suggested.

'Yeah but if he sees it, it's like we've left a calling card for him.'

Alfie then turned to Franny. 'You want to do your party trick then?' he said, knowing that she'd been able to pick locks almost before she could walk on account of her father, who'd been a number-one face, teaching her. And now she was somewhat of an expert, to say the least.

'No problem,' Franny said as she looked at the combination lock.

She pulled on it, applying a constant downward pressure from the padlock's silver shackle to the body of the lock as she tested each wheel to find the one with the most resistance. She bent down, listening carefully for a click as she then turned the top wheel and felt the lock move down slightly. She repeated the process for each wheel until there was a final click and the silver shackle popped out of the lock. 'Hey presto,' she said.

'Too slow,' Alfie replied, winking at her but clearly impressed by her skill as usual.

They moved quickly inside the outhouse and pushed their way past an old tractor to get to the main part of the building. Vaughn looked at them both. 'Let's each take a part of the place. You take the left side, and Franny take over there and I'll take this side but we have to hurry. We're looking for a trunk – that's what Tia said he stored it in. Make sure you're as quiet as you can.'

Without replying, Franny and Alfie rushed to their

designated areas and began to search, carefully moving boxes and crates, old rusting equipment and empty sacks all the time listening out for anyone approaching the outhouse.

Fifteen minutes later, a despairing Franny walked across to Vaughn. 'I've searched the place three times over and I still ain't finding anything.'

'It must be here. Just keep on looking.'

Alfie walked over to join them. 'But where? There ain't anywhere else to look. Maybe he's moved it. Come on, you said yourself that it was only a vague remark Tia made. I knew you should've spoken to her before we came here.'

Irritated and stressed, Vaughn barked at Alfie, 'Look, I didn't see you coming up with any good ideas, so don't fucking have a go at me for trying.'

'Yeah but this ain't a good idea, is it?' Alfie retorted.

'Alf, at least he's trying,' Franny said.

'Oh, and I'm not?'

She sighed. 'Did I say that? No, I didn't. I didn't say anything.'

Alfie glared at her. 'No, but you often don't say anything. You often keep things to yourself, don't you?'

'I don't know what you're getting at, Alf, though I think I can guess. In case you've forgotten, we are in the middle of nowhere looking for bags of coke and you're talking about me and Carter.'

Alfie was incensed and yes, he knew of all the times and places this *certainly* wasn't the time but the pressure of Wan and the girls and Harry was getting to him, and the guilt he felt over what happened to Sasha after she came to talk to him and Rachel was overwhelming. So, like he often did when he was angry and hurting, he transferred his pain into other issues. 'Oh so there *is* a you and Carter?'

Angry and wanting to shut him up, Franny shook her head as she hissed at him, 'There is no me and Carter, but there was sex, good sex mind, but that's all it was. There is nothing between us, cos as you keep telling me, I do love you and I want to be with you. Happy now? Is that soft and romantic enough for you?'

He stared at her, wanting to kill her himself. He clenched and unclenched his fists, but he managed to turn away, marching towards the door, stomping across, but then he suddenly stopped. He tapped his foot on the ground and then he tapped it again. The floor felt different, sounded different and dropping to the ground, he moved a broken crate out of the way.

'Quick, come over here! There's a wooden flap.' He lifted it up to reveal the way down to the basement.

With his heart racing, Alfie stepped onto the ladder and carefully began to make his way into the darkness followed by the other two.

At the bottom of the ladder, he started searching the area, lighting up the room with his torch.

For the next ten minutes the trio searched the room, moving and squeezing past empty wine crates, piles of old boxes and bags, looking for the trunk. Then, getting to a pile of tarpaulins in the corner, Alfie kicked them out of the way, revealing a cupboard with another padlock on it.

He glanced across at Franny. 'Fran?'

She nodded and bent down and was able to pick the lock just as quickly and easily. Hurriedly, she opened the cupboard door to reveal a trunk. Holding her breath Franny slid it out slowly.

'Alf, you want to do the honours?'

Alfie bent down alongside her and flicked open the catches of the trunk, pushing up the lid. He grinned as he saw what they were looking for. He turned to Vaughn. 'That's a nice stash of coke there . . . Maybe, it wasn't such a bad idea after all.'

56

It was just before 6am and back in Soho, Vaughn, Alfie and Franny sat in Franny's blacked-out Range Rover.

'You sure you'll be all right?' Vaughn asked.

'Yeah, absolutely, there's nothing strange about me going into the club; in fact it would be strange if I didn't. I'm usually there at this time when they're all locking up . . . Why don't I meet you back at my house? Here's my keys . . . let yourself in. I'll see you soon.'

'Be careful, cos don't forget, there are a lot of people who want your head on a plate,' Alfie said.

She leant over and kissed him. 'Thank you, and I will.'

Inside Wan's club, Franny walked around, nodding hello to the cleaners and various other men who worked for Wan. Nothing unusual, nothing different, which was perfect.

Walking into the back office, Franny closed the door

then quickly rushed over to a cupboard. She opened it to reveal a safe and knowing the combination as quickly as she could she unlocked it.

Glancing at the door to make sure no one was coming, Franny went into the satchel she was carrying, pulling out one of the kilo bags of cocaine they'd taken from Harry's. She placed it in the safe then closed it, hurrying out, before making her way down the stairs to Wan's office.

Knowing he wouldn't be there but knocking on the door just to be on the safe side, she waited and, getting no answer, opened the door.

She moved quickly inside and went to a large, expensive wooden cabinet. Going into her satchel again, she pulled out the remaining two bags and carefully pushed them, jamming them in behind the cabinet.

Smiling to herself, she closed her eyes letting out a sigh of relief. If the girls couldn't nail Wan, she hoped that this would. And by her reckoning he'd be going down for a long time . . .

'Well, what did Carter say, Fran?' Vaughn asked as he sat in the expensive hand-crafted white kitchen of her house.

Pouring herself a glass of freshly squeezed orange juice, Franny looked at both Alfie and Vaughn, the surreal sense of the three of them being back together – for *now* – not being lost on her. There was no way only a few weeks ago she could ever have contemplated being in the same room as Vaughn without wanting to kill him there and then, but for now at least, she knew they had to put their differences aside.

'He said he could get a unit to the club within the hour. They're going to raid it and he knows exactly where to look. So now we just wait. He's going to call me when it's done but that's not going to be until much later, cos no one can know that we're involved. He's just going to put it down as a tip-off by one of his sources, so he won't be able to call me from his work phone. He'll have to wait until he's home. But it'll be worth the wait. He'll be able to arrest Wan straight away and the amount of coke we hid, well, Wan's looking at a hell of a lot of time behind bars.'

Vaughn nodded as he smoked his cigarette. 'And Milly? What did he say about her?'

'He's going to come and talk to us as soon as possible, you know, try and work out what the best thing to do is . . . I know it's hard but *please* try not to worry. We'll find her.'

'How though? Dead or alive?' The room fell silent.

Half an hour later and the wait was killing Alfie. He paced along the kitchen floor, waiting for news about the raid. But with the pressure getting to him he made his way into the bathroom and pulled out a carefully folded piece of paper from his pocket.

He placed it on the marble surface, opening it just as carefully as he'd folded it. Then he pulled out his credit card from his wallet and tapped the contents – the couple of grams or so of cocaine he'd siphoned off Harry's stash – out of the paper onto the grey vanity unit.

He began to chop it up with the side of his bank card before separating it into several, thick lines. Eagerly he rolled up a twenty-pound note and bent over it, greedily snorting one line after another. But then he frowned and immediately snorted up another line . . . and another . . . and another.

'*What the fuck?*' Suddenly he raced out of the bathroom and down the stairs where Franny and Vaughn were still sitting. Charging into the room, panicked, his words tumbled out. 'That coke, that coke we took from Harry's place, I don't think it's coke at all.'

'What?' Franny said as she stared in bewilderment. 'What are you talking about?'

'Look at me, I ain't got a buzz, not a sweat, not one damn fucking note of a high.'

'So?'

'Well that's what I'm trying to tell you – I've just tasted the goods, and it ain't cocaine.'

Vaughn stood up and, like Franny, he stared at Alfie. 'You sound fucking high to me, cos you ain't making sense.'

'Look, maybe I shouldn't have but when I was putting the bags of coke in the satchel for Fran, I just took a little bit for meself. Don't fucking look like that, Vaughn, cos the rights or wrongs of me doing that ain't the point. The point is, that is not coke. Which means—'

'What we hid in Wan's club ain't coke,' Franny said, filling in the gaps.

It was Vaughn's turn to begin to pace. 'Maybe it just wasn't mixed properly – you know as well as I do that they put all sorts of shit in coke to stop it being so pure. Maybe you just got a part that hadn't been blended in properly.'

Alfie stared back at Vaughn. 'I think we need to get in touch with Carter, call it off, cos if they raid the place and only find dummy cocaine then not only will Wan still be walking free, but he'll also know he's being set up and it won't take him too long to work it out who it is. Then not only are the girls fucked, but so are we. At least if we stop Carter going in, Franny can get back the coke and we can get it tested, I dunno, something like that . . .'

'Maybe Alf's right, maybe we should call Carter, but we can't, can we? *Shit*. The only number I've got is his personal phone,' Franny said, looking worried.

Looking just as worried, Alfie began to pace again. 'What about we go round to the club? We stop him going in.'

Angrily, Vaughn yelled, 'Then we'll all be fucked. It'll hardly be discreet will it? Us all turning up at the club. We might as well put a sign around our necks telling Wan we turned him over.'

'Then you tell us what we're going to do cos whatever way I look at this, we're fucked. How could we be so stupid not to know it wasn't coke?'

'Stop being so fucking dramatic, Alf, of course it's coke. What else would it be? It's not like Harry's Mary Berry, is he? He's hardly going to have bags of fucking self-raising flour locked away. Look, I tell you what, just to shut you lot up . . .' He stopped and pulled out his phone, dialling and waiting for it to be answered.

'Tia, hey sweetheart, it's me . . . Listen I need to ask you something. You know that coke that Harry has, well I need to do something with it, so I was wondering if I could . . . What? I don't understand . . . Are you sure? No . . . no, no it's fine, don't worry . . . Okay, listen I have to go, I'll talk to you later.' Vaughn clicked off the phone and stared at the other two. His face was pale and worry was etched in his eyes.

'You were right, Alf. Tia's just told me that the cocaine wasn't cocaine at all. She swapped the bags so if Harry did look in the trunk at least there was something there. What we took was essentially just white powder. It might as well have been self-raising flour after all . . . which means we need to stop Carter, *now*!'

Franny looked at Vaughn and then at Alfie. 'But that's the point, Vaughn, we've got no way of contacting him at all.'

57

'You fool, you fucking fool. Didn't it occur to you to check what gear you were planting? Didn't it occur to you to talk to Tia?' Franny screamed at Vaughn. 'And as we couldn't stop Carter raiding the club, you've now alerted Wan that he was being set up. You might as well have killed those girls yourself – he knows we're on to him.'

'He doesn't know for sure,' Vaughn shot back.

'Well how the fuck long do you think it will take for him to know? You have fucked everything up, not to mention fucking Carter about too.'

'Just shut up! Just shut the fuck up!'

Franny, distraught at the implications of the massive blunder over the raid, glared. 'Who do you think you're talking to?'

'*You*, now fuck off out of my way,' Vaughn said as he

tried to storm out of the house even though she blocked his way.

'You ain't going anywhere, Vaughn, until we sort this out, sort out what we're going to do. It ain't any good you splitting. Milly is out there, don't forget. We need to come up with a plan.'

He leant right into her face and growled. 'I said get the fuck out of my way.' As he said it, he grabbed her, smashing her against the wall, where she elbowed him in the face, busting his nose open as he shoved her harder.

'What the fuck!' Alfie roared and charged at Vaughn, diving at him and getting him into a headlock before pummelling him with a fist in his face, but Vaughn twisted his body, managing to get out of Alfie's grip.

He turned around to hit Alfie but Franny got there first, throwing an uppercut punch to Vaughn's chin, making him stumble to the side and giving Alfie the opportunity to kick him hard, buckling his legs, causing Vaughn to fall to the ground.

As he fell, Alfie stumbled and fell on top of him, giving Vaughn a chance to slam his fist into Alfie's face and throat, making him cough and splutter. Not to be stopped, Alfie managed to knee Vaughn, splitting his lip open and bringing his fists down as Vaughn struggled underneath him. But then Franny's voice cut through the air. 'Stop! Stop! Enough, that's enough! Alfie, no more!'

Spitting out the blood from his mouth, Alfie, exhausted, stopped. He looked at Franny and then down at Vaughn and panting his words he said, 'She's right – we can't do this. This ain't going to help anyone. We need to work together. So this stops, *now*.'

With Vaughn and Alfie having gone out to get some food, Franny stood in the shower letting the water pound against her skin, letting the heat sting it. She couldn't believe what had happened. She was angry with Vaughn. No she was more than that, she was fit to bursting but Alfie was right – it was no good them tearing each other apart, not now anyway. The girls were more important than their fight and certainly bringing Wan down was what they need to focus on.

'I'll think I'll have that cup of tea now.'

Franny spun around and there, standing with a grin on his face, was Harry. He whistled at her as he regarded her naked body. 'I can see why Alfie still sniffs around you. With a body like that you'd give a dead man a boner. I might try a bit myself before I do what I've come here to do.' He stopped talking and placed his hand on his groin. 'What do you say, Franny, fancy a bit of action before you meet your maker?'

'Go to hell.'

He laughed. 'No, I think that's you, not me.' He grabbed her suddenly, pulling her out of the shower so quickly that she slipped on the soapy floor, tumbling onto the marble tiles. Immediately, Harry got on top of her, his heavy, muscular body pinning her down.

He pulled at his trousers with one hand as his other hand roamed over Franny's body. She struggled, fighting to get away, but the way he had her pinned down made it almost impossible for her to move.

She hit at his face and pulled at his hair but he just laughed. 'You won't get any complaints from me. I like it rough. Keep on pulling, darlin'. It always turns me on when—'

'You fucking bastard. I'm going to kill you!' Alfie stood behind Harry with his gun pressed against the back of Harry's head.

'No, Alfie! Don't kill him, *not yet*, because we need him first.'

Harry sat tied to a chair in one of the spare rooms in Franny's house with Vaughn and Alfie standing opposite him as Franny held Harry's phone in her hand, having taken it out of his pocket.

She stared at him. 'Now I want you to call Wan. I want you to say exactly what I told you to.'

Harry looked at her, laughed, then spat, only just missing her. She slapped him around the face but he chuckled and winked. 'Like I told you, I like it rough . . . I don't suppose there's a chance of a quick blow job before I meet me maker – you know, give me my last rites . . .'

'You want it rough? How about this for rough?' Alfie said as he slammed his fist in Harry's face, splitting his nose and lips open. 'Now do as she says. Call Wan. *Now.*'

With his front tooth having been knocked back from the force of the punch, Harry rolled his tongue over his mouth, tasting the pouring blood. 'No, jog on, cos you're going to kill me anyway.'

Alfie bent down to him and grinned. 'You're right we are, but as you know, there are different ways of killing people. Quick and painless or long and painful, and if you don't call Wan, I am going to make this the longest motherfucking killing on record. You'll be seeing in Christmas before I'm done with you. How about I start with your toes. One after the other. Chop, chop, chop.'

Harry twisted his face up in anger looking at them all. 'Fine, fine, I'll do it.'

Alfie winked. 'I thought you'd say that.' He nodded to Franny who pressed Wan's number and held the phone up against Harry's ear.

'Now make it sound natural, understand?' Franny snarled as she switched the phone onto speaker.

Harry just stared but almost immediately the call was answered. 'Wan, it's Harry . . . Listen, er . . .' He stopped to look at Franny who nodded at him, pushing him on to say what she'd told him to.

'Yeah, er . . . I heard about the raid. It's fucked up, but I need to see you. It's about . . . Ellie and Sasha.'

'What about them?'

'I saw Ellie and she's spouting a lot of shit about Sasha. She was all over the place . . . I think we need to talk about what we're going to do with her. You know, she seems to be mouthing off a lot and I really don't want her to start mouthing off about me . . . but I don't want to talk on the phone, so I think it's best we meet up at the farmhouse cos I reckon the Old Bill will be watching your club now.'

'Yeah okay. What time?'

'Say about eleven tonight?'

'Sounds good, I'll see you there.'

The call finished and Vaughn winked at Harry. 'Impressive

356

– you made that sound real, but then you've always been a lying cunt, ain't you.' He turned to Alfie and Franny. 'Ready?'

'Ready,' Alfie said and with that they screwed silencers on their guns.

Franny smiled and nodded. 'Ready . . . One for all and all for one.'

At which point all three of them pulled their triggers, blowing Harry into bits.

58

It was late and Vaughn, Franny and Alfie watched as Wan's car headlights appeared up the main driveway of the farm-house. 'You still all prepared to do this? You know they'll be after us after this,' Vaughn said.

Franny glanced at Alfie and smiled. 'I'm okay with this. If it gets Wan off the streets, it'll be worth it. We'll have to hide, maybe go to Spain.'

Vaughn nodded. 'They'll still come looking for us but that ain't a problem, once Milly . . . well, once we find Milly, I'm sure Tia would be more than happy to get out of the country with the kids. There's nothing keeping her here now. And you're all right with it, ain't you, Alf?'

'Yeah, if it means the girls are safe and I'm with Fran, I'm happy to go wherever . . . And I never said this before but, I'm fucking choked up that we're back together . . . This is how it always should've been, hey Fran?'

'Yeah, sure,' Franny said but her eyes didn't hold the sentiment.

Nothing more was said as they watched Wan's car getting nearer. But as it approached, Vaughn narrowed his eyes as he made out the outline of another person in the car. 'Shit, he's got someone else with him . . . two other people . . . Fran, why don't you quickly go to the top of the courtyard and, Alfie, why don't you go over to the trees? I'll stay here, then at least that way we've got him at all angles.'

Alfie nodded. 'Good idea,' he said as he dashed over to where Vaughn had suggested, disappearing into the darkness as Franny did the same.

Holding his gun close, Vaughn stared as the car pulled up only feet away. He watched as Wan got out and saw his two men getting out on the other side of the car. Readying himself he suddenly stood up and shouted. 'Wan!'

Wan turned to look at Vaughn as Franny and Alfie blasted holes into the two other men, but as Vaughn went to pull the trigger his gun jammed, which gave Wan the vital split seconds he needed to dash behind his car and into the bushes, running into the night.

'Fuck!' Vaughn yelled as he gave chase, hearing Franny and Alfie rushing up behind him.

'What happened?' Alfie said breathlessly.

'I dunno, the gun didn't go off – maybe I've got a dud load. *Fuck,*' he said as he discarded the round of bullets in his gun on the floor, changing them for a new round that he pulled out of his pocket.

'Look, we need to make sure he doesn't get off the

property, cos if he does then we'll never get him,' Vaughn said as he double-checked his gun again.

'Do you want to split up?' Franny asked as her eyes darted around.

'No, let's stay together for now. Come on let's go . . .'

The trio dashed through the grounds, looking and stopping at every noise and sound, running behind trees and bushes looking for Wan as they came to the barn. Suddenly, Franny put her arm up, gesturing for them to stop. 'Listen, can you hear that?'

Alfie nodded. 'That scraping noise, yeah, it's coming from the barn.'

'Come on, let's go . . . but let's be careful,' Franny said as she moved forward along the side of the barn, stepping over bits of old farm machinery and rusting lengths of discarded barbed wire, but as they crept along further Alfie suddenly let out a yelp. *Fuck! Fuck! Fuck!*

Franny turned around to where Alfie had dropped to the ground. 'What's happened? What's the matter?'

'My leg! My fucking leg.'

She stared closer at it and saw a bent piece of sharp rusting steel had cut into his leg, severing through his flesh.

Quickly she took off her jacket, wrapping it around his leg, trying to stem the bleeding.

'You stay here; me and Vaughn will go and see what it is. We won't be long. Will you be all right?'

Through his pain he smiled at her as she got up and edged forward with Vaughn towards the entrance of the barn.

At the doors of the barn, she paused as she held her gun in her hands. She nodded at Vaughn. 'You all right?'

He nodded back. 'I'm good . . . How about we go in after the count of three?' Without waiting for a reply he began to count down. '*Three . . . two . . . one . . .*'

They rushed inside holding their guns in front of them but Franny suddenly froze. 'Oh my God!' There in front of her tied to a chair with a gag over her mouth was Milly.

She ran over to her calling her name. 'Milly! Milly! Milly, it's me, sweetheart.' Ripping her gag off and untying her hands, Franny could see how bruised and bloody she was, her face and lips swollen. 'Did Wan do this to you?'

Crying hysterically Milly threw her arms around Franny, shaking. 'No, it was my dad! He brought me here. He said that I needed to be taught a lesson but I thought he'd come back, I thought he'd come back.'

Franny held on to her, rocking her gently, knowing that Harry taking her, forcing her here before Wan had found her, had ironically saved her life. 'What about the baby? Can you still feel it moving?'

'Yeah, it's been kicking.'

'That's good, that's good.' Franny smiled. 'We'll get you out of here soon but for now, you need to stay here . . . Oh, this is Vaughn by the way. Vaughn meet Milly.'

Vaughn – overwhelmed by not only what Harry had done to her, but also by the fact that he was meeting his daughter for the first time – fought back the tears as he spoke. 'Nice to meet you, Milly; your mum's going to be delighted we found you,' was all he managed to say.

'Vaughn, listen, why don't I go and get Alfie to stay with her? His leg is bad, but that don't mean he won't be able to pull the trigger if he needs to.'

Vaughn thought for a moment. 'Yeah, okay and I'll go and look for Wan.'

'Okay and once I've got Alfie, I'll come and find you.'

Vaughn crept along, staying well hidden and crouching behind the old oak tree. He held his gun up, listening as he continued forward.

Slinking quietly towards the pond, a sound coming from the left had him whirling around but not before a bullet was suddenly fired at him. He ran, rushing through the trees, ducking down as he saw the figure of Wan approaching in the darkness of the night.

Vaughn aimed his gun, firing back as Wan dashed out of sight. More shots were fired out from the darkness as Wan hid behind the trees, though with no light Vaughn wasn't certain where they were coming from.

He sprinted along the gravel path and diving for cover he pressed his body against the wall. Breathing hard he listened again but this time he couldn't hear any sound. As he crept forward again, a shadow suddenly loomed near him. He heard the crack of the gun and he dashed forward but he felt a pain in his leg, burning into his calf. He yelled out as he threw himself down the ditch, readying himself for Wan to appear at any moment.

Groaning in pain, Vaughn gritted his teeth as he pressed his hand down on his leg trying to stop the flow of blood. He pulled himself up, dragging his body into the darkness, and as he did he saw Wan going into the main house. Although the pain was rushing through him, as if his whole body was on fire, he knew there was no way he was going to let Wan get away. Staggering up on his feet, Vaughn made his way across to the house.

Inside the farmhouse, Vaughn slowly crept along the hallway, peering carefully into each room, his finger hovering over the trigger of his gun.

Getting to the lounge, he looked about, his eyes darting from one side of the room to another. But suddenly he stopped. He could hear footsteps coming from above him. Wan was there, just a few feet away . . .

Slowly, Vaughn made his way up the stairs, pushing himself once more against the wall. He could feel his heart racing and the sweat pouring down his back along with the blood that oozed from his leg.

Coming to the landing, Vaughn stood and looked through the crack of the door. Seeing Wan, he stepped forward, aiming his gun but at the last moment, Wan, hearing a noise himself, spun around and began to raise his gun. Without hesitation, Vaughn squeezed the trigger, emptying all the bullets from his gun one after another.

'Oh my God, you got him.' Franny's voice came from behind Vaughn.

Staring down at the body Vaughn let out a sigh. 'Yeah, at least that's one problem out of the way. We'll have to stick together now, Fran. The Triads will be after us.'

Franny smiled as she walked forward and looked down at where Wan was lying in a pool of his own blood. She was pleased he was dead – more than pleased. He was scum and at least now the girls would be free of him.

She blinked then slowly raised her gaze to look at

Vaughn. 'You mean the Triads will be after *you*. First you kill Wan's brother and now you kill him . . . They won't like that.'

'Well that's what I'm saying – we need to be tighter than ever now.'

Franny chuckled. 'You know it's true what they say: a common danger does unite even the bitterest enemies, but now that the common enemy is dead, that only leaves the bitterest of enemies. And I once told you that when you're least expecting it, you'd be a dead man. I haven't forgotten that you tried to kill me, Vaughn, and all this mess is because you set me up in the first place . . . The best thing about this is no one will ever know. I'll just tell them that you shot Wan. I can make you a hero, if you like?'

'What the fuck are you on about?'

'Don't worry, I've got it all worked out. You shot him but not before he shot *you*. Then you died of your wounds . . . Don't look like that, Vaughn, I'll bring your favourite flowers to the funeral. Lilies, ain't it? I'll get Milly to do a reading as well and I'll make sure you can have one of those wreaths that says "*Dad*" in the funeral car. I would get a couple of horses to carry your coffin, but I know you ain't too keen, I know you're allergic . . . Anyway, hark at me talking.' Franny raised her gun and smiled again though the smile certainly didn't hit her eyes. She pointed the gun, jamming it against Vaughn's head and drawing back the trigger she whispered her words. 'Now get ready to say die . . .'

'No! Franny, no! Don't do it!' Carter shouted from behind her.

She turned her head and glared at him. 'What the hell are you doing here?'

'Alfie called me.'

She nodded but turned her attention back to Vaughn. 'Get out, Carter, this is between me and Vaughn.'

'Franny, listen to me: you don't have to do this. You can draw a line under it. Wan was the enemy, not Vaughn . . . I said I would protect you and I will. I will keep that promise. I will make sure that what's happened here won't be connected to any of you. If you go now, all of you, you can get away. Nothing will happen to you because we had a deal . . . But the Flying Squad are going to be here in about ten minutes, so you need to go now.'

'It won't take me that long to shoot him.'

Carter stepped into the room. He looked at her warmly, his eyes pleading with her. 'Just put the gun down, Franny, because if you don't, if you shoot him, I will *not* protect you, because that was not part of the deal. Killing Vaughn was not our agreement and whether I want you to or not, whether I care about you or not, I will make certain that you go down for the rest of your life. So go on, tell me: what's it going to be, Franny? Make your choice . . .'

Acknowledgements

A huge and loving thank you to Katie Loughnane who has championed me from the moment we met and who is simply an awesome editor and person. Will miss you. Thank you to the Avon team who are just a lovely bunch, it's been fantastic working with you on so many books. Thanks to my agency, and of course a big thanks goes to my loyal and new readers. And as always, a big shoutout to family and friends and my bunch of amazing animals. Happy days.

Before, there was just bad blood running
through her veins. But now, there is poison . . .

Available in paperback and ebook.

Betrayal and lies come with consequences, and
old sins cast long shadows . . .

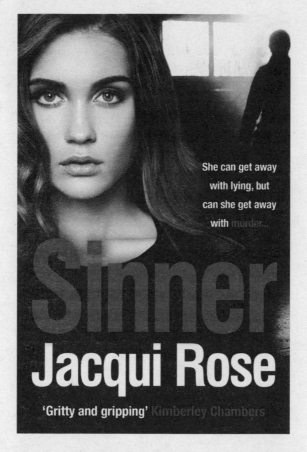

Available in paperback and ebook.

An eye for an eye.
A tooth for a tooth.
A daughter for a daughter . . .

'Gritty and gripping'
KIMBERLEY CHAMBERS

Love can save you,
but it can also be…

Fatal

Jacqui Rose

Available in paperback and ebook.

Bree Dwyer is desperate to escape her husband,
take the children and run. But he's always
watching. And she always gets caught.
Until now . . .